FIRE RIDER

FIRE RIDER

THE RILLION BOOK 1

T M Miller

T M Miller

Copyright © T M Miller 2018

ISBN: 978-1-9993245-0-6

First published in 2018 by Hatchinscope.

PO box 1023, Horsham,
West Sussex, England. RH12 9TW.

To my parents and big bro.
And why I was such a dreamer.

1

The City of Tiara floated on a bed of low mist. Graceful, white-stone towers rose high into the night sky and gave off a ghostly radiance in the moonlight. By now, the torches placed along the top of the city wall had burnt down to nothing more than smoking husks. Only one light was clearly visible, and it came from just beyond the perimeter. Here, a shorter tower sat inside a high-fenced yard, its top balcony bathed in a flickering glow from within.

Through the open doors, a boy could be seen pacing back and forth by the light of a lantern. He wore a crumpled nightshirt and walked with an uneven gait. As he limped across his sparsely furnished room, he ran a hand through his dark brown hair in an agitated manner. Back and forth he went, passing his bed, with its blanket thrown to the floor, three more times. At last, he stopped short and threw up his hands in a futile gesture. Turning, he stepped out onto the terrace. He cut a scrawny silhouette with his thin limbs and mussed hair. The boy's name was Jaron, and the tail end of his own scream had woken him from his nightmare.

Jaron unbuttoned his nightshirt in an attempt to cool the sweat from his chest before resting his elbows on the balcony wall. The Plains of Wake were spread out before him, the moon still high enough to bathe them in a blue-tinged haze. Thin wisps of cloud, pushed by a gentle breeze, dimmed the moonlight at intervals, and turned the sluggishly swirling mists that covered the plains into a mirage sea. In the distance, he could see the shadow of the Notresia mountains that bordered their northern edge. Jaron sucked in the cool night air, glad to be out of his stuffy room. Not for the first time, he gave silent thanks for being given the floor at the top of this tower, and not only for the view. The terrace doors had thick glass, so at least up here no one else could be disturbed by his nightmares, even if he woke himself.

Sprague, the trainer, had moved him to this tower not long after taking Jaron on at the yard, saying it would help force his fitness having to tackle the stairs. Jaron suspected it was rather to stop him from waking the other workers, although Brill was the only one who had complained, and that was no surprise coming from him. Climbing the steep winding steps had been painful at first, but Sprague had been right; they had helped his tighter left hip to become more mobile. Yet at the end of the day, and when he was especially tired, Jaron still needed the help of his hateful stick to make it up to his room.

The three floors below Jaron's were used for storage. At ground level there was a feeding room with a thick butcher's bench for cutting up meat and a tack room for saddles and bridles. In here, two crossbows hung on the back wall ready for emergencies and with firing bolts to hand. The other riders and grooms lived in a block at the far end of the yard, just past the exercise pens and next door to Sprague's house.

Jaron didn't mind being so isolated. This last year he had found himself becoming more and more of a loner anyway. He cupped his chin in his hand and sighed. For five months he had been sleeping well and had even begun to hope he was free of the nightmares, at last. Caught up with training, Jaron had fallen into bed at the end of the day too exhausted to dream of anything. It could only be the rumours that had reignited them; whispers of how the Raken and their monstrous flying firedrake were coming to Tiara to protect the city's stores. *Protectors,* he thought in disgust. He turned his head to look westwards, to where the huge dark blocks that were the grain barns sat at the start of the bare fields.

Jaron knew the soldiers would be waiting there hidden in shadow, as they had been every night since the harvest. *Why couldn't the Tiarian soldiers deal with the raids? Anything rather than have the firedrake here.* The Raken may have been cleared of any blame after the attack, but all Jaron knew for certain was he couldn't face having those beasts anywhere near him, wild or not. Not after knowing what they were capable of – and not after losing Teel.

He still missed the man who had been as a father to him. Teel had seemed invincible, but not to firedrake fire, nothing was. Not a day had passed that Jaron hadn't thought of him: his kind brown eyes, the bad jokes, his strength.

A tear escaped and slid down Jaron's cheek, slowing as it met the trench of his scar. He angrily brushed it away and shook his head, disgusted. 'They'd better not come here,' Jaron warned the glowing moon. His anger had made him speak out loud, forgetting for a moment where it was he stood.

In answer, a deep-chested rumble sounded, rising up from one of the two barns in the yard below. They faced each other across a wide path, thinly shrouded now in mist. The barns had no white-stone walls; instead, thick bars ran from ground to tiled roof. At the end of the nearest barn, a large shadow moved, as big as one of the cart horses that pulled the grain wagons. It came closer to the bars and pressed against them.

Jaron bent over the balcony wall as far as he dared. 'It's

alright, Caliber,' he called down softly. There came another
low rumble, before, apparently satisfied, the shadow backed
off and was lost within the dark interior of its cage. As Jaron
straightened, a sudden wave of heavy weariness washed
over him.

Enough. Pushing off from the balcony wall he returned
to his room, taking care to close the doors softly behind him.
Inside, it was still too warm, and he would have liked to
leave them open, but he couldn't run the risk of disturbing
the kelpra below should his nightmare return.

Falling onto his bed, Jaron left the blanket where it was
on the floor. He sat up to put out the lantern on his little table
and, with a tired sigh, laid back down. Spreading his arms
and legs wide in a bid to stay cool, he closed his eyes.

Next morning, early, it was already warming up in the yard.
The kelpra were out in their separate high-fenced pens after
slurping up an offal breakfast swimming in blood, the sun
picking out the patches or stripes on each kelpra's coat that
marked them from afar. The large beasts were similar in
shape to a horse with a wedge-shaped head, a slightly shorter
neck than you would find on a pony, complete with mane
but with a tufted long tail and rounded ears. Each pen had a
thick scratching post and while working off their bloody
morning tonic the kelpra would run their long claws down
its length or gnaw at the wood with their sharp teeth.

Inside the barns, the mucking out was in process. Straw
was tossed and pulled up to air the metal floors of the cages.
The two barns faced each other across a small yard and
within the slanting rays of sun dust spores danced and
twirled.

Sprague arrived, at an unusually late hour for him. The
trainer called to his workers to stop what they were doing.
When all five had stepped into the yard, Sprague's bushy

dark eyebrows knitted as he pointed a thick finger at Brill, a tall gangling youth. 'Monty's tack was in a right grubby state last night. How come you didn't clean it after training?'

Brill pouted. 'I did clean it, Sprague.'

The trainer grunted. 'Not by my reckoning, the stitching was terrible. Look after your tack, Brill – how many times?'

Brill scowled and turned away into Monty's cage.

'I've not finished yet,' Sprague called after him. Muttering under his breath, the youth let his fork fall with a clatter before turning back. 'Listen up, all of you.' Sprague ran a hand over his shining bald head. 'All riding is to take place on the training track only, no going out onto the plains.'

The workers looked at one another.

'Because of the thefts,' Sprague explained. 'Blasted Ernots have been at the grain stores again.'

'But Sprague,' Sanra was tying up her thick black curly hair to cool the back of her neck, 'they'd never catch us on the kelpra.'

'They came too close to the yard last night,' Sprague said. 'I met the soldiers carrying a dead Ernot when I unlocked the yard gates at dawn.'

Tucker gasped. 'A mountain man! Are they as big as they say?'

'Massive, I heard.' Liam got in before Sprague could answer. He was the oldest of the workers and Sprague's second. 'My brother's a soldier. He says it takes six of them to carry a dead Ernot and they're covered in hair all over, like fur.'

'Really?' Tucker's eyes widened even more. He was the latest recruit, the youngest, and the most excitable. Not a good combination with the kelpra but then hands were hard to find due to the danger of getting them bitten off if you didn't know how to handle the beasts. The others still took care to always accompany Tucker, just in case.

'Lord Bell,' Sprague resumed, frowning at their interruption, 'summoned me just after. He thinks they're getting too brazen. And he's fed up with those creatures taking up too much of the army's time.'

'The Ernots wouldn't stand a chance against the kelpra,' Brill muttered.

Sprague shook his head. 'They've broken the locks on the grain barns more than once and if they got in here all it would take is a spear through the bars. Lord Bell doesn't want to run the risk of losing any of them with the race festival so near.' He looked at Jaron as he said this, who felt a strong sense of unease rise up inside of him. He didn't like the way this was going.

Sanra folded her arms. 'I still don't see why we have to stick to the track, Sprague,' she argued. 'Everybody knows the Ernots only attack at night. The kelpra'll get bored.'

'Boring or no, that's my order, or rather, Lord Bell's.' He hesitated, seeing their downcast faces. 'Look, it won't be for long. His eyes flicked to Jaron and away again. 'Maybe just 'til the Raken get here.'

They all gasped, except for Jaron, who felt his heart give a little judder.

'So, the rumours are true,' Liam said. He looked quickly over at Jaron, who couldn't stop himself:

'Raken?' he rasped.

The trainer's usual fierce glare softened. 'Yes, Jaron. I saw Lord Bell yesterday. He told me they've agreed to come – now they've got a good enough offer,' he added with some disgust.

'The Raken are coming!' Tucker was bouncing on his feet. 'I've never seen a firedrake!'

'Jaron has, haven't you?' Brill's loud mocking voice.

'Shut up, Brill,' Liam said, a little too quickly.

Jaron kept his chin up but felt the scar on his left cheek burn.

6

'I still don't understand why they would come,' Tucker said.

'For protection, as guards,' Sanra answered.

'Weren't you listening, Tucker?' Brill was more impatient.

As Tucker's face went as red as his hair, Sprague answered, not unkindly. 'We lost too much to the Ernots last year, they would never dare raid the grain with the Raken as sentries on those flying beasts.' He rubbed his short beard. 'So, when they get here, training on the plains will resume. But until then...' he frowned at them all, 'absolutely *no* riding out on the Wake, got that?'

'Yes, Sprague,' they said as one.

'Right, back to work, you lot.'

They returned to mucking out cages. As they worked they talked excitedly about the Raken and their flying beasts. Jaron couldn't join in with their enthusiasm. He piled up the straw and forked up a gnawed thigh bone and the calf bladder Caliber had left from last night's meal. Now it was confirmed, he was dwelling on the news with dread in his heart. A prickle of heat washed over his body that was nothing to do with the temperature. He reached up to work a finger under the thin scarf he still wore about his neck.

'Jaron?' Sprague was standing at his shoulder. 'You alright?' He spoke in a quiet voice so the others wouldn't hear. 'They won't come anywhere near the yard, nor the kelpra. They'll have me to answer to if they do.'

'I'm fine,' Jaron lied. After last night's nightmare wrenching him from sleep, he felt weary of it all. Sprague must have sensed he didn't want to talk and, left alone, Jaron dug his fork back into the straw with some force. It was as though his village being destroyed didn't matter at all here in Tiara. A year and a half ago, he would have been as excited as Tucker. He would have run outside with his friends to watch in awe whenever a Raken beast flew overhead. As Jaron banked up the bed, working to toss the straw up the sides of the cage, his mouth twisted in bitterness at the memory.

2

A warm sunny afternoon three days later and Jaron was on an errand to the racetrack. Over one shoulder he carried a sack full of grooming tools. He had offered to spare Tucker another journey but if truth be told, it was really to escape the excited chatter back at the yard as the day of Tiara's race festival drew ever nearer. His nerves were jangling enough as it was. He and Caliber had raced three times now, but the Great Wake Trophy was the most prestigious race in all the Corelands. Jaron still had to pinch himself to believe it was happening at all.

It made a nice change being away from the yard. As he passed into the large square, he looked about him with interest. It was only half-full of people as it wasn't market day, which was one of the reasons for Jaron choosing to take a short cut through it today. Despite the lack of crowds, he noticed a couple of people staring at his limping gait and he dipped his chin down so his hair fell over his cheek scar.

As he reached the middle of the large square, he couldn't resist looking up now and then to gaze at the beautiful facades of the white-stoned buildings that surrounded it. Tiara was renowned for its graceful architecture. Suddenly, the back of his neck prickled – just as a huge shadow sliced across the sunlit faces of the buildings to his right. Somebody screamed and, jerking his head round, Jaron saw an arm pointing skywards. He looked up, and gasped.

The huge silhouette of a firedrake flew low above the square, the sun picking out the network of thick veins threading through the wing membranes as they thrust through the sky with a heavy *whoosh*. Dropping his sack, Jaron pivoted on his heel towards it. Shielding his eyes from the sun with one hand he kept it in his sights amidst the cries and surprised shouts from all around him. Fear clenched his chest. The beast's long narrow neck stretched forward as the huge reptile passed over the square. He just caught sight of the face of its rider looking down before it flapped out of sight over the rooftops, its long tail slicing after it through the warm afternoon air.

Amidst the exclamations of awe from people at what they had just seen, along with some mutterings, Jaron stood staring up at the now-empty sky with the bitter taste of fear still in his mouth. Shaking his head in disgust, he bent down to retrieve his fallen bundle and limped unsteadily on his way.

'They are awesome, really amazing.' In the cage next door, Tucker's eyes were shining but his enthusiasm was wearing. 'I would love to ride one. Dad said the riders are really friendly.'

Jaron gritted his teeth and concentrated on brushing the dried sweat off Caliber's velvet ebony coat, watching how from under the bristles the thin blue stripes shone through.

'And how does your dad know that?' he heard Liam ask as Caliber, sensing Jaron's sudden mood, turned his head around as far as his chain allowed to look back at his rider. The kelpra's eyes; bright amber, were placed more forward than a horse, and now they gazed at him intently. Jaron reached over to stroke a hand down the long nose that ended in a wide muzzle like a cat, where two gleaming fangs protruded below the upper lip.

'He works in the kitchens and takes them food sometimes. I might go with him one evening; perhaps I could get a ride, do ya think I could? He said there's one called Val, his firedrake's called Motch and–'

'Motch?'

'Yeah, so I thought–'

'Strange name for a beast like that.'

'What's this?' At Sanra's voice Jaron looked over. She stood beside Liam in the cage doorway where the red-haired boy was mucking out. Undoing her riding helmet, she pulled it off and shook her black curls free.

'I was talking about the firedrake. They're great, aren't they?'

'Oh.' Her eyes went to Jaron who quickly returned to his grooming.

Brill, pulling down Monty's straw bed opposite, had been listening. 'Yeah, they're great,' he called across now. How are you feeling, Jaron? You looked white as *ash* when you came back from the track the other day.' Jaron stopped brushing and turned to eye Brill. From within the empty cage, Brill sauntered over to the doorway and grinned across the yard at him. 'Frightened you're going to get *burnt*, Jaron?'

Sanra gasped. 'Brill!'

'Shut up, Brill,' Liam growled at him.

'Just saying,' Brill sneered.

'Well, don't,' Liam said.

Jaron stared at the older boy as cold anger flared in his chest. He had got used to Brill's jibes – but *this* was going too far. Carefully, he climbed down the set of small steps he used to reach Caliber's back for grooming.

'Hey... Jaron?' Liam's uncertain voice called through the bars.

Jaron didn't answer as he limped across the yard. He stopped directly in front of Brill and glared up at the tall, lean youth. Brill's blue eyes widened in surprise for a moment before his mouth screwed up into a leer. He snorted with laughter. 'Thinking of taking me on, Scarface?'

Without giving himself time to think, Jaron swung his

arm, putting all the force he could muster into his punch. His knuckles slammed into Brill's jaw with a satisfying *crack* and Brill's head snapped back. *Ow.* Shaking his hand out and grimacing in pain, Jaron was just in time to see Brill straighten up, his mouth twisted with rage. He came at Jaron so quick he had no time to jump aside. Brill's weight cannoned into his chest and knocked him flat to the ground. Next moment Brill was straddling Jaron with his knees. Jaron struggled, hitting out and with legs kicking, but Brill was sat on his stomach, looking down at him with mad triumph in his eyes and blood on his chin. Behind him, someone shouted something but Jaron took no notice, only just managing to block the first hit to his face with his arm. The next punch landed on his side, making him grunt with pain. Another hit him on his other side, where his scars were, and he groaned aloud.

Just as a loud grating snarl ripped the air, coming from behind.

Brill looked up, and his clenched fist froze level with his shoulder while his face blanched in stark terror. A long, low menacing growl sounded next. *Oh no.* Jaron squirmed out from underneath Brill and flipped over onto his stomach despite his sore body.

Caliber stood in the cage doorway, the broken chain dangling from his metal-banded leather headcollar and with rounded ears folded flat back. As Jaron stared, the kelpra lowered his body into a predatory crouch, his amber eyes still staring at Brill's face with dark intent. His thick tail lashed back and forth, the tuft on the end raised and quivering.

Jaron swallowed. *Calm, keep calm.* 'Caliber,' he called quietly. 'I'm alright, boy.'

Caliber flicked his gaze down to where Jaron lay on the floor, then back up to Brill. His upper lip lifted, revealing more of his gleaming fangs. At Jaron's eye level, long black claws, curved and deadly, slid out from their sheaths in the neatly rounded paws.

Jaron levered himself slowly to his knees, his eyes never leaving the kelpra. Behind him, he heard Brill whimper. Trying not to grimace from pain, Jaron carefully got his feet underneath him. 'I'm alright, Cal, see?' He slowly straightened up, only dimly aware of the others, who had taken refuge inside the next cage with the barred door slid firmly shut. Jaron licked his dry lips and whistled the lilting tune he sometimes used on the kelpra to calm him. Pricking his ears up at the sound, the hard light in Caliber's eyes faded just a little as he looked at his rider.

'That's a boy,' Jaron dared to take a step forward. Carefully, he reached for the dangling chain to grasp it. Whistling the tune again, he brought his hand up slowly and rubbed the blue blaze shaped like a question mark in the centre of the wide forehead. The kelpra blinked then huffed at him, and Jaron smiled.

'Alright, let's just back up now...' He stepped to one side to put a hand on Caliber's shoulder.

He heard a scraping sound behind him as Brill chose that moment to get to his feet. With a snarl, Caliber suddenly lunged forward.

'*No!*' Jaron cried, yanking hard on the chain, his voice lost in Brill's short scream of terror, a piercing sound in the metal-floored cage. Strangely enough, it saved him. Caliber's ears flattened for protection as the beast stopped short, crouched on his haunches.

Jaron quickly stepped between them. 'Cal! *Leave him!*' His voice came from somewhere deep in his chest and had a timbre like it wasn't his own. To his astonishment the air between boy and beast seemed almost to shimmer for a brief moment. With all his focus on Caliber, Jaron mentally dismissed it and dared to meet the kelpra's stare in challenge as he looked down at his rider, eyes wide. He knew it was a risk to look the beast directly in the eye but Jaron could only go with his instinct and it had never failed him before. After a tense moment, Caliber lowered his head and his whiskers tickled Jaron's hand. 'Good boy,' Jaron murmured, relieved. 'Back now.' He pushed at the kelpra's shoulder for emphasis and was grateful Caliber obeyed him and started to retreat from the cage doorway.

Once in the more open space of the yard and talking softly all the while, Jaron turned the kelpra and led him back to his cage, his hand clasping the chain directly under Caliber's chin. He took care to keep the beast's head slightly ahead of him. Once inside, and noting the claws were now pulled in, Jaron gave him another pat. 'There's a lad.' Still facing the kelpra he bent carefully to pick up the fallen steps, unclipped Caliber and slowly backed out, sliding the barred door shut between them.

He let out a breath and turned to see the others all stood staring at him in a line.

'That was… amazing,' Tucker said in awe.

'Are you hurt, Jaron?' Sanra asked.

'Is *he* hurt?' Brill muttered. He was standing half bent over as he tried to control his trembling body. When he lifted his face, it was to reveal it drained of all colour, the blood from Jaron's hit a bright red smear on his chin. '*He* started it,' Brill pointed a shaking finger at Jaron, his voice unnaturally high, 'and *I* was almost killed because he forgot to close his mad beast's door!' His black hair was stuck full of straw.

'Cal snapped his chain.' Liam's voice was hard. 'Because of what *you* were doing to his rider. You're lucky Sprague wasn't here, he would have banned you from the yard for fighting. If you do *anything* like that again…' Liam stepped closer and gave him a hard stare, 'I'll punch you myself and it will hurt. Very badly.' It was not an idle threat; Liam was shorter than Brill but much more muscular.

'Idiot,' Sanra added in disgust. Jaron leaned against the door for a moment as his legs started trembling; a delayed reaction as the adrenalin left his body. Sanra wasn't done yet. 'What did you expect?' she said to Brill. 'We all heard the talk about how bad that attack was, Jaron's people *died* – are you so stupid you can't think before you open that big fat mouth of yours?'

Jaron glanced over at her in surprise, then caught the sudden look of shame on Brill's face just before the lips curled up into the usual sneer. It was enough. Seeing Caliber was calmly rubbing his nose on his knee, Jaron turned and limped unsteadily up the yard. As he passed Tucker he said, 'Put some meat through the bars for Caliber, would you?'

Staring at him, the boy dumbly nodded.

'Jaron?'

He didn't stop at Liam's call. He left, the weight of their stares at his back.

3

Jaron sat in the stronghold's massive kitchen, set in the bowels of the palace. His mother stood across from her son, kneading a large lump of dough at the table with her strong hands.

'Don't look so worried,' she said. 'You're the lead rider now, so of course Lord Bell wants to show you off at the festival dinner.'

'Show me off?' Jaron waved a hand vaguely at himself. 'Give the other riders more confidence, you mean.'

His mother stopped her kneading and gave him one of her looks. 'Stop talking yourself down, Jaron. You know it's tradition, the lead riders of the Great Wake go along with the trainers.' Something caught her eye over Jaron's head. 'More salt than that, Leena,' she called. 'Really rub it into the skin.'

'Yes, Mistress Rella,' said a girl's voice from behind him.

'And I hope you're being careful, handling those beasts,' his mother muttered. She had always worried about him working with the kelpra and had even gone to visit the yard to see for herself, to her son's acute embarrassment.

'You know I am.' Jaron thought it best not to mention the fight and Brill nearly being attacked four days before. Brill hadn't spoken to him since, and that suited Jaron just fine. Brill had never forgiven him for winning the star ride on Caliber, who had arrived in the yard unsettled and suspicious of them all. To everyone's surprise, it was Jaron, the quiet new boy, who had won the kelpra over. For Jaron's part, he had always been able to calm the feistiest of colts when breaking horses with Teel, who had always said he had an extraordinary way with animals. Helping his stepfather to train difficult horses had led to Sprague taking Jaron on when all the horse stables in the city had taken one look at this pale, lame boy and turned him away. That, and the scarcity of finding those willing to work with the kelpra.

Becoming Caliber's rider had led Brill to point out to Sprague (more than once), that Jaron would lessen their chances with his weaknesses. Yet in doing so he did Jaron an unintended favour. Determined to prove Brill wrong, Jaron had gritted his teeth and thrown himself into training. It had hurt, but inch by sore inch over the months Jaron had moved the stirrup leathers up to the next hole, gritting his teeth against the pain of the thickened scar tissue on his left hip. That little bit of extra speed meant everything in a race. Now, he could finally ride like a proper race rider – and fall like one. You didn't want to do that, not in the Great Wake Trophy, not with all those strange kelpra entered from the other Coreland cities coming up behind ready to snap you–

Abruptly stopping his thoughts, Jaron watched the kitchen workers, some walking past laden with pans, others bent over the work tops. Huge ovens sat against the far wall next to a fireplace so big it housed a whole skewered pig that roasted slowly on a spit. The palace kitchens were set below ground level to help keep them cooler, but it was uncomfortably hot now. Despite the heat, it was a great bustle with his mother at the centre of it all and not missing a thing.

Her cooking skills and strong will had soon brought her to the attention of the palace chief. Now, the kitchen was very much her domain. For Jaron's part, he was only glad he no longer worked here scrubbing pans.

He ran his fingernail along a split in the aged wood of the table. 'This dinner tonight...'

'Again?' His mother sounded exasperated. Tendrils of

FIRE RIDER

hair had escaped her bun and were stuck to her forehead in the heat. Jaron had inherited his mother's thick dark hair and small build, but whereas her eyes were a rich hazel; his eyes were an unusual silver-blue.

Jaron cast a cautious look at the other cooks working at the long bench where he sat and lowered his voice. 'They'll see me... they'll see this.' He lightly touched his left cheek.

Rella banged the dough down onto the table so hard her son jumped along with most of the staff. She stalked around to where he sat and he flinched as she grabbed his arm. Pulling him off the chair she led him out of the kitchens. As they left, he could feel the eyes of the staff burning a hole in his back. His mother yanked open a door and stopped when they stood in the small area at the bottom of the stone steps leading up to the courtyard. She pulled her son round to face her.

'I won't have you do this to yourself. Never, ever feel you are anything less than them.' Her voice was low but Jaron caught the determination in it.

'Sorry,' he muttered.

'For what exactly?' she asked in an even voice. 'For acting like a prize gooseberry for not believing a word I say, no matter how many times I say it? Your face isn't all about your scar, Jaron, and *you* are not all about your burns.' Jaron lowered his head. He wished now his mother would drop the subject. 'You think I would lie to you? About this?' her voice hissed. Dough-encrusted fingers caught his chin and tilted it up so he was forced to look at her again. Her hazel eyes were glinting with anger. 'Be proud, Jaron. You've earned the right to be there tonight – more than those merely born into privilege.'

He tried to nod but it was difficult with his chin trapped. Her eyes searched his before she released him and folded her arms. 'There's something else troubling you, isn't there?'

'Nothing,' he mumbled, picking bits of dough off his chin.

'You hurting? I've got some Limpan jelly in the kitchen. I could take a look at your burns if you are.'

'Mum, I said I'm fine.'

She cocked her head, studying him. 'It's the Raken being here, isn't it?'

Jaron grimaced. 'And what came with them,' he admitted. 'Doesn't it bother you? After – after what that firedrake did?'

'It was a rogue, Jaron, a wild firedrake.' Her voice was gentle now. Reaching out, her hand gripped his and gave it a squeeze.

'I still think I saw the shadow of something, or someone, on its back.'

She dropped his hand and folded her arms across her chest. 'It was night,' she replied, suddenly sounding tired. 'You told the captain of Tiara's Guard its underside looked blue in the light of the fires – the wild firedrake are all blue. And there was no girth strap for a saddle, the captain asked you that.'

'I... might have been mistaken,' Jaron muttered defensively, 'about the girth strap.' He swallowed. 'It flew over so fast.'

'You have to let it go, son, for your own sake.'

Jaron set his jaw and looked down at his feet. It was true that he couldn't be sure. The beast had only made two overhead passes that moonless night; all it had needed to raze Harnt to the ground. The wild blue firedrake were still about, although not many were left, and the Raken firedrake were all green or red. There was no one else to ask: Jaron had been the only survivor – thanks to Teel thrusting him under the porch of their little cottage. Jaron's mother had been away from the village that night on her monthly market run and he would be forever grateful for that. But with the

Rakens' coming it had all painfully resurfaced in his mind.

'I just don't think those beasts can be protectors,' he said at last, still unwilling to drop it.

His mother didn't reply; when he looked up it was to see her face was drawn and tired. They hadn't spoken much of that terrible night since, not once Jaron was able to give a report to the captain. After Jaron's long recovery, both mother and son had tried to move on with their lives and carve out a new life in the city. Keep going forward. It was all they could do.

'The Raken won't allow their firedrake to kill.' When his mother spoke again it was slowly, as though she were trying to etch the words into his mind. 'I understand how hard it is for you but the Raken protect the lands, Jaron. They are trusted.' She laid a hot hand on his cheek, the one unmarked. 'Such a thing had never happened before. The Raken would have hunted down that firedrake and killed it. The captain came and told me the leaders of the Corelands had demanded nothing less after Harnt being attacked.'

'Then I hope it suffered before it died,' Jaron growled.

'If only you could really know their firedrake,' she whispered, holding his gaze. 'The link they have with their riders, so much more than what you have now – you would see what they can be. And their coming here might just be that chance.'

He looked away, 'I'm sorry, Mum, but I can't help how I feel.'

'Jaron,' he heard her voice catch as her hand slipped from his face. 'You know they were my people.'

How he wished it were otherwise: his mother was of Raken blood. After her own mother had died, Rella had left the Raken to go and live with her aunt. He first learnt this from his grand aunt, clutching her hand while they stared up at the huge fearsome beasts flying over; a rare sight to behold in their isolated hamlet. 'And with you still a babe in her belly, Jaron,' she had croaked down at him, and shaken her head. Not long after that, his mother had packed their belongings and moved them on, leaving her aunt behind. They settled in Harnt. As the years went by and he grew more into his childhood his mother would talk to him about the Raken and the firedrake when he badgered her, but she never mentioned why he didn't have a father like the other village children and he never quite got around to asking. Then big, bear-hugging, joking Teel arrived in their lives. Soon they became a family and the need to ask simply faded away for Jaron.

Now, looking back up at his mother, he caught the sudden guarded look in her hazel eyes but he still couldn't voice the question he sensed hung between them now; not yet anyway, not with how he now felt about the Raken and Teel's death still so raw. 'Teel was a father to me,' he muttered at last.

His mother moved closer to him and for just a moment Jaron turned away from her. 'I miss Teel too you know, he was a good man, the best. Jaron,' her voice whispered, pleading now. 'Please try, for your own sake.'

He gave it up and folded into her arms. It was stupid to allow the Raken and their beasts to come between them, he reasoned – that murdering firedrake had done more than enough damage already. When they parted he gave his mother a weak smile then turned and began to slowly climb the steps to the courtyard above.

Her voice wafted up after him. 'Come and see me tomorrow, I want to check you over.'

'I'm fine,' Jaron said over his shoulder. The last thing he wanted was for his mother to see the bruises he still had from Brill's battering. He carried on up the steps, head down. Behind him, he heard the door close as he stepped into the kitchen courtyard.

A strangled gasp escaped his throat.

The red firedrake, crouched on the cobbled stones, heard it and swung its head round to find the source as it half-opened its wings. Jaron staggered back with a low cry, only just missing falling backwards down the steps again.

Its eyes fixed on him, a bright, luminous yellow with narrow black slits for the pupils. Jaron instinctively froze. With its wings held out it nearly filled the large courtyard. Beast and boy stared at each other, neither moving, Jaron's brain still trying to register the huge reptile. Its scales glinted like jewels in the midday sun and the top of its neck bristled with raised plates fanning out to frame the massive head. More scale plates protruded between its narrow ears and ran down the top neck ridge.

Jaron noticed all this with astonishing clarity in his silent terror. He couldn't look away, couldn't drop his eyes as he knew he should do. With a slithering motion, the thick, tapered tail slowly slid over the cobblestones and tucked against the firedrake's side, the end coming to rest over its scaled front paws, but not before Jaron had noticed each of them was as big as the pig roasting on the spit in the kitchen. The narrow tip of its tail quivered and raised slightly off the cobbled floor as the boy stared, revealing curved black claws as long as his forearm. He saw the ridged nostrils quiver as the beast took his scent. It blinked and with a rustle folded its wings, snaking out its head – and to his horror reaching out towards him with its nose. Carefully, Jaron's searching foot found the top of the stairs and he retreated down one step. For the first time, he noticed it wore an empty saddle on its back.

The beast suddenly pricked its ears. Raising its neck high it swung its head to one side. As it did so the sky-blue scales on its chest were revealed. Jaron's eyes narrowed.

Through an open door a man stepped into the courtyard. His head was bare, revealing short-cropped brown hair. He walked with long strides across the yard, heels ringing on the cobbles. He wore a leather jacket, open at the front to reveal a worn leather tunic, and in the crook of one arm he carried a helmet. As the man reached the red beast's head, he turned in the act of putting it on – and saw Jaron for the first time.

'Hello,' he said, lowering his arms again.

Jaron didn't answer. He saw the chiselled, tanned face frown a little, the deep-set eyes narrow. Without saying a word, Jaron slowly turned and carefully walked back down the steps, one hand on the stone wall to support his trembling legs.

4

That night, the palace dining hall was packed with Tiara's finest and their guests. The atmosphere was merry after the first two courses and bubbling chatter and laughter fueled by fine ale and rich wine rose up to the high beams of the large hall.

'Watching your diet, eh?' Sprague leaned in towards Jaron and nodded in approval at his unfinished beef. 'I usually have to get the jockeys to hold off devouring everything on their plates on these occasions.' His broad face was red and sweating as Sprague was already on his fourth tankard.

The truth was Jaron didn't feel hungry at all. The race was only two days away now and his stomach was in knots most of the time.

'Well, your rival doesn't seem to be bothered about *his* weight,' his other neighbour leaned in to whisper and gave a meaningful look to where Pache, Jaron's main competition and rider of Teller, sat. Teller was the favourite entry of neighbouring Kyrinda and for two years had been the winner of the Great Wake Trophy. Pache sat swigging at a tankard of ale behind his empty plate. He was tall for a jockey, lean as a whip, and even slouching in his chair exuded a predatory air. His sharp eyes narrowed as they studied Jaron without smiling.

'He looks like he could eat me too,' Jaron whispered back, and when his neighbour chuckled looked at him properly for the first time. The young man had shoulder length brown hair and a smooth, clean-cut face that was evenly tanned. He met Jaron's gaze and grinned, teeth startling white against his browned skin. He stuck out a hand. 'I'm Flick,' he said.

Jaron took the offered hand. 'I'm—'

'Jaron, yes, I know. I heard you getting yelled at on the track the other day by your trainer.'

'Did you?' Jaron was surprised.

'I get a good view from Tarp's back.'

'Tarp?' Jaron asked, not understanding.

'Not much escapes us from up on the roof.'

'Oh?' Then Jaron understood. He stiffened and looked down at his plate.

Sprague had heard and shifted towards Jaron's other elbow and frowned across him at the young man. 'You're one of the firedrake riders, aren't you?'

'Yes, that's right.' Flick sounded proud.

'Well, you want to keep away from my jockeys when they're training.'

Jaron looked up in time to catch the young man's smile fade a little.

'We always do, sir.'

'We are very careful not to upset the locals,' a deeper voice interjected, coming from a man in his forties sitting opposite. His face, like Flick's, was deeply tanned but his skin had a leathery quality to it.

Flick extended a hand towards the other firedrake rider. 'This is Val.'

Val nodded to them but seemed disinclined to further conversation. Not so Flick who tapped Jaron's arm to get his attention again.

'The Plains of Wake make great flying.'

He grinned at Jaron, eyes alight with good humour, and despite himself, Jaron couldn't help smiling back. He found he felt no animosity against this friendly young man. 'Yes, the plains make good riding too.'

Flick shook his head. 'You want to see it from the air. There's nothing quite like it.'

Val coughed and eyeballed his younger colleague. Flick ducked his head and smiled at Jaron. 'Sorry, I'm not boasting or anything. I bet it's great going out there. What are the kelpra beasts like to ride?'

'A challenge,' Jaron answered. 'But great when they want to work for you.'

'Huh,' Pache interrupted. 'A good jockey, he has to be determined more than anything else. Make them work for you, don't ask them if they feel like it, or you'll never get the best effort. They need a master's touch.'

'Now, now, Pache my lad, don't you go giving the competition advice.' The Kyrindian trainer put a hand on his jockey's arm.

Sprague's mouth thinned. 'Not that we need it,' he said with a huff. 'I wouldn't be so sure this year if I were you, Tam.'

'Really, my old friend?' Tam replied, smiling. 'Teller is in the finest form, so he is, the best form.'

'Getting on a bit now, isn't he?'

'In his prime, Sprague, in his prime.'

The evening wore on. As home lead rider and trainer, Sprague and Jaron had the honour of being seated directly below and side on to the raised platform where Lord Bell's guests sat at a long table facing out over the proceedings. Jaron recognized Lord Varne, an avid racegoer, and lord of the western city of Kyrinda. His fine long white hair had thin bands of silver woven into it for the occasion, as well as his beard. He was a lean man with a face so white it made him look insubstantial. As if to compensate he wore a heavy white fur cloak over his embroidered tunic, seemingly oblivious to the heat in the dining hall.

In contrast Lord Bell, leader of Tiara, sat next to him sweating profusely on his ornate carved throne. His blond hair and beard were just beginning to frizz in the heat, mingled with his own damp sweat. On the other chair next to Bell sat a very beautiful woman wearing a velvet red dress. Her hair was a mane of heavy, long black curling locks. Her skin was an unblemished creamy white and Jaron had noticed the men at his table often cast sneaky glances up at her.

'That was a very satisfying meal you laid on there, Bell.' It was Lord Varne who spoke and his thin voice floated down to Jaron's table. He watched as the Lord of Tiara grinned and raised his tankard, spilling half of it in the process down his beard.

'Yes, indeed, my compliments to the chef. In fact, let's get her out here. Lale!' he bellowed. An elderly servant creaked through the tables towards his master.

'My lord?'

'Get the woman, what's her name? The head cook! Out here. We want to pay our compliments.'

'Yes, my lord.' The servant turned and began to weave his way through the tables.

Jaron watched him go then frowned up at the table, more than a little annoyed at Lord Bell for calling his mother 'the woman.'

'So, the firedrake are to protect the grain this year, I hear,' Lord Varne said to Bell.

The Lord of Tiara grinned. 'Yes, a fine show your riders put on the other night, Lord Carna.'

Jaron hadn't heard the Raken lord speak at all so far, although he had been casting surreptitious glances of dislike at the rider of the red beast, for it was the very same man he had seen in the courtyard that afternoon. Sitting next to the lady, he didn't seem to have dressed up for the occasion and wore the same worn leather tunic with muscled tanned arms bare. Now Carna merely nodded at Lord Bell, who tried again.

'Only complaint I've got is you didn't kill any of those damned Ernots.'

Carna shrugged. 'My men reported they started running, so why kill them?'

Jaron, on hearing this, was surprised. He stared up at the rider of the red firedrake. Feeling his focus on him, Carna looked down at his table, and their eyes locked. Jaron broke first, looking down to pick at the cheese on his plate.

The lady spoke then. 'Tell me, Lord Carna, is it only the Raken who ride the beasts?' She twisted a lock of hair in her hand and smiled at him.

'Yes, Lady Roser,' Carna's reply was short.

Lord Bell leaned over the table. 'My son here has been pestering me for a ride on one of your firedrakes. Indeed, I should think all the boys in Tiara would like to have the chance to fly such a beast.' He didn't look best pleased at this even as he said it.

Not this boy, Jaron thought to himself. He caught the flush of excitement that suddenly spread over Lord Hawke's face from further down the table. He had his father's shock of blond hair but was, in stark contrast, thin and tall.

The Raken lord had made no comment and Bell studied him, now with narrowed eyes. 'But surely you would give a ride to my son, Lord Carna,' he pressed. 'After all, I heard you arranged for my advisor to get a ride back to Tiara.'

Carna's neighbour, who Jaron had assumed was another firedrake rider by his tanned face and similar attire, flashed a look at his silent lord and answered for him. 'It is the firedrake's choice, not ours. Should the firedrake have not allowed the elder on his back, then it would not have happened.'

Lord Bell raised his eyebrows. 'Oh, come now…?'

'Wing Commander Nave, my lord.'

'Well, Nave,' Jaron noticed Bell didn't use the man's title, 'surely the choice is the rider's? After all, who is the master here, the beast or the man?'

Lord Carna put his elbows on the table and turned his head to stare at the Tiarian Lord. Nave suddenly shot a look down at Jaron's table and the boy caught Flick and Val exchanging glances. Val raised his eyebrows at the younger Raken and Jaron heard Flick sigh before he pushed his seat away and stood.

'You can have a ride on Tarp – if he doesn't mind.'

Hawke clapped his hands and laughed in delight. 'Thank you…?'

'Flick, my lord.' The young man slumped back down in his seat, looking glum.

Jaron noticed then the old servant returning, and behind him came his mother, walking with her head held high between the tables. He saw she had taken off her apron and untied her thick dark hair, leaving it to fall across her shoulders for the occasion. She still looked hot from the kitchens, but on her it seemed more of a glow. He felt a surge of pride. Someone from the crowd whistled, and he frowned.

Bell clapped his hands. 'Ah, here she is, my head chef. Come closer, my dear.'

Rella approached and stopped before their table. She gave the shortest of curtseys.

'My lord.'

A tankard slammed down from the top table, making Jaron jump. He saw Lord Carna had sat up straighter and was openly staring at his mother. Jaron glared up at him.

'My compliments to the chef, we very much appreciated the fine food.' Lord Bell raised his voice to the hall. 'Didn't we, friends?' At this there were calls of agreement and some clapping.

Rella dipped her head. 'My lord is very kind.'

To Jaron's surprise Carna spoke then. 'Yes, in Rakenar we do not have such a wide range of dishes. I am sure our kitchen is missing one such as you, my lady; a mistress chef.' He held her gaze and the lord's normally hard look turned just a little too eager for Jaron's liking, who stared at him and then at his mother. He was shocked to see a smile playing on her lips just before she looked down at her feet.

'It is very good of you to say so, my lord Carna,' her voice was low, husky even.

Carna continued to stare at her and when she looked up again to meet his eyes, a slow smile stretched across his tanned face. Jaron wondered how she knew the lord's name. Kitchen gossip, he supposed. He missed what Lord Bell was saying for a moment until Flick nudged him.

'…and her son there is my star jockey for the race. Stand up, boy.'

Jaron looked horrified at Lord Bell and Sprague had to elbow him in the ribs to get him to move. 'It's tradition,' the trainer hissed in his ear. Jaron stood, gripping the table hard, but it would be rude to drop his chin in an attempt to hide his scarred face.

'He's very small,' Varne said. 'And quite pale. Do you think he will make the race to its end, Bell?' Jaron flushed but then noticed his mother eyeballing him. When she saw she had his attention she lifted her chin a little. Jaron did the same and she winked at him, causing a smile to touch his lips.

Bell grinned through his beard. 'Sprague speaks very highly of him.'

Sprague stood up. 'I do, my lord. He trained horses with his stepfather before coming to Tiara and Caliberion wouldn't tolerate anyone else on his back. He's young, but one of the best rider's I've had.'

Jaron, surprised by the usually gruff trainer's praise, shot a grateful look over at him. Sprague gave the slightest of winks.

The lady in the red dress was smiling kindly at Jaron. 'Are you looking forward to the race, boy?'

'Yes, very much, my lady.' Jaron was pleased his voice sounded clear when his heart was hammering so.

'And do you think Tiara has a chance this year?' Varne asked. 'Against my Teller?'

Jaron looked the Kyrindian Lord in the eye. 'Yes, I do, my lord. Caliber is very fast.'

There was a ripple of clapping from the Tiarian guests at this.

Varne merely smiled. 'I am glad you are so devoted, boy. I only hope you will not be too disappointed when you lose.'

Jaron kept his chin up. 'Then I will do my best to avoid that outcome, my lord.' Laughter from the guests but also applause and rumbles of agreement. Bell clapped his hands for silence.

'All the lead riders from the lands entered, stand up with their trainers.'

At this there was a scraping of chairs as riders and trainers stood from various tables around the room. Tam nudged Pache who unfolded himself from his chair with feline grace and stood up next to his trainer. He towered over Jaron and grinned derisively.

Bell raised a tankard and stood.

'Here's to a good race, a clean race, we remember the Camorian entrant who died last year.' Bell nodded along the table to the elderly lord of Camoria who inclined his head. There was silence in the hall as people bowed their heads in tribute.

After a moment Lord Bell raised his arms. 'And the best of luck to Tiara!' he bellowed, and the cry was echoed by those Tiarians in the hall. Bell raised his tankard to Jaron before taking a long swig.

'May Lady Luck be with us,' Sprague whispered and took a drink from his tankard.

Jaron looked over at his mother but Rella was smiling up at the top table, oblivious to the old waiter trying to get her attention to leave. Jaron followed her gaze straight to where Carna sat. The Raken lord was not looking at his mother, however, and with a jolt Jaron saw he was now staring directly at him, with a frown on his wind-tanned face.

S

After the banquet, the next day was a rare morning off for Jaron. He dressed late and threw open the windows to his rooms before stepping out on to the balcony in his socks. He searched the sky warily, but no firedrake flew there and he could relax. The Plains of Wake shone golden in the morning sun and to the north, the Notresia range rose up in a blue haze. He closed his eyes and raised his face to take in the sun's rays with a smile.

'Hey!'

He started in surprise and turned to look back into his room but the landing door remained closed.

'Jaron!'

Jaron frowned; it wasn't a voice he recognized. He bent over the balcony but the walkway to the stables far below was empty.

'Up here!'

Jaron turned, looked up – and gasped. The balcony wall pressed against his back and there was nowhere to go.

A green firedrake was making its way down the roof directly above him, the scales on its head catching the sun in an iridescent blue and purple sheen. Carefully, it placed one forefoot then the other on the steep gradient, wings held half out to balance itself. Green reptilian eyes looked directly into his, the pupils' narrow vertical slits in the bright morning sunlight. Jaron couldn't move. Stark terror left his limbs frozen like a rabbit before a hawk.

'Morning. Lovely day, isn't it?'

It was only then Jaron saw a face peering over the beast's

shoulder at him. His stricken mind remembered then, the rider from last night... *Flick*. Next moment a roof tile, dislodged by the firedrake's weight, slid down the roof and smashed onto the balcony next to Jaron. Yet still he didn't move nor take his eyes from the great beast; he couldn't seem to make his legs work.

'Oops, sorry about that.' Flick looked genuinely upset. 'Tarp!' He slapped his firedrake on the neck. 'Be more careful, would you?' Tarp rumbled from deep in his chest and cocked his head at Jaron. 'Tarp says sorry,' Flick said. 'Hey, where are you going?'

Jaron didn't answer; able to move his limbs at last, he was already through the balcony doors and stumbling into his room. He fell on the bed, panting while he tried to still his hammering heart. The sound of another tile smashing onto stone caused him to flip over with a start. A scream threatened to form in his throat at what he saw next.

The firedrake's head now filled the balcony door frame as it peered in at him. Its blue tongue flicked out then in, and it gave a strange hiccupping sort of squeak. Jaron cried out and back-pedalled over the bed until he fell off the other side with a thump.

'Tarp! Let me in, would you? Get back, you great lump!'

Jaron peered over the bed in time to see the firedrake's head pull right back. It was now hovering outside the balcony, wings beating, its clawed forepaws gripping the balcony wall to keep it in place. Flick came into view, standing upright on the point of the beast's shoulders. He ran lightly along its neck, arms outstretched for balance and with neat footwork avoiding the raised scale plates. Crouching, he dropped down onto a foreleg and swung himself onto the balcony. The young Raken sauntered through the open doors but stopped short when he caught sight of Jaron's face from behind the bed.

'What are you doing down there? Are you alright?' he

asked, concerned.

'Um, yes.' Jaron stood up slowly, stealing a glance past Flick at the now-empty balcony doors.

'Ah, sorry we startled you. Didn't mean to but we've been waiting ages for you to wake up and Tarp got a bit impatient.' The young man studied him for a moment with a level gaze. In daylight, Jaron noticed his eyes were an unusual green, although not quite as vivid as his firedrake's were. When Jaron didn't say anything in reply, Flick wandered off to stick his head into Jaron's little washroom. 'Quite a nice den you've got here,' he said, looking around.

'Yes, I like it.' Jaron's voice sounded unnaturally high and he coughed, trying to mask it.

'Did we disturb you in the early hours?' Flick asked, turning back.

Jaron stared at him blankly.

'The Ernots tried another raid on the barns,' Flick grinned, 'but we got them running soon enough.' This last was said with some pride.

Jaron shook his head dumbly and stole another look at the balcony. It was still empty and he felt his faculties returning. 'How did you know where I was?'

'Didn't you know one of our postings was on your roof?'

Jaron stared and shook his head slowly.

'We can see the storage barns from here.'

'Oh.' He hadn't realised the stable tower was a regular post. *Just brilliant, out of all the places they could be stationed in the whole of Tiara.*

Flick was wandering around the room again. He hadn't bothered with the helmet the riders usually seemed to wear and, being tall, had to duck his head to avoid a low beam. Jaron stayed where he was, keeping the bed between him and the balcony, one eye on the open windows should the firedrake return.

'I thought you might like to come and watch Lord Hawke

have a ride this morning.' Flick was standing at Jaron's shoulder now, having apparently finished his inspection of his room.

'Err, I'm alright, thanks.'

'Well, I thought it might be a chance for you to have a flight down there on Tarp?'

Jaron tore his gaze away from the window. 'Sorry, what did you say?'

'I said,' Flick was frowning at him now, obviously wondering if Jaron was all there, 'do you want a ride on Tarp? Down to see Lord Hawke fly?'

Jaron stepped back before he could stop himself. 'No! I mean, thanks but I'm fine, lots to do, you know, before the race.'

'I thought I heard your trainer give you today off?'

'A half day,' Jaron corrected, remembering Flick and the other Raken – Val? – had been following them out when they left the dinner last night. He thought quickly. 'Got to clean my tack and get ready.'

Flick looked disappointed. 'That's a shame. Lord Carna is taking your mother, she seemed quite keen to ride Madrag.'

What? 'Madrag?' Jaron stared at him.

'My lord's firedrake.'

'My mother is riding Lord Carna's firedrake?' *Surely, he's mistaken.*

'Yes.'

'The big red one?'

Flick cocked his head at him much like his firedrake had done; he was obviously now utterly convinced Jaron was a bit slow. 'Yes, that's right. So, you up for it?'

Jaron knew he wasn't. But the thought of his mother and Lord Carna being so friendly staggered him. It was obviously Carna making a play for her and Jaron was suddenly determined to be there. She was too spirited for her own good sometimes. Jaron had visions of her being flown off to the Raken mountain city, never to be seen again. Or perhaps she hadn't *wanted* to ride the red firedrake but didn't feel she could refuse the lord of the Raken. Yes, that would be it. Jaron felt a surge of anger. He looked up at Flick, who stood watching him with one eyebrow raised.

'Where is Lord Hawke flying from?'

'The Lake of Ra, there's a good flying spot on the flattened hill just above it. I think it's called–'

'Barton Hill,' Jaron cut in. 'I'll see you there.' He sat on the bed and started to pull on a riding boot.

'But I said I'll take you.'

'Um, I have to look at the racing track where it cuts out onto the plains – Sprague's instructions. I'll be riding a kelpra so I'll see you there.'

'Oh.' Flick didn't seem to believe anyone could pass up the chance of a ride on a firedrake. 'Well, if you're sure.'

'I am, thanks.'

'Alright then.' Flick turned to leave. 'Doesn't sound much like a morning off to me though. See you later.'

Jaron didn't reply, busy with pulling on the other boot. He heard Flick whistle and looked up to see the young Raken rider standing on the balcony wall. To his amazement, he jumped off – and fell.

Horrified, Jaron ran in his half hopping gait out onto the balcony. Leaning over, he saw with relief Flick below soaring away on Tarp's back as the firedrake flew low over the city wall towards the grain barns.

Jaron shook his head. These Raken were mad, quite mad. He pushed away from the wall and went inside to get his tunic.

Before long Jaron was trotting away from the yard on Caliber. Tucker, allowed to be alone in the yard for washing out the feed bins, had held Caliber for him as he mounted up, all the while giving Jaron odd looks. Impatient to leave, he had ignored the younger boy's staring.

Caliber cantered between fields, bare now as the harvest was finished. Jaron let him stretch his neck in walk for a bit then pushed him on again. Caliber was only too willing; his ears were pricked and Jaron could tell he was enjoying being away from the track for a change. Jaron was grateful Sprague hadn't been in the yard or he would have questioned why he was riding on his morning off. As it was, Sprague wouldn't be pleased to have the star ride being ridden without him being present. Jaron was definitely going to get a telling off, but he was willing to face that for his mother's safety.

'Good boy, Cal.' Jaron patted the smooth arched neck as they moved into canter.

He hoped they wouldn't be stopped by anyone. Not that anyone would dare to get too close and this path out the back of the city was quiet. Caliber's ebony coat was sliced with thin blue stripes that ran widest across his muscular chest and shoulders but at a distance he looked solid black. Being horse-shaped meant they might just escape notice from afar. It still amazed Jaron the kelpra allowed a rider on their back at all. He smiled to himself. And now, seven months on, here *he* was; a rider on the favourite entry for the most prestigious race in the Corelands.

They were galloping around the white-stoned perimeter of the city wall when the Lake of Ra at the back of Tiara came into view. It was a huge lake, and its calm surface mirrored the clear blue sky. Jaron could see Barton Hill to one side of it and he tried to ignore the flip his heart did on seeing the great red beast already there, wings furled. He seemed to almost glow in the sunlight and it served to enhance Jaron's feeling of misgiving. Along the lake edge stood a few Tiarians clustered into little protective groups, watching the firedrake.

They were cantering towards the path that ran around the

lake when Caliber jerked up his head, ears flickering back and forth. Next moment, a shadow flashed over them and Jaron instinctively crouched in fear over Caliber's thick crested neck, looking up in time to see the green firedrake's pale brown underbelly momentarily blocking out the sun as it flew towards Barton Hill. When the firedrake had passed over it dipped slightly lower over the water and moved its body from side to side, waggling its outstretched wings. It was flying low enough for Jaron to see the bare-headed rider twist round and wave at him: Flick. Jaron gritted his teeth and muttered an oath under his breath. He pushed Caliber on, hearing the low warning rumble the kelpra made as he passed by the people that stood exclaiming. Thankfully, they were far down on the lake bank with their backs to them as they watched the green land, and Jaron was grateful to see the path ahead was empty; he was only too aware how dangerous it could be should someone be silly enough to come too close.

Heading for the clump of trees at the base of the low hill, Jaron stopped Caliber and slid off. Unclipping the chain (a thicker one this time), about Caliber's neck, he ran it around the mature oak's trunk and clipped the other end to the ring on the kelpra's thick leather headcollar, itself reinforced with an inlay of metal chain-link. It wasn't really done to leave such a beast unattended, and especially not the city's main hope for the Great Wake Race but it was another risk Jaron was willing to take for his mother's sake. He could only hope Caliber would be content after his blow-out to stand still and wait for him. At least they were far enough away from the firedrake watchers. He tested the chain; it should serve the purpose. 'Wait here Cal, won't be long,' he said and patted the kelpra. Caliber blew out through his nose and stepped forward to rend his claws down the trunk. 'Yes, have a good rake and I'll be back in a mo.' Jaron turned and ran, forcing his left hip to keep up in a hopping gait.

On reaching the base of the hill, he paused. He could see Flick's green firedrake was landed. Jaron looked back towards Caliber but the blue and black striped kelpra now had both forelegs wrapped around the trunk and was rubbing his chest up and down the bark, showing his fangs in full as he grinned in contentment.

Jaron took a deep breath to steady his sudden hammering heart and concentrated on getting up the rise of Barton Hill as quickly as he could. His room being on the top floor of the stable tower had stood him in good stead, and although his limp began to feel heavier as he climbed, he was halfway up before he knew it. Jaron deliberately hadn't been looking up at the firedrake to keep his courage, so he started in surprise when a voice spoke so close.

'Good morning.'

Lord Carna stood directly in front of him. The Raken's eyes were a strange light flint, Jaron saw now, and as they stared down at him the boy felt his heart quail under that piercing gaze. Standing slightly further up on the slope only added to the height and size of the Raken lord. His shoulders were broad but his wide chest tapered down to a flat stomach and long legs. By the time Jaron had remembered he was supposed to bow, the man had put out his hand. The boy stared down at it. He was a lord, however, and it wouldn't do to offend him.

Reluctantly, he took the offered hand and his own was immediately engulfed. The palm was rough and he winced a little at the strong grip. Carna smiled and Jaron looked away as he removed his hand, suddenly not caring if he was being rude.

'I didn't mean to startle you, Jaron.'

Surprised at the use of his name Jaron now saw the lord was studying his face gravely. For just an instant Carna's gaze shifted down to his neck and up again. Unbidden, Jaron's hand flew up, his eyes widening when his worst fears were confirmed; in his haste and panic this morning he had forgotten to put on a scarf. Flick must have seen as well, although he had given no indication. No wonder Tucker had stared at him earlier.

Defiantly, he raised his chin to expose the rippled neck further. *Look if you want. Look and see what your beasts can do.*

'You've come to watch Lord Hawke fly?' Carna asked, without batting an eyelid. 'A beautiful day for it.'

'Your rider told me my mother was here. I wanted to make sure she was alright.'

The Raken lord frowned down at him. 'Rella is fine. I would not allow any harm to come to her.'

Now he was calling his mother by name. Jaron glared up at him, lord or no.

'You can trust us Jaron, we are not barbarians.' Carna turned away to look up the hill.

Jaron stared, surprised at the remark. He followed Carna's gaze, saw Rella – and sucked in a sharp breath. His mother was dwarfed by the red beast and standing far too close, right in front of the wide blue scaly chest. He walked past the lord, his eyes raised to his mother. The firedrake turned its head towards them and Rella raised her arm and waved enthusiastically, apparently completely unconcerned that she stood directly under its nose. Jaron broke into an awkward, hopping run, ignoring the pull on the thickened skin as his left hip and thigh were forced to work more. He had to get to her before she lost her arm. *What on earth was she thinking?* Barton Hill rose more steeply and once he staggered, the muscles in his left leg trembling now beneath him; he wished he had his stick, but he forced himself to keep going.

'Mum!' he panted as he drew close, eyes on the huge firedrake towering above her.

'I'm glad you've come, son,' she was smiling and looked

unharmed, if a little flushed. Without replying he pulled her away from the beast.

'What are you *doing*?' he hissed.

She smiled innocently. 'I'm enjoying this beautiful sunshine. I did wonder if you were going to laze about in your room all day, but I think the fresh air is doing you good.'

Jaron stared. Her eyes were shining. It irritated him she could be so unaware of her own safety. 'You didn't leave me much choice, did you?' He was angry now and frightened being this close to the firedrake. The big red looked even bigger out in the open than in the courtyard. Taking his mother's arm again, he began to pull her further away from the monster.

She put a cool hand on his to get his attention. 'Jaron,' she smiled, 'it's fine. You must believe they will not hurt you.' Her voice was low and soothing.

'How can you say that? After everything we've been through! Did he force you, Mum, make you come here?'

'Carna? Of course not!' His mother pursed her lips.

'I won't allow you to get on that beast's back, Mum.' Jaron kept his voice low.

She stared at him. 'I've already done it, Jaron, and as you can see I have come to no harm.'

'What?' Jaron spluttered.

Carna had now reached the top of the hill and moved to stand beside his beast's shoulder while he watched them. Flick walked over to join him. Jaron found he didn't care if they heard or not.

'What did you expect me to think, Mother?' She knew he only called her that when he was angry. He eyed Tarp lumbering after his rider. 'I hear you're riding a firedrake, it has a blue chest. *Blue!* After all that we went through that night, that terrible…' He nearly choked on her betrayal and saw his mother's eyes suddenly moisten.

ogle。

'Darling Jaron,' she whispered. 'I am so sorry to have upset you. All red firedrake have the same blue chest. The captain of the guard told you that when he questioned you, remember?'

Jaron stared at her, stubborn, angry, and frightened all at the same time.

'But I can assure you Madrag is not a killer.' She reached out to grasp him by the shoulders. 'You have to accept the Raken were cleared of any blame and move on, son.'

'Accept them?' Jaron muttered, incredulous. He roughly shrugged off her hands, 'you want me to accept...' He looked up at the firedrake and anything else he was about to say froze on his lips as he saw the huge red beast take a step towards them over her shoulder. It rumbled from deep in its chest and swivelled its great head one way then the other to eye him with its bright yellow eyes half-lidded.

Jaron quickly stepped around his mother and kept her behind him as he walked slowly backwards. The beast followed his retreat by stretching out its neck. It lowered its head until its nose was level with his. As he froze and stared in wide-eyed horror it puffed directly into his face and he nearly choked in fear and disgust at the ash smell of its breath. Careful not to make any quick moves, Jaron tried to step further away but behind his back his mother resisted. To his disbelief her hands gripped his shoulders again, this time preventing his escape.

'He will not hurt you,' she said in his ear, her voice calm now, soothing. 'Don't let his size put you off – Madrag has always been a gentle soul with those he likes.'

Carna moved to his firedrake's head. 'No Raken firedrake would harm a human, Jaron, unless it is the case of defending their rider or it is directly under threat itself.'

Jaron didn't reply. He felt his mother's hands squeeze his shoulders. The red blinked its terrible eyes and pulled back, shortening its neck.

Flick joined them, quickly glancing at his lord. 'Hey, you made it.' He was smiling even though he must have witnessed Jaron's fear. Behind him, his green firedrake huffed. 'And Tarp greets you too. You're honoured, it's not often they take a shine to strangers.'

Jaron said nothing. His legs felt weak and he didn't trust himself to speak. Anger was replacing his fear. How could his mother put him through this? He shrugged off her hands and as he turned saw Rella exchange a concerned look with the Raken Lord. Jaron couldn't understand it. It was as if she was consulting with the man about him. What was anything he did to do with this man? He felt his hands bunch into fists.

Just then, Flick let out a loud sigh. 'Here he comes, your Lord Hawke.' The young Raken looked across at his leader, pleading with his eyes.

'Let's get this over with,' Carna said. 'It won't happen again, you have my word on it.'

Hawke paced up the hill dressed in his finest riding gear, eyes shining with excitement. He stopped short when he saw Jaron and Rella, obviously wondering what they were doing here. Carna approached him then and he gave a slight bow to the Raken lord. 'Good morning, Lord Carna.'

Carna merely nodded. 'Lord Hawke, we have Tarp here for you to ride, Flick's mount.' Carna indicated Flick who stood arms folded as he leant back against Tarp's shoulder. Carna stared over at the young rider and Flick sighed again, pushed himself straight and bowed to Hawke, who clapped his hands in delight.

'I am so looking forward to this!' Hawke said, forgetting to acknowledge Flick. He whipped out a pair of fur-lined green velvet riding gloves from his belt. They matched his tunic and breeches exactly, while the boots were polished and buffed. His cloak was fur-lined in the finest ermine; the young lord had obviously dressed up for the occasion, Jaron thought.

'Well, first you have to meet Tarp,' Flick said.

Hawke didn't deign to even nod in reply and eyed up Jaron and Rella, who Jaron had pulled safely away to one side. Rella dropped a short curtsy while Jaron kept a hand covering his neck as he bowed. Hawke kept his kelpra, Dash, at the yard although Jaron suspected it was more for prestige than any real interest in the beasts. He hadn't ridden since Dash had snapped at him a month ago, leaving Sanra to exercise him. Hawke's loud voice and imperious manner unsettled the beasts and put them all at risk. Sprague didn't encourage him to visit often.

'Why aren't you at the stables?' Hawke called across to Jaron now and pulled on his riding gloves while he waited for an answer.

'I've been given this day by Sprague, my lord,' Jaron answered, thinking that if only Hawke could read his thoughts he would know he would rather be anywhere else but here.

Carna took a few steps over to stand at Rella's side. 'I invited the boy and his mother,' he intoned, staring at Hawke.

Jaron stood passively as Hawke stared at him. The young lord was distracted then as Flick led a lumbering Tarp over with a hand under his firedrake's chin. They were more ungainly on the ground than Jaron would have thought.

Hawke strode impatiently towards Tarp. The firedrake stopped short at his confident approach and raised his head high on his long neck.

'Best stand still, my lord, and let Tarp have a sniff at you,' Flick said. He clicked at Tarp who cocked his head at his rider and lowered himself again. Flick led him right up to Hawke who did as he was told, looking in awe at the firedrake. Jaron didn't envy the young lord his ride. It felt surprisingly familiar, however, to hear Flick click to his firedrake just as he did to Caliber.

Tarp lowered his head and sniffed delicately at Hawke. He blew out a huffing snort and took a step back. Flick encouraged him forward again, but Tarp refused to lower his head nor even look at the lord. 'He won't take him,' Jaron heard Carna murmur. He raised his voice to call over. 'Lord Hawke, I'm afraid it won't be possible to ride Tarp today.'

'What?' Hawke was astounded. 'Why not?'

'The firedrake will not allow you on his back and we have to respect his wishes.'

'*His* wishes?' Hawke flapped a hand at Tarp. 'But he is just a beast!' He glared at Flick. 'Surely as his master you must insist he take me!' It looked to Jaron like he might even stamp a foot but he didn't. 'I demand you exercise your right as his rider!'

Flick froze and his eyes went flat.

Carna strode over, hand held aloft to the young Raken rider. 'You have no such rights, my Lord Hawke, where a rider and his firedrake are concerned. I am sorry,' he said, looking anything but.

Hawke gave the Raken lord a disgusted look. 'You are here at my father's request, I think you will find I have every right.' Then, before anyone could react, he had sprung to Tarp's side and grabbed hold of the stirrup that hung down next to the firedrake's belly.

Tarp gave an unearthly screech and reared up onto his hind legs, wings spread wide as he leapt away. Jaron gasped in fear and grabbed his mother's hand, pulling her further away down the hill. She let him do it, transfixed by the catastrophe unfolding on the hilltop.

Flick was trying to calm his firedrake but Tarp was too incensed to be placated. Swinging his neck round, he snapped at Hawke with a flash of long pointed teeth, but the young lord, eyes wide now with terror, flattened himself against the firedrake's side and was mercifully too close to Tarp's body; the teeth missed him by inches. Carna leapt to grab Hawke but Tarp gyrated away again, twisting and bucking in fury. Hawke seemed unable or too frozen with fear to let go of the stirrup leather. Tarp suddenly opened his wings and threw himself from the hill into the air, taking the young lord with him. Jaron could see Hawke's legs flailing as he was lifted away and felt his own heart quail in horror.

'Tarp!' Flick shouted, skidding to the plateau edge.

'Oh my,' Rella muttered, sounding remarkably calm. 'Stupid boy.'

'Scorched scales!' Carna swore. 'Flick!' He ran to his firedrake, Flick a step behind him. Carna jumped onto his red's lifted foreleg and swung himself up on Madrag in one fluent motion, grabbing Flick's outstretched arm to pull him up behind him. The red firedrake opened his wings, crouched, and gave an almighty leap into the air, sweeping his wings down in one powerful beat that caused Jaron and Rella to protect their eyes from the gust. When they lowered their arms Madrag was up, sharply angling his body as he banked on one wingtip to turn and pursue Tarp.

Tarp was terrible to hear – the green firedrake screamed and roared, dove and twisted in the air as he tried to dislodge Hawke. Rella eagerly dragged Jaron back up the rise to get a clearer view and, feeling a little calmer now the firedrake had lifted off, Jaron shielded his eyes with one hand as he watched, wondering how much longer the lord could hang on for.

Not much, as it turned out. Madrag was catching the smaller firedrake up as they flew over the lake when Tarp dropped a wing and, with a cry, the young lord lost his grip. Jaron gasped as Hawke fell like a stone, arms and legs thrashing madly. Carna put his firedrake into a dive after him, but it was too late. Hawke hit the water with an almighty splash, leaving Carna to level out just in time before they followed him in.

Mother and son stood side by side staring at the spot he

had gone into the water. 'There!' Rella said and pointed. 'See his head?'

Jaron squinted against the sun and could see Hawke's head bobbing up and down, his arms flailing. They listened to his faint shouts and cries.

'Oh my,' Rella said. 'Looks like our lord can swim, at least.' They looked at each other and Rella burst out laughing. Jaron felt the last of his adrenaline fizzing out of his fingertips.

'And you say they won't hurt us?' he said incredulously.

Rella's laugh cut off and she looked seriously at him. 'These won't, if you treat them right. I was brought up with the Raken, you often choose to forget that, darling.'

They watched a fishing boat rowing slowly out to where Hawke was still shouting and waving from the middle of the lake. Tarp had flown over to join Madrag and the two firedrake were now flying side by side. Jaron squinted from under his hand; he could make out Flick leaning over towards his firedrake on Madrag's back. Tarp moved to fly right below the big red. Then Flick leant even further out and suddenly fell from behind Carna.

'Oh!' Jaron said in surprise, but Flick landed safely right in the middle of Tarp's back. In fact, Jaron was certain Tarp had adjusted to make *sure* he caught his rider. He realised he was even thinking of the beasts by their names now. He shook his head, disgusted with himself. Then he remembered something and turned to his mother. 'You said something about Carna's firedrake.'

'Yes?'

'That he was always…' Jaron hesitated, hardly believing he was going to say this out loud to describe a firedrake. 'A gentle soul.'

His mother smiled. 'That's right, I always liked Carna's firedrake.' So, she had already known the Raken lord in her previous life. Jaron stared at his mother as he digested this.

T M MILLER

She must have noticed the look on her son's face for her own turned serious. 'I keep telling you, Jaron, the firedrake are not all like that wild rogue that burned our village. I spent many years with the Raken and for us the firedrake were part of our lives.'

'Us.'

'Hmm?'

'You said 'us' so you think yourself as one of them,' he pointed with his chin to the two firedrake who were now hovering over the fishing boat that was in the process of hauling Hawke, legs kicking, over the side. Rella didn't reply immediately and he tore his gaze away from the firedrake to look at her.

She stood facing him, arms folded. 'I do, Jaron, I always have done.'

Jaron swallowed. He made to turn away but she pulled him back towards her. 'I am of Raken blood, Jaron. They are my people and they are yours too.' She dropped her hand from his arm and gazed at him, waiting for him to digest her words.

'Oh,' Jaron said. He felt his throat constrict. 'I'm sorry, you stayed away because of me.' How could he not have seen this before, the sacrifices his mother was making for him?

She put her arm around his shoulders. 'Don't be, never be sorry. I don't regret it, of course I don't.' She stepped back and ruffled his hair, pushing back his fringe. 'You are my life, Jaron, and will always come first. I just knew you weren't ready.' She hesitated. 'I look on the firedrake coming here as a blessing, Jaron.'

A blessing. Jaron watched the firedrake flying back towards them. 'I thought he had asked you and you didn't think you could refuse, him being the lord of the Raken.'

'What?' She sounded angry for a moment, but then, unexpectedly, she smiled at him. 'Yet you came to rescue me, even though you were terrified.' She hugged him. 'You are very brave.'

'It will always be difficult,' Jaron said, his words muffled by her dress. 'I can't just change how I feel about them. And – and I don't see why I should, Mum.'

She held him away and looked him in the eyes. 'Jaron, I want you to be happy, son, regardless of how it turns out.'

The firedrakes' shadows fell across them. The beasts were pulling their wings out to brake. Jaron felt the fear fizz again and tried to ignore it. 'I thought they were going to fly you off,' he said and heard her laugh.

'As though I would leave you. Anyway,' his mother sighed, 'there's the race to get over first. I want you to concentrate on that, Jaron, give yourself every chance.'

Jaron nodded. 'Yes, I'll–' his eyes widened. 'Oh, Caliber! I've got to go.' He made to leave then hesitated. 'Mum? Coming with me?'

She looked over at Carna as his firedrake landed. 'I'll be heading off to the kitchens after you, son.' When he still didn't move she looked at him and smiled. 'I'll be fine, Jaron. Off you go.'

He had left Caliber too long as it was. With no other choice Jaron was forced to leave her with Carna and set off down the hill as fast as he could, his left hip jarring his knee at every step.

Caliber was fine, although the oak's trunk looked pretty shredded by now. The kelpra turned his head on hearing him approach. There was a thick log in his mouth and it splintered in two with one crunch of Caliber's strong jaws.

'Good boy,' Jaron said, relieved to see him still there. He managed to get onto the kelpra's back by standing on a rock. It wasn't easy, and his left hip felt heavy after all the running about he had done. He was grateful Caliber stood still and waited for him.

As he was cantering back along the length of the lake, he

came across a bedraggled Hawke being helped from the fishing boat to shore. Hawke glared at him with unsuppressed rage and Jaron studiously averted his eyes from the young lord as he passed.

When they approached the yard gates Jaron wondered how he would ever be able to conquer this fear; he wasn't sure that he wanted to. Something his mother said had been nagging at him and he turned their conversation over in his mind, searching for it as Caliber stopped of his own accord near the mounting block. Then he remembered what it was. She had said she wouldn't leave him. *'First, there was the race to get over.'* He wondered what was coming next and felt certain once the Great Wake was done she *would* leave, return to the city of Rakenar. And because he was still so scared of the firedrake he was going to be left behind.

6

In front of the packed stands, three horse races had already been run that morning in the growing heat. As was the pattern in Tiara, the plains sent blessed relief at noon in the form of a strong wind that now pulled at the flags spaced at intervals around the circular track. Tiara's own flag, red with a black bull and a sheaf of barley, stood tallest. There was palpable excitement in the air now as a wall of faces looked on in expectation of the highlight of the day: the Annual Kelpra Great Wake Trophy. Even the stewards earned applause as they started to lift the temporary fencing at one end of the track to open up the exit for the beasts to follow the cross-country part of the race. When the kelpra began to be released into the arena, the stewards retreated behind narrow protective walls of thick wood that stood at intervals around the edges of the arena. When Brill galloped in on Monty, the cheering swelled to a crescendo.

The noise didn't help Jaron's nerves any from where he waited in the kelpra racing yard. He was mounted up ready on Caliber, who now started jogging on the spot in his excitement. As the home favourite, they were the last to leave. The wait had been unbearable as the other entrants had been let out of their cages one by one and ridden out. Sprague and Liam's faces were now running in sweat from under their helmets. They both wore protective stiff leather armour to protect them, just in case.

'Ready?' Liam's red face was grinning up at him, a metal-banded glove pressed against Caliber's shoulder.

Jaron swallowed. 'As I'll ever be.' He pulled down his

goggles and shortened the reins.

Sprague had his elbow jammed into Caliber's neck on Jaron's other side and was straining with the effort of pitting his considerable brawn against the kelpra. 'He's eager, I'll say that,' he grunted.

Sanra and Tucker were waiting for them at the gates and pulled them open as the entourage approached. As Caliber jogged through they fell into step beside Jaron. 'Good luck,' Sanra said, her eyes shining with excitement.

Jaron thought his voice might betray his nerves so all he could do was smile his thanks. Tucker's red face looked like it was about to explode and he was too excited to even speak.

As they jogged up the tunnel, Sprague gave last minute instructions and Jaron tried to concentrate over the noise coming from the stands. 'Let him have a canter as you go in, you won't be able to stop him when the crowd welcomes you. He'll have a better chance of settling if he's moving through all that noise. Remember what I told you, keep your distance and don't be swept up with the crowd, don't lose your head and don't push him – you're not even a third of the way through at that point so conserve his energy.'

They were nearing the entrance.

'Watch out for that Kyrindian jockey, sneaky bugger,' Sprague continued. 'Tam always tells his jockeys to do whatever it takes. Remember the real race starts when you leave the stands behind.'

Caliber snorted as they looked out into the arena, still hidden from the crowd. Jaron felt the kelpra's body tremble beneath him. He tried to calm his own hammering heart and failed: he was too keyed up. Sprague held on while Liam checked the girth yet again. Jaron stared at the wall of faces opposite them on the other side of the track. From where they stood he could see two of the kelpra already in the arena. One bolted out of view and another was bucking in a frenzied fashion. Jaron's palms started to sweat and he wiped one then the other on his breeches; it wouldn't do to let the reins slip. He wondered from where his mother would be watching. *'Be safe,'* was all she had been able to manage earlier on before nearly squeezing the life out of him and making a quick exit, wiping at her eyes.

'I want all the details when you get back,' Liam winked. Jaron couldn't reply; his throat felt suddenly dry and his tongue like a wad of cotton.

'Alright?' Sprague asked Liam, who nodded. *'Now.'* They both let go at the same time and just managed to get clear as Caliber leapt forward. When he hit the ground, he was straight into a dead run.

They careered out onto the track. The crowd greeted their home favourite with a burgeoning roar. The biggest welcome of the day had been reserved for them and Caliber's ears flattened. For a moment Jaron lost all control of his kelpra as they galloped wildly across the arena. Fighting Caliber, he caught sight of a wall of faces looking down at them. The colours, the noise, it was incredible – and nothing like the other races they had taken part in. For a moment, Jaron clean forgot everything Sprague had taught him. He saw other kelpra leaping and rearing, shaking their heads and resisting their riders trying to hold them back. One bolted clean across their path and Jaron had to quickly jerk Caliber's head away before he went after it. But Sprague proved to be right: the wall of sound that continued to roar from the crowd at last caused Caliber to slow and Jaron took the opportunity to regain control; he nudged him up to the resistance of the bridle then kept him between hand and leg. At last, the kelpra eased back into canter – Jaron could breathe again.

Concentrating on Caliber had helped his own stage fright a little and Jaron cast about for the first time as he took proper stock of where the other kelpra were. The bolter was now being trotted in small circles by the rider in the

Lugasian colours but the Camorian kelpra was cantering towards Caliber, its rider still fighting for control. Caliber's ribcage vibrated as he snarled at this stranger. Jaron turned his head away and quickly sent him forward at a short gallop to get him out of its path. Looking over his shoulder he was relieved to see the other kelpra carry straight on.

Shouts of 'good luck' came from the crowd but Jaron didn't dare take a hand from the reins to acknowledge the support. Caliber snorted at all these other kelpra on his home turf and let out a huge roar that caused Jaron's body to shudder in the saddle. The audience laughed and clapped. There came an answering roar and Caliber stopped dead – causing Jaron to nearly go over his head – before he whipped around to look for the challenger. From the grassy area in the middle of the track Jaron saw the black and tan striped Teller with ears pricked and nostrils flared while he danced on the spot. Even from this distance Jaron could see Pache's sneering grin.

Jaron pushed Caliber on. 'Come on boy, settle down,' he pleaded. He moved closer to the jumps to give Caliber a chance to see them and caught sight of Pache waving to the crowd as Teller reared and pranced. Jaron envied the Kyrindian jockey his confidence.

Slowly the crowd's shouting subsided to a more bearable level and he felt Caliber's tense muscles begin to relax a little. Jaron eased him back into trot and headed towards the start where he could see most of the other kelpra circling. As he approached he saw two beasts rear up against each other, their noses wrinkled as they snarled, front claws reaching. The crowd oohed but an armoured steward darted between them and whipped the chest of one before ducking back out. The beast, distracted, came down and squealed. It whirled to kick out, missing the steward by a narrow margin. The kelpra had a hard pad set on their back heels, like a flat hoof that packed a heavy punch if they had to defend themselves from behind.

Two more stewards ran to help and the beasts were led away from each other. There was a ripple of applause at the man's bravery and he bowed in acknowledgment.

'All riders, line up!' a man resplendent in red uniform and feathered hat shouted from the wooden platform that was at the start line. His cloak whipped against his stout frame as he pointed the rolled flag to the ground in front of him.

The riders got into two lines and nosed forward with a lot of growling and baring of teeth from the kelpra, who were more interested in challenging each other. Jaron could see Brill and big, brown-and-white patched Monty up the front next to Pache on Teller. He kept Caliber in the thinner row behind and the kelpra shook his head as he fought the resistance, displeased with his rider. The starter unfurled the flag and slowly held it up with outstretched arm, Tiara's emblem rippling in the breeze.

The stands went eerily quiet in a collective holding of breath. The only sounds were the flapping of the flags around the arena and the occasional kelpra snort and snarl.

Jaron's arms were aching with the effort of keeping Caliber held; he felt the kelpra's haunches bunch up, lowering, and just as he was certain his mount was going to rear up on him, the flag swept down and the lead row surged forward.

The crowd roared anew and Caliber leapt into a dead run. In no time at all he was on the heels of the kelpra directly in front and track dirt was flying up into Jaron's face. Desperately Jaron tried to get his mount back; as they rounded the first bend he could see the hurdle coming up, fast. He pulled more on the reins, trying to get Caliber to take notice. Then there was no time left and Jaron had no other choice but to swing him out to one side of the racing group or get caught up with the kelpra in front. They just managed to keep in line with the hurdle enough to jump it. Caliber leapt flat and when the kelpra's front legs hit the ground he had already overtaken the leading row.

The crowd roared even harder.

'Too fast!' Jaron thought, he had to slow him up, conserve something. He put more pressure on the reins, but now Caliber had the bit between his teeth. 'Cal, ease up,' Jaron cried. Still they hammered on. In desperation, Jaron jiggled the reins, pulling one side, then the other in quick succession to get his attention. *Slow down, please Cal.* Amazingly, he felt his mount release his clenched teeth on the bit as though he had heard his thoughts. *At last.* Jaron rewarded him immediately by giving the reins a little as he went back into racing position. 'Good boy, good boy,' he chanted. His heart was pounding but there was no time for terror as the next fence was looming and Caliber took it without breaking pace. Jaron heard the thunder of the racing herd behind him as they landed. When they flattened out he swung Caliber to the outside lane again, keeping him away from the crowded inside track as they took the bend. A kelpra came past, its jockey wearing the blue and white Rapan colours and Jaron saw Brill and Monty the other side of him along with the rest of the runners. He could smell the earthy odour of kelpra sweat as the beasts ran shoulder to shoulder. Intent on running hard, all snarling and snapping had stopped.

The racers took another hurdle and Jaron, still on the outside line, saw one kelpra go down, tripped up by another that had got too close behind. The crowd gave a collective gasp.

Sensing danger, Jaron looked across and saw a rider-less kelpra running next to them. He risked moving his mount even further off the racing line and threw a glance over in time to see the kelpra fling out a foreleg to catch the back leg of the beast in front. The scream was terrible as the leader tripped and went down with its jockey, the loose kelpra falling on top; Jaron heard its loud snarl behind them merge with a human scream.

A sudden rush of bile came into his throat. His knees trembled, and not just from supporting his weight with his behind lifted off the saddle. Then the next hurdle was coming up and he was hard pushed to get back together for it. They jumped clean, however. Suddenly Teller was right next to Caliber. The crowd, which had been silent at the fallen rider's scream, roared even harder.

Jaron hoped the wall of sound would slow Caliber down but as Teller pulled ahead the stallion ran even faster.

'*Look to the bigger picture*,' Sprague's words came into his mind. '*Don't get swept up with the crowd...*'

'Cal, no!' But his mount lowered his head and set his neck against him. Jaron sat down and leant back in the saddle, using his weight to pull harder – but this time Caliber was having none of it. The blue-blazoned kelpra accelerated after Teller, who passed the two Rapan entries and one of the Camorians. Teller was now leading up ahead and as they, too, passed the other kelpra Caliber's ears were pricked; he had the Kyrindian kelpra in his sights, Jaron realised. For Caliber, this was the home straight.

In no time at all they were at Teller's tail, past his striped pounding haunches and then Jaron was right up alongside Pache. The Kyrindian jockey flashed him a look that froze his blood. Then Pache grinned and bent lower over Teller's neck; he was going to take him on for the crowd.

They met the fifth hurdle together and Jaron felt the bunch, then the thrust of the hind quarters, the incredible lift that sailed him over the jump. Lean back, take the jar from the landing that runs up the shoulders, watch the head come up, collect the reins, feel the back condense as the hind legs work underneath, fold your body and get back into position. *Go with him*, he decided – too much energy would be used by both of them if he fought the kelpra now.

He bent low and gave the reins, just a little bit.

And Caliber took wing and flew for him.

It felt like Jaron was floating; it felt like everything slowed. Caliber lengthened and travelled at such speed over the track his stride seemed to eat up the ground. He hardly slowed to take the last hurdle and they landed with no other kelpra near them.

Jaron became aware for the first time the arena had fallen silent in what seemed to be shock. It was short-lived, however, for just then the spectators erupted into such noise as he had never heard before. Caliber's ears meshed further flat to his head but he didn't slow as they flashed past what would be the finishing line when they entered the arena for the last time. He looked over his shoulder to see Teller at least eight kelpra lengths behind him. The crowd were applauding and chanting Caliber's name as they galloped under the decorated archway and out onto the Plains of Wake.

The kelpra slowed significantly and Jaron let out an explosive breath. The boy lengthened his reins and took the chance to let Caliber stretch his neck down and blow out before the others caught up with them.

'It's not over yet, boy,' he said as he patted him, gathering up the reins again.

Pache passed them just then without casting a glance Jaron's way. Teller's neck and shoulders were covered with frothed sweat and Pache's long thin face was etched with rage and disbelief. Now they all knew what Tiara's favourite could do. Jaron grimaced and wondered if Pache would make him pay, but more importantly, would Caliber pay, his endurance spent on that last run?

His left hip was aching. It felt sore too and Jaron sat down in the saddle to slip his foot out of the stirrup iron to stretch the thickened scar tissue. A kelpra came up alongside, quite close, and Jaron had to hurriedly scrabble with his toe to find the stirrup again.

It was Brill and Monty. The huge patched beast looked in good shape after the first part of the race. He had a keen eye and his ears were pricked forward as he cantered easily beside his yard mate. The two had squared up against each other in the past, with threatening growls and some snapping. Now, with so many strange kelpra about, the two appeared more willing to accept each other. That was only the kelpra of course.

Brill lifted his goggles and looked over, his face covered with track dirt and rivulets of sweat. 'You might well have just run your race, Scar,' he said to Jaron. 'A more *experienced* jockey, a *stronger* jockey, would have been able to hold him.' While Jaron stared at the older boy he sneered back before kicking Monty on ahead.

Jaron watched them cantering away. Not much hope Brill would watch his back then.

There were no more spectators, they were all banned from watching the cross-country part of the race for their own safety. As the pack followed the bright yellow markers placed at intervals along the route Jaron welcomed being away from the noise of the arena. Out here, the only sounds were the odd creak of leather and the heavy breathing of the kelpra, along with the occasional warning snarl if they inadvertently got too close to one another. The scream of that fallen rider broke into Jaron's thoughts. With an effort, he pushed it out of his mind. *They all knew the risks.* Without the kelpra, Jaron would still be scrubbing pans in the palace kitchens.

By the time the pack had left the Plains of Wake behind and entered the dense Rotarn Forest that nestled at the base of the Notresia Mountains, the riders had all lifted their goggles to cool down, and Jaron was grateful to pass into blessed shade. The forest sat at the edge of the plains and marked the northern border of Tiara's lands just before the mountains. Sprague had told him it was the first time it had been included as part of the race, and the route would involve the River Not. 'Let him drink his fill there,' Sprague had said. 'Some think it does them no good to run on a stomach full of water but I've never had a problem with that. Better he's refreshed fully.'

Caliber was skittish in the woods, they were eerily silent and no birdsong came to Jaron's ears. Amongst the trees large rocks and boulders were dotted, evidence the Notresia mountains sat at the forest border. The Camorian mount suddenly darted forwards and nearly got a hind foot in the face from Teller. Pache's mount was sweating more than any of them and Pache whipped him often when he slowed too much.

Suddenly, the kelpra all speeded up, ears pricked and nostrils flaring as they scented the air. The pack burst out of the woods onto the bank of a wide silver ribbon flowing sluggishly through the forest. They spread out as they eagerly entered the river, lowering their heads to drink from the cool water. The riders, too, were leaning half out of their saddles as they hung over one side to reach down with cupped hands.

Jaron pushed Caliber further out until the water lapped around the kelpra's stomach so he could reach and quench his thirst. He leant over to one side, hanging onto the saddle for support, and noticed how the water was so clear he could see the river bed. He reached down and dipped his hand into the cold water, cupping his palm. It tasted clean and eased his parched throat. Jaron wished he had time to dip his sore hip into the river.

Suddenly, with an unexpected hard shove on his shoulder, he got his wish. With a heavy splash – he was in.

Cold water shocked his hot body and Jaron came up gasping and thrashing. More water forced itself into his mouth; he gurgled and spat then realised he was being towed, his arm caught in the reins as Caliber, panicking, had leapt further out into the middle of the river. They were now so deep the kelpra was swimming against the current, his head held just out of the water as he snorted loudly. The water pushed the boy further back towards Caliber's rump and frantically he kicked and scrabbled to grab hold of the saddle flap, one arm still caught in the reins. His boots were full of water, their weight pulling him down. Gasping, Jaron fought to grope his way up towards the saddle pommel. At last, his fingers clutched hold and he frantically tried to get some leverage. The buoyancy of the water became his ally and he managed to haul his chest onto the saddle and throw a leg over to sit astride, his damaged hip muscles burning with the effort.

'It's alright, boy,' he gasped, grabbing hold of the reins again, even though they were anything but. In answer, Caliber, still swimming, rolled a panicked eye back at his rider. Jaron turned Caliber's head towards the bank and encouraged him forward with his heels. As the kelpra swam closer, Jaron searched with some difficulty for the stirrup leathers as they floated with the current. At last, he managed to slot his feet into the irons just before Caliber got a paw hold and began to lurch and leap to get clear. His head was held high and Jaron could see the kelpra was losing his nerve. He shortened the reins and assumed command, steadying himself and stroking a calming hand on his mount's neck before urging Caliber on towards the bank. Once there, the kelpra stood trembling, his flanks heaving.

'Easy there,' Jaron stroked the thick dripping neck. He looked around and was relieved to see the bank further upriver where the kelpra had first entered the water. It was empty of the other entrants. They had not been carried so very far down after all thanks to Caliber's strong swimming. Jaron set his jaw; he didn't doubt it was Pache who had pushed him, since Jaron had passed him as he had gone deeper to quench his own thirst. Well, he might just do the same to him when he caught up with the bully.

Once Caliber had regained his breath, they splashed along the shallows until they reached the bank where they had come in. Looking down, Jaron could see the paw prints of the others and where they had left to continue into the forest. He nudged Caliber with his heels and the kelpra broke into a canter. Jaron bent low over his neck as they followed the path, showering water droplets onto the leaves as they passed.

It was horrible riding in wet clothes and squelching boots. As he rode, Jaron got more and more angry. He could have drowned but they had all left, including Brill. For the first time Jaron started to wonder whether the race was really worth all this. Again, he remembered the jockey's terrible scream from back in the arena; horses would not have tried to eat their riders.

Just then, a kelpra roar filtered through the trees ahead. Fuming, Jaron sent Caliber faster. He bent low to avoid a branch and ground his teeth – when he caught up with Pache…

Caliber galloped round a narrow bend. His head went up, ears pricked, and Jaron gasped in horror. Just in time Caliber jumped to avoid trampling the kelpra that lay flat out in their path, a long spear protruding from its side. Horrified, Jaron twisted in the saddle to look back at it, in time to see a spear slice across the path behind them, whistling past Caliber's haunches. Throwing up his head in panic Caliber charged forward. They entered a clearing, and the kelpra skidded to a halt.

A body lay face down in front of them.

7

The Rapan entrant lay on his face, legs and arms sprawled at sickeningly odd angles. Jaron lifted his shocked gaze to see tall, bulky figures attacking the kelpra with spears and axes. They wore only rough woven tunics and were wide-shouldered with arms and legs covered all over in hair, like fur. They could only be... *Ernots!* Shouts and screams of the riders rent the forest air mingled with kelpra snarls and the guttural battle cries of the mountain men. For a stark moment boy and beast froze. In the clearing, the Ernots had the kelpra separated and were clustered around each one. Jaron pulled Caliber's head round, intending to escape into the woods, then hesitated; he couldn't find it in himself to run and leave the others, not even Brill.

'Help me!' a Lugasian rider, a boy not much older than Jaron, ran towards him, his eyes wide with terror. Without a thought Jaron turned Caliber back and kicked him on, not daring to call out encouragement lest he draw attention to them. The boy stumbled towards him, blood trickling down his face. He kept on shouting and Jaron saw an Ernot spin towards him.

'Come *on!*' Jaron urged, bending lower over Caliber's neck, hand outstretched. Caliber was closing but the mountain man moved quicker than his bulk suggested. The boy saw him coming too and faltered, his face a mask of horror. The Ernot's bulk blocked the boy from Jaron's sight.

A wrenching scream.

'No!' Jaron rammed Caliber into the broad back, knocking the Ernot flying. Beyond he saw the boy was down, not moving. Another Ernot ran towards them. Jaron tried to turn his mount, but it was too late and a large hairy hand caught hold of Caliber's bridle. The kelpra screeched and reared. Jaron looked down to see a blunt face with a heavy forehead covered in brown hair and black teeth grinning up at him through the beard. In desperation, he slashed his whip across the Ernot's hairy face and the man snarled as he tore the whip from his grasp. Under the bulbous forehead deep-set eyes flashed with anger as he reached for him. But the Ernot had taken his attention off Caliber, who twisted and threw out a foreleg, claws primed. It raked down the neck and chest of the Ernot who made a gurgling sound as he toppled to the ground, Caliber's bridle still in his hand. Snorting, the kelpra clawed his twitching body.

Another Ernot came running across the clearing. Caliber saw him too and roared as he turned to meet him. Jaron saw the mountain man lob an arm forward. He desperately tried to nudge Caliber over with his knee – but without a bridle it was all too slow. A sudden, shocking pain caused him to scream and clutch at his thigh. *A knife...* He nearly came off as Caliber whirled to meet the Ernot's charge. The kelpra lunged and clamped his jaws around the neck of the Ernot, whose thick hands flailed and punched at the kelpra's nose. Jaron saw his eyes widen in terror as he clawed desperately at the beast's chest. Caliber shook him, hard, and wet spots spattered over Jaron's face before the broken body was slung aside. Swaying in the saddle, Jaron looked down in disbelief at the knife protruding from his left leg. Bile rose in his throat along with sick, gut-wrenching pain. More Ernots came. Thick-fingered hairy hands reached for him, trying to get a hold. He screamed, but Caliber suddenly broke through a gap, Jaron slipping to one side and only just in time managing to save himself by grabbing a handful of mane. The kelpra galloped across the clearing but here there was a large rocky outcrop just beyond the scrub: they couldn't get past. He skidded to a halt and spun round on his haunches to face his enemies. Beyond them, Jaron caught sight of Monty galloping past, blood on his haunch, Brill low over his neck. The huge kelpra cannoned into an Ernot that tried to stop them, knocking him flying. They flashed into the trees and were gone.

At least one had got away. From his slumped position, Jaron could only watch as the Ernots approaching them slowed. They were shoulder to shoulder, half-crouching with knives and axes held ready. Seven. Too many, there was no way through. And the valiant kelpra was nearly spent, his flanks heaving.

'Good boy,' Jaron whispered to him. 'Brave boy, Cal.'

The Ernots stepped closer, axes held ready. The kelpra snarled, lowering into a defensive crouch. They moved forward another step, more cautious with this one. Jaron closed his eyes, for a moment seeing his mother's face in his mind. He opened them again to see Pache being dragged from Teller on the other side of the clearing. Teller was down on his knees, an Ernot's arm snared in his jaws. Another Ernot swept up an axe, and brought it down.

Pache screamed.

And a sudden channel of fire roared down from above. The Ernot holding the axe simply disappeared, engulfed by flames.

Jaron instinctively threw up his arms, the Ernot's screaming ringing in his ears. Caliber reared – and he fell backwards, rolling over the kelpra's rump and hitting the ground, a tortured cry wrenching out of his throat as the knife sticking out of his thigh tore at his flesh as it was knocked out. Weak from pain, he lifted his head.

A huge red firedrake was flapping into the clearing, tearing the leaves from the trees with the force of its wings. It slowly circled in the air, letting loose another roaring channel of fire that slammed into the Ernots running towards it with axes and spears raised. Terrible screams rent the air and Jaron saw the sickening sight of bodies thrashing wildly on the ground amongst the flames. Another two came at the firedrake from the back, but a long thick tail whacked into them, sending them flying backwards and right into a beam of flame that suddenly razed down from above.

Jaron squinted through the smoke now curling up. Lord Carna, sitting tall in the saddle. And Madrag. He felt relief course through him. But then the terrible smell of burning flesh that he remembered so well reached his nose and he nearly gagged.

But he was not saved yet. An Ernot, fleeing from the red beast, was running towards him. Alarmed, Jaron flipped over and found the strength to yell, 'Caliber!' But the kelpra was off to one side, caught up with twisting the head off an Ernot. Jaron frantically dragged himself backwards through the scrub, but his back came up against rock. Glinting eyes fixed on him. An axe swept up. He screamed.

Something snaked down so fast it was a green blur. There was a flash of teeth, and the Ernot was snatched around his torso and flung away like a rag doll. His guttural scream abruptly cut off as he slammed into a tree and dropped to the ground in a broken heap.

Jaron blinked. Small stones suddenly cascaded down onto him and he raised his arm for protection as he twisted painfully to look up.

A firedrake's head was hanging directly above him, wings flapping as its claws scraped on the outcrop of rocks. Its position seemed familiar somehow. And looking over his shoulder was a face... Jaron tried to focus. It was Flick's face... and Tarp. He looked back across the clearing and saw the red beast had landed. Carna was leaning over in the saddle, his head turning, searching.

'He's here!' Flick's voice shouted from above. Carna's head jerked round towards them and Madrag's neck folded in. His fire eyes fixed on Jaron.

Caliber slunk across to stand next to his fallen rider, flanks heaving. 'It's alright, Cal,' Jaron said. He wondered if the kelpra had even heard him, his voice was so weak now.

The red firedrake took a step towards them, long claws digging into the earth. Incredibly, Caliber moved forward, snarling a challenge. Madrag's nose curled up in a return snarl so loud it reverberated round the clearing. Caliber backed up slightly, ears pricked.

'Please don't hurt him,' Jaron called weakly. 'He's only protecting me. I wouldn't be alive if it wasn't for him. Please.' Carna stared at him, then at the kelpra.

'He won't leave the boy's side,' a calm, deep voice called down from above the clearing. A green was hovering in the air there, its rider looking at Caliber.

Carna's gaze shifted to above Jaron's head. 'Flick, can you lift the beast?' he called out. 'Will Tarp do it?'

'Yes, if I get him by surprise,' Flick replied. 'Tarp lifts all the time in the games… slightly different cargo though.'

'Okay, get him ready,' Carna tapped his firedrake's neck on the right side. It snaked its head over, luminous yellow eyes never leaving the kelpra. Caliber growled anew and stepped aside from Jaron to follow the firedrake's movement.

Suddenly, more stones showered over Jaron from above, who flinched then stared in amazement as the green firedrake, boosting down from the rock, grabbed the surprised beast around his middle in a vice-like hold with his scaled front legs, wings flapping. Jaron threw up an arm against the draught then watched, astonished, as his mount was lifted into the air, struggling against Tarp's chest, legs thrashing and screaming with rage. He tried to bite, but Tarp had him under the armpits and he couldn't reach anything. Tarp's wing beats were laboured as Flick brought him to hover over Carna, who shouted up at the young rider with a cupped hand, 'Get him to the Plains – if Tarp can bear it – the beast can find his own way back from there.'

Flick nodded and with a last look over at Jaron he turned Tarp. With their yowling, snarling cargo they flew away over the forest.

The boy flopped back, relief flooding through him. Caliber at least was safe – terrified, but safe. He closed his eyes.

'Jaron?' a deep voice said, surprisingly close.

'I'm alright,' Jaron murmured. Strong fingers caught his chin and tilted his head back. Liquid poured into his mouth. He swallowed painfully at first, then, as the cool water soothed his throat, his eyes snapped open.

'Easy now,' the voice said as the water bottle was taken away. The Raken lord's tanned face was directly in front of him, the steely grey eyes regarding him solemnly. 'Jaron, where else are you hurt?' The boy felt fingers probing his chest through his thin racing shirt and winced with pain. 'Bruised ribs, I think,' Carna said to someone at his shoulder. Carna's hand moved to his leg and gently peeled back his torn, blood-soaked trousers.

Another face swam into view. *Leathery...* He recognised it from somewhere. *Val, yes, that was it.* 'Not too deep, looks like knife rather than spear,' Val said. 'It can't be poisoned or he'd be dead by now.' There was a tearing sound just before Carna's hands gently lifted his thigh. Val wrapped a rough strip of cloth around it and Jaron grimaced at the pain as he felt the makeshift bandage pulled tight.

'The others...' he began, but Carna cut him off.

'It's alright, Jaron, we're seeing to them.'

'How...?'

'We were following you at a distance, but lost sight of the kelpra under the trees. Thankfully, Madrag has sharp eyes. Try not to speak for now, I'm going to lift you. I'll be as gentle as I can.'

Jaron nodded. Carna lifted him gently, but still he couldn't stop a small groan escaping. He ached everywhere, and his thigh throbbed with renewed vengeance while his head swirled in a thickening red mist of pain. Carna carried him across the clearing, crowded now with Val's green landed next to the red. Another green landed on the outcrop of rocks that Tarp had recently vacated. The clearing was a terrible sight. Riders, some laying deathly still, others stirring and moaning, were dotted amongst bloody kelpra bodies and the smouldering blackened carcasses of Ernots. Jaron saw Val was now kneeling over Pache, who sat with one hand to his head, his face turned towards the body of Teller, a hand laid on his mount's blood-matted shoulder. The kelpra lay on his chest, eyes closed as though he were only sleeping.

Carna's firedrake lowered his head towards them as they approached and Jaron tensed, staring at the red beast. If Carna felt his body go rigid in his arms, he ignored it and didn't pause as he strode over to his huge 'drake.

'No, wait,' Jaron protested weakly. 'I can't–'

'You must, there is no other way, Jaron.'

He was suddenly hefted onto a shoulder, groaning as his ribs jarred him. With his head hanging over Carna's back as he stepped up, Jaron caught sight of Pache being pulled up onto Val's firedrake.

'No. Wait,' he protested.

But now his body was being slid back down. For just a moment he was nose to nose with the Raken lord. His own wide eyes must have shown his terrified fear, but Carna's gaze was completely calm and seemingly unaffected by all the horror around them. The lord gently placed Jaron sideways in front of him, careful not to touch his injured thigh. A strong arm went about his shoulders to hold him against Carna's chest. 'You will be quite safe, Jaron.'

Mind frozen, Jaron couldn't reply. Carna clicked with his tongue, and Jaron's stomach fell away as the great beast leapt into the air with what seemed impossible speed. As the firedrake's wings snapped fully open, Jaron's stomach lurched back into place again. The boy tried to breathe but it came out in short panting gasps. Where he sat the front ridge of a great red wing rose and fell beneath his dangling feet, and he could see a single large hooked claw at the front fold of the wing, gleaming in the sun. He looked away and saw Val on his firedrake already up in the sky, Pache sat astride in front of the rider and clinging to a neck scale with both hands.

They circled over the clearing and Jaron stared down at the battleground of bodies amongst the curling smoke. It wasn't until the green below lifted off, with another rescued rider slumped over the front of the saddle, that the wing beside him suddenly rose, blocking everything below from Jaron's sight. They were turning.

Jaron stretched his neck to see round Carna's arm. The other two greens were behind them now – and getting smaller, he realised. They were flying away from them. *Why were they going in the opposite direction?* some part of his frayed mind asked as the forest canopy passed by far below. The Notresia Range, with its stark jagged mountains, slid past underneath. They were definitely leaving Tiara behind. He wanted to ask why, but as another wave of nausea took him Jaron couldn't manage it. He turned his face away into Carna's chest. On top of his pain, and after the strain of the race and the attack – it was all too much. The boy finally gave it up and let the red swirling mist thicken and draw him down.

8

Jaron stirred and snuggled further under warm blankets. He felt so comfortable he dozed for a while longer; the bed was so unlike his own hard bunk in his room. As this thought sunk in, he frowned against the feather-soft pillow. Still reluctant to come fully awake, he rolled over on to his other side.

Pain jabbed from his thigh and with a low cry he opened his eyes and sat up, hand flying to his ribs as they protested the movement. Exploring his leg, his fingers came up against stiff cloth under what felt like woollen trousers. Jaron lifted the blanket and peered through the half-light, tugging up the trouser leg. Clean bandages swathed his left thigh. Jaron stared at the dressing, remembering the knife. He pulled the blanket back up and winced again at his ribs. The shirt he was wearing was unfamiliar.

Raising his gaze Jaron saw a large lantern burning softly from where it was set in the wall, throwing flickering shadows across the rough stone. There were no windows and Jaron tilted his head back to look up at a rounded stone hewn ceiling. He was in a cave, he realised then, but not of the damp, dark variety. A wide, soft leather chair sat in one corner with a colourful blanket thrown across the arm, a wooden table next to it with legs carved in a leaf pattern. On the other side was another lantern, its candle burning. A set of drawers stood against this wall with a jug resting on top along with a neatly folded cloth.

Jaron sat up carefully. His head swam even with that small effort and he waited, eyes closed, until it felt the room had stopped moving. His ribs were sore but not too painful now he wasn't lying prone. Propped up on his pillows, Jaron stared across from his bed to two enormous wooden doors that spread the width of the room. Set within these was a smaller, normal-sized door. Jaron eyed it for a bit then threw back the blankets, swinging his legs out with a grunt as his sore ribs protested. His feet landed on a warm fur rug and he wiggled his toes against the generous hair while rubbing at his thigh. Carefully, he stood up, his injured leg sending another dart of sore pain as the pierced muscle was forced to strain. Despite his swimming head there was no faintness although his knees wobbled and he wondered how long he had been unconscious. He took a step forward and nearly fell over when his damaged leg remained left behind. Regaining his balance, he tried again, this time just managing to lift his stiff hip enough to clear his foot from the floor. Hobbling badly, Jaron made it across to the chest and found water in the jug. He looked for a vessel to pour it in and saw it back on a little table by his bed that he hadn't noticed; a tankard that he assumed must be already full. Not having the energy to retrace his steps instead Jaron picked up the jug and drank deeply from it, feeling a small measure of strength returning to him as his thirst was quenched.

Leaning against the chest and wiping his mouth with the cloth, he stared at the small door. Setting down the tankard and cloth, he lurched over to the wall to use it for support. When he reached the door, breathing hard even with the short effort, Jaron tugged at the handle. The door wouldn't give and the panicked thought crossed his mind that he was shut in. He pulled harder still, and to his relief the thick wood swung open with a creak. A blast of cold air rushed through, so unexpectedly powerful it nearly knocked him over. He managed to catch himself and poked his head out into the wind.

A rock ledge spanned out from the door, wide and worn

smooth. The view beyond it was of an alien landscape and Jaron stared in disbelief. Mountains rose up against a cloudless blue sky, bunched close together like rotten teeth, and he counted four from where he stood. Each seemed to be made up of layers of different coloured stone and all along the lighter ridges were holes, like burrows that had been bored into the mountain face at various levels. Or like caves, he realised, caves like the one he was standing in now – with no way out or off. Fear clenched his throat. Was he in a prison of some sort?

He held onto the door frame for support against the wind before leaning out for a better look. His shirt plastered flat against his skin and he shivered in the cold blast, not trusting he would even be able to manage the step. Craning his neck, he saw a wide grassy basin nestled in front of the mountains with a river meandering through it that opened into a lake. There were small figures of people moving alongside the wide ribbon of water. The mountain air was so cold and crisp it burned his nostrils. Jaron tried to keep calm. *Prison would not have such a soft bed*, he told himself, *nor take care to make him well again, there was no need to panic*.

Just then, he saw the firedrake. It was wheeling in the air above him. With an open mouth he stared at it in disbelief. He saw another coming over a mountain, soaring into the air above the grass plateau. As he watched it angled its wings and dipped lower, riding the wind. Before he had time to let his breath go there came another, and another – until the air was full of screeching green firedrake. They wheeled in clouds so thick they darkened the sky and Jaron stared, mind still trying to register what he was seeing, his ears assailed by the volume of their calls. Now and then one would peel off to land on one of the ledges, until the whole flock was moving, separating out to land at their various caves. Jaron saw riders dismounting and walking inside while their firedrakes furled their wings and settled out on the ledges.

'Rakenar,' the word came out in a hoarse whisper. He was in the northern mountain city of the Raken, at a ledge where firedrake came in to land.

Next moment he was turning, ignoring the pain. Nearly falling, he saved himself by grabbing the door edge. Fear gave him extra strength and with an almighty push he managed to get the thick door shut and leant against it, eyes closed as he held his ribs while his breath came in short strangled gasps.

'Jaron?' He lifted his gaze to see his mother standing in the room. With tears in her eyes Rella lifted her arms and her son stumbled across to fall into his mother's clutching embrace.

'But why are we here? Why didn't Lord Carna take me back to Tiara?' Jaron was back in bed and Rella had pulled up the chair to sit beside him.

'Carna wanted us both here, Jaron,' she paused. 'He blames Bell, as do I.' When Jaron stared at her, uncomprehending, she sighed. 'I don't know why Bell thought to put the racecourse so close to the Ernots' territory, it was asking for trouble.' She pursed her lips. 'In his usual self-important way, he thought the Ernots were beaten after their raids were thwarted by the firedrake. He gave little thought to the danger he put you all in.' She brushed her long hair away from her face and Jaron thought how drawn and tired she looked. He squeezed her hand where it lay entwined with his on the blankets.

'I'm sorry,' he whispered. 'I thought of you, when it looked like it was all over...' He closed his eyes, remembering. 'All those riders... I saw one die right in front of me. I tried to reach him. Mum, it was terrible.'

Rella's hand stroked his cheek and rested there, her hazel eyes haunted. 'Such a waste of young life.' Jaron nodded, he remembered how he had come to the same conclusion. 'I saw a rider killed, Jaron,' she whispered. 'Right there in front of my eyes in the arena. You were racing next to that kelpra at one point.'

So the jockey hadn't survived. His mother continued in the same strained low voice. 'And the crowd, it wasn't long before they were cheering again. It felt like we were throwing you all to the lions, as if you were mere fodder for our entertainment.'

'Was Brill alright?' Jaron asked.

'Yes, we waited and the crowd were getting impatient. When he came riding into the arena, the beast was stumbling and they both looked exhausted.' Rella sat straighter, her eyes shining now with anger. 'The crowd cheered then, and Lord Bell stood up and shouted that Tiara had won the Great Wake. Even I could see something was wrong, but they were all blind, or refused to see. Even after we got the full story it didn't seem to cross Bell's mind to take back his claim.' She shook her head in disbelief.

'Carna said he was following us,' Jaron said. 'Did you know?'

'He offered to.' She watched him. 'Thank the Gods.'

Jaron silently agreed. 'How many survived?' he asked in a small voice.

'Four, including Brill,' she swallowed. 'And including you,' her eyes suddenly filled with tears and she leaned in to press her forehead against his. After a moment, she sat back and wiped at her eyes. 'Sorry, I said I wouldn't do this when I spoke to you.' She took a deep breath. 'When we heard what had happened, Bell didn't even stop celebrating.' This last was spoken in disgust. 'That nice young rider, Flick?' Jaron nodded. 'Came to find me and flew me straight here. He said you were injured, but alive.'

'Did Flick bring Caliber back?' Jaron asked, but Rella stared at him, uncomprehending, and he felt his heart sink. 'Tarp was carrying Caliber.'

His mother shook her head. 'Flick didn't say anything about the kelpra. You can understand I wasn't too concerned about that beast, I had you on my mind.'

'But he saved me! Mum, if it hadn't been for Caliber I wouldn't have made it. Is Flick here? I've got to find out what happened!' He made to get out of bed but his mother gently pushed him back against his pillows. She pulled the blankets back in place and tucked them in.

'Shhh now, there'll be time for that later. I want you to rest some more. Can you eat anything?'

'I don't know,' Jaron frowned, distracted.

'Well, you've been out of it for days. You must eat something. I'll get you some soup.' His mother stood and ruffled his hair, then bent down and wrapped her son in her arms. Jaron breathed in her familiar jasmine scent as they held each other in silence.

At last, Rella released him and stood up, tucking her hair back and smoothing her skirt. Jaron saw her eyes were wet but she forced a smile. 'Won't be long,' she said and went over to pull at a curtain hung in a back corner of the cave he hadn't noticed. As she swished the curtain back, an entrance was revealed carved into the rock. She gave him another smile over her shoulder before being swallowed by shadow.

Alone, he stared ahead at the huge wooden doors at the end of his bed while terrible images flashed across his mind. *Only three others.* His throat tightened and he swallowed, took a shaky breath. And Caliber hadn't made it back. What had happened? He felt terrible, like he had abandoned his mount. You never did that, Sprague had always said look after your animals first. But Brill was okay, that was something. He wondered too about Carna offering to follow the race, then sighed. Answers would have to come later. In the meantime, despite what his mother had said, there was no way he was going to stay in Rakenar, no way at all.

When Rella returned, Jaron saw there was someone

standing behind her, lifting the curtain to make way. His mother walked across to the bed holding a tray with a steaming bowl and a plate of bread but Jaron's welcoming smile for her died when he saw it was Lord Carna who followed.

He strode over to stand by Jaron's bed, across from Rella who placed the tray on the blankets.

'I am glad to see you are awake, Jaron, how are you feeling?

'Much better, thank you.' He hesitated, it didn't seem enough. 'I'm very grateful you took the trouble to follow us, my lord. If you hadn't–'

Carna batted his thanks away with a raised hand. 'I am only glad to bring you back alive. It's a terrible business.' As he spoke his tanned smooth face grew dark and Jaron saw a flash of anger cross the grey eyes, turning them instantly to hard flint. Jaron lowered his gaze. 'Our healer has been pleased with your progress,' he heard Carna say. 'The wound has cleaned up well, but it is deep and you need rest.'

Out of the corner of his eye Jaron saw his mother shudder.

'The bleeding helped to clean the wound,' Carna continued. 'Rest assured our healers are the best and it is mending well. You are both very welcome here, consider Rakenar your home from now on.' This last was said with a slow smile for Jaron's mother.

Their home! 'Oh no, we couldn't possibly impose any further on you, my lord,' Jaron forced himself to speak calmly. 'As soon as I am well again we will return to Tiara.'

The lord's smile faded and now he stared down at Jaron.

Rella jumped in. 'That's a long way off yet, son, you must give yourself time to heal.'

'Until I'm well enough,' Jaron muttered. He looked up at Carna and forced a smile. 'Thank you.' He was a lord after all, Jaron supposed, and had saved Jaron's life and spared his mother unbearable sorrow. It wouldn't do to look too ungracious, and Jaron was grateful.

9

Flick came to visit him the next day. The young firedrake rider gave a loud cough and popped his head round the curtain before sauntering over to the bedside chair. 'At last you're awake.' He sat and crossed his long legs. 'You're looking much better, pale as a sheet you were. We were very worried about you.'

'Thank you for all you did, Flick, and please pass my thanks on to Val.'

'No need for that, we're just glad you're alright.' His mouth tightened. 'Looked awful from the air. We didn't expect to find anyone alive.'

Jaron nodded. More than once during the night he had woken with a start and felt wet tears on his face. He shook his head to push away such dark thoughts and realised Flick was quietly watching him.

'I'm sorry, I didn't mean to remind you about all you went through,' the young rider said. 'You're safe now and getting better.' He uncrossed his legs and reached to put his hand on Jaron's shoulder.

'You didn't,' Jaron lied. He looked down at his hands resting on the blankets, clasped and unclasped them. 'Flick, what happened to Caliber?'

Flick frowned as he sat back. 'Caliber?'

'Yes,' Jaron stared at him now, anxious. 'My mother said you didn't come back to Tiara with him?'

'Ah yes, the kelpra.'

Jaron tried to keep his annoyance in check. Why did nobody acknowledge what Caliber had done for him? It was as though they had forgotten about him already.

'I tried to hold him all the way, or rather Tarp tried.'

Jaron went cold. 'You dropped him.'

Flick was indignant. 'Of course not, Tarp would never do that.'

'I'm sorry.' Relieved, Jaron quickly apologised. 'He saved my life, Flick. It was amazing the way he fought for us. I wouldn't be here otherwise.' He paused, realising how that sounded. 'I mean... you all did. What happened? Please tell me.'

Flick smiled. 'Of course, I can understand you're worried.' He settled back in the bedside chair. 'We got clear of the forest and were just entering the Wake, but by the shades did your beast wriggle! And you should have heard the noise! Growling and snarling the whole way,' he paused while Jaron listened anxiously. 'Got spunk, I'll say that. Tarp started to grumble a little and at one point I thought he might bite the devil, he got so fed up with him.' He held up a hand on seeing Jaron's face. 'Of course, Tarp wouldn't do that, not with cargo anyway, but he was quite a weight and we flew lower and lower in the air until Tarp was looking back at me, telling me he couldn't manage much further – so we had to let him go.'

'Let him go?' Jaron squeaked.

'In the middle of the plains, as I said, and releasing him was pretty hairy too. Tarp wouldn't land, wisely as it turned out. Your kelpra was facing away as we held him but as soon as Tarp let go, he landed on all fours and immediately turned and went for him.' Flick shook his head in wonder, remembering. 'He leapt up at Tarp as we rose and I distinctly heard his teeth snap.'

Jaron sat back against his pillows and breathed a sigh of relief. *Caliber was alright*. He smiled at Flick. 'Thank you.'

'So, will you please stop worrying now?'

Jaron laughed then flinched as his sore ribs protested.

'Which direction did he go?' he asked, an arm across his chest. 'Towards Tiara?'

But Flick shook his head. 'As we flew on I looked back and he was running east.' He leant forward, putting his elbows on Jaron's bed. 'I should think your beast can look after himself pretty well.'

'I suppose,' Jaron said, doubtful.

'Perhaps he feels like a bit of freedom, Jaron.'

'Yes, I'm sure you're right.'

'And now you are in Rakenar,' Flick said, 'you'll find it quite different. It's fabulous country, wilder than the Corelands – and great for flying, best seen from the air.'

'Hmm, you're not going back to Tiara on sentry duty?' Jaron asked.

Flick shook his head. 'Lord Carna was all for pulling the firedrake out completely, he was so mad at Lord Bell, but Thorel managed to talk him round.'

Why would he be so mad? Jaron thought. 'Thorel?' he asked out loud.

'Thorel Rand, he's chief advisor here. He said Rakenar still needed grain from Tiara and it was enough that Carna had taken Lord Bell's chief cook and lead jockey away.'

Jaron shifted in his bed. 'It won't be long before we're back. As soon as I'm better.'

'S'pose so.' Flick seemed noncommittal. 'Your mother sided with Thorel so Carna dispatched three more firedrake and kept me, Val and Nave here. I tell you,' Flick grinned, 'I'm pretty happy about that. Sentry duty is soooo boring.'

Jaron said nothing; he was still digesting the news that his mother had spoken up against Lord Carna, the lord of all Rakenar – and sided with his advisor. A respected man, by all accounts. It surprised him she had been present at their meeting at all.

'And have you seen your fabulous view?' Flick was waving a hand towards the closed double doors.

Jaron managed to keep his smile. 'Yes, I've seen. Um, bit wild.'

Flick grinned. 'There's so much I want to show you, when you're well enough, of course. And the weather is so warm today! Why don't you get some fresh air?' He stood up and made to move towards the doors.

'I think I need to rest please, Flick. I'll do that much better with the doors closed.'

'Oh, alright. I'll leave you to sleep then.' He made to go then turned back. 'Your mother's nice, fits right in. I didn't know she's a Raken.'

Jaron stared. 'Yes, a long time ago, before she made Tiara her home,' he replied, putting an emphasis on 'Tiara' and 'home.'

'You've not been at Tiara two years, she said to me,' Flick waved cheerfully. 'I'll come and see you again.' With a swish of the curtain he was gone.

Jaron chewed his bottom lip. His mother had made no secret of the fact she had been brought up with the Raken. He wondered again why a lord would offer to follow them to ease his mother's mind. And *why* had Carna even been talking to his mother in the first place? Jaron frowned. Carna was definitely making a play for her. *I have to get her away from here as soon as possible.*

The weather turned warmer over the next week. Jaron knew this because Flick, a frequent visitor, said he should enjoy the air and insisted on opening up the large double doors for him. 'Get some clean mountain air in your lungs. Believe me, this warm weather doesn't happen often in Rakenar.' Of course, that now meant he could see firedrake flying past with distressing regularity.

Surprisingly, the Raken lord himself often came to visit, asking him how he was. The tall lord would hover by the chair but Jaron never invited him to sit. Their conversations were short and awkward and Jaron always sighed with relief once he had left.

The healer was a short, stout man, but spoke in a strange breathless voice that made him seem older than his middle years. He was pleased with the progress of his patient's bruised ribs and injury but voiced his concern over Jaron's tight left hip. 'It's stiffer than I would like,' he said in a rasping wheeze to Rella, who was sitting in her customary position at her son's bedside. 'The thigh muscle is healing well but without exercise his old injury is too stiff.' The healer was manipulating his leg by stretching it out fully then folding it back onto Jaron's chest, who couldn't help but grimace as his muscles complained. 'Have you been doing the exercises I prescribed, young man?' When Jaron nodded the healer looked to his mother. 'Walking in his room is not enough, tomorrow he must get out and about.'

Rella frowned. 'I forgot your old stick, Jaron, it's still in Tiara.'

'Perhaps I should get better there,' the smile Jaron gave her was innocent.

She shook her thick mane of hair. 'You're not well enough to travel yet, I'll ask one of the carpenters to make one for you.'

Jaron grunted as the healer pulled his leg to full stretch again and twisted it. Laid on the pillow his face was still towards his mother and he noticed she didn't look so drawn now. If anything, she was more beautiful than ever and he frowned, wondering what the change was. Her eyes were bright and clear and she had lost the dark shadows that had formed under them. Her rich dark hair was shining and she seemed to be almost glowing to her son's eyes. The dress she wore was of dark velvet blue with a cream lace on the front and a cloak to match it, pinned with an ornate gold brooch at her shoulder. It was quite a change from her kitchen garb and all became her very well. Jaron couldn't think when he had ever seen her wearing such a beautiful dress and they had never been able to afford jewellery before. Of course, she wouldn't be so worried about him now, but there was something else... something that was nothing to do with her son getting stronger.

It's being here in Rakenar, Jaron thought, and no doubt Lord Carna had something to do with it as well. With a sinking heart, he turned to stare up at the ceiling while the healer continued to work and allowed himself to acknowledge what he had been trying so hard not to; his mother was happy, the happiest he had seen her for years. *How can I possibly force her to give all this up?*

Jaron knew he couldn't.

10

The next evening, Rella came to his room with an armful of clothes, and something else.

'For you,' she said, and handed him a walking stick.

Of course, the handle was carved in the image of a firedrake head. Jaron sighed and took it then hefted it in his hand, raising his eyebrows. It was surprisingly light and so beautifully carved he had to take a closer look despite himself. The head was intricately detailed; the forehead smooth with jewelled deep-set eyes and its mouth breathed a plume of fire that formed the tapering end of the curved handle. The neck arched into the rod and the posture reminded him of Caliber, when the stallion was showing off and prancing with his chin pulled in.

'The detail… it's beautiful,' he murmured, running his hand over the polished wood. It felt warm to the touch and his fingers traced the ridges of the ears carved flat against the curve of the handle and worked their way down the scales that were painstakingly detailed, curling around the wood in a firedrake tail. A gold metal tip sealed the end with a dark material on the bottom that yielded just a little when Jaron pressed it with his thumb. He looked up at his mother. 'Who did this?'

'Oran,' she smiled down at him. 'He was an apprentice when I left, but now he's the master. He set straight to it when I asked him. He was carving most of last night and this morning. It's chestnut, light and strong. The wood to trust, Oran said.'

'Will you thank him for me?'

'You can tell him yourself when you see him.' She turned to retrieve a bundle of clothes she had put on the chair. 'Want me to help you get dressed?'

Jaron pouted at her and she smiled and moved to the door. 'Give me a shout when you're ready.'

Jaron pulled on woollen brown leggings and a crisp white shirt, thin but made of warm wool. He buttoned the plush brown velvet tunic and wondered at the quality of the cloth. He had never worn such well-made clothes before. His boots looked new too, made of soft dusky brown leather that pulled on easily and were a perfect fit. When he had finished dressing he picked up the staff and leant on it as he stood. It felt made for his hand and he experimented with a few steps. With the exercises the healer had given him these last few days his foot moved better now. It still pulled on his scarred hip to lift his injured leg when he took a step, but the boots were stout yet wonderfully light, supporting his foot well and making walking just a bit easier.

'My, what a handsome young man you are,' Rella was standing at the door, appraising him.

'Too much?' Jaron asked. 'I feel a bit… conspicuous.'

His mother laughed and shook her head. 'Come on, it's time to stop hiding.' She held out her arm and her son placed his hand on it. Slowly, they walked out of his cave.

Jaron was surprised to see beyond his curtain was a narrow, dark tunnel carved into the stone. He hadn't known what to expect, but he admitted to himself he felt a little disappointed. Rella moved in front, holding her hand back to him but Jaron found it easier to lean on the cave wall. His hip was even stiffer with the enforced rest, his thigh still sore, and he was mindful not to put too much pressure on it. Inside the tunnel it felt cold and the dark narrow space made Jaron uneasy. *Is the whole of the mountain like this? Do the Raken live like underground creatures?* The thought dismayed him. But the tunnel was short and, looking past his mother, Jaron saw soft orange light up ahead. 'What's that?' he asked, suspicious.

'You'll see,' Rella said.

They got closer to the end of the tunnel and his mother stepped out and turned to smile back at him with her hair glowing in the warm light. Jaron made to follow her – and stopped short. He could hear the faint babble of many voices.

'Come along, Jaron.' His mother beckoned him closer.

He stepped out – and gaped.

The mountain was hollow. A huge cavern yawned before him with row upon row of walkways set against the walls. All the paths were lit by brightly coloured lanterns, most hanging outside doors that were dotted at intervals along the walkways. He could see people, in groups or alone, some leaning on the railing looking down as they chatted with their neighbours, some passing into tunnels he judged were of a similar size to the one he had just stepped out from. He noticed there was a faint tinge of burning wood in the air.

'Incredible, isn't it?' his mother said.

Jaron nodded, his eye travelling along the tiers of iron-railed paths with steps linking them to the floors above and below. Lowering his astonished gaze, he saw they were on a similar walkway, wide enough for four men to walk abreast. Tilting his head back to look up, he saw there was no tier above them; on this side they were on the top floor and the ceiling overhead disappeared into darkness. It amazed him that somehow the Raken had hollowed out a whole mountain.

'Come closer, Jaron, it's quite safe.' Rella was holding out a hand to him and he unsteadily moved towards her. He clutched at her hand for balance and felt it give a squeeze. Looking behind him at his tunnel he saw it had its own door, now swung open on its hinges. Next to it a large glass lantern was hanging from the wall, its glass tinted a deep orange that gave off a warm glow.

His mother drew him towards the iron railing and beckoned his gaze down. Peering over, Jaron saw more walkways below. At ground level and far below them, the cavern floor glowed white. With so much grey rock around here, he was surprised and wondered if it was made of the same stone Tiara was built from. Tiny figures of people were walking about down there. Half of the cavern was covered in a large number of tables and chairs placed in rows, more people walking in between them. He squinted, trying to see better and saw they were laying out plates and dishes. *A feeding hall.* As he watched, he was startled to see a green firedrake fly in. It landed to dispatch its rider at the beginning of the hall. As its rider walked away it jumped back into the air, making Jaron jerk back from the railing. As he warily peered over again it was to see the firedrake still far below him, flapping heavily as it turned before flying out again. Curious now, Jaron edged further along the railing to see where it had flown in from. A huge mouth of another cave tunnel came into his view, so big it yawned large enough to have two firedrake Tarp's size fly in with wings spread fully.

'Amazing,' he muttered. Clutching the railing, his gaze travelled along the huge hall. The centre was dominated by a statue that even up here Jaron could see was of a red firedrake with wings half-opened. He couldn't see the head for its neck looked to be tucked under. The statue flickered with the reflections of the torches burning in their alcoves and it glowed in a disjointed way like a many-faceted jewel, although he was too high up to see why that was. Around it people chatted, clustered in groups, or took their places at the tables. Jaron could see they were becoming laden with dishes, with yet more being brought in by servants through a cave entrance at the back of the hall.

'Come on,' Rella looped her arm through his. 'You're

supposed to be exercising that leg.'

They proceeded at a slow pace, occasionally meeting groups of Raken who, on seeing his limp and stick, stood to one side to let them by. Rella thanked them and Jaron cast a surreptitious glance at their faces. Ordinary men and women, no different from the Tiarians, except they had a tanned, outdoor look, which he assumed was from riding firedrake. They looked at him with interest and some smiled when they met his gaze. Mindful of his facial scar, he ducked his head and limped on by. Soon they were halfway round the walkway and as he walked, leaning on his stick, Jaron watched the hall below fill until every seat was taken and the dinner was in full flow. Faint chatter and laughter bubbled up.

'Did you want to join them?' He had noticed his mother often looked down at the diners.

'I'm not going to leave you,' she said, patting his arm. 'Anyway, I ate earlier.'

They continued on. Jaron grunted as his stiff hip and sore thigh began to jar him. He could feel beads of sweat standing out on his forehead with the effort. He hadn't realised he had got so unfit.

'Want to rest?'

'Just for a little while. Mum, how long was I out for?'

'Three days.'

Jaron stared. 'So long?' That meant he had been bed bound for almost two weeks; no wonder he felt so stiff.

'The healer gave you something to make you sleep. We stirred you for water and some soup, don't you remember?'

Jaron shook his head.

As he rested, a man came walking along the walkway towards them. He was tall and moved with a graceful gait unusual for a man. His head was shaved yet his face was surprisingly young. Jaron squinted as he drew closer. His eyes looked to be lined with black and his lips were an unnatural deep red. Jaron blinked. His face reminded him of the high ladies in Tiara when they put rouge on and made themselves up for special occasions. The man caught him staring and winked. Embarrassed, Jaron dropped his eyes.

'Ah, so the patient is out and about at last,' he heard the man say in a rich deep timbre. Surprised, he looked up.

His mother was smiling. 'Hello, Oran.'

'Rella,' he bowed and took her hand in his then brushed his lips against the back of it. 'Lovely as always.' He straightened and reached for both her hands, swallowing them in his own large ones as he spread her arms wide. 'I do like that dress, my dear, good choice – royal blue becomes you very well.'

His mother laughed. 'The years haven't changed you much, Oran.'

'Nor you, my dear. Your beauty is as radiant as ever.' He looked over at Jaron who was silently watching them.

Rella moved to stand next to her son. 'Jaron, this is my very old friend Oran, you remember I told you he carved your stick?'

Jaron nodded but he didn't need her prompt – the man was strange and he wasn't sure he liked his over-familiarity with his mother, but he did want to express his gratitude. 'Thank you for carving it for me, it's beautiful.'

'It's my pleasure.' Oran tilted his head to one side and smiled slowly. 'He becomes you very well, Rella, he has your hair but not your eyes.'

Jaron looked away, not sure how to take such a compliment from a man. Couldn't he see his scar?

'Now, Oran,' Rella's voice had a slight bite to Jaron's ears although he saw she was smiling. 'Stop teasing.'

Oran was appraising Jaron's walking stick. 'It might be slightly too long for you. Stand up a little straighter please, so I might see.' Jaron did so and Oran held one large hand flat against his shoulder and seemed to be counting with the other. 'Hmm, no, I think that will do, how does it feel to walk with?'

'Fine, thank you.'

'Try a few steps please.'

Feeling self-conscious, Jaron walked along the walkway a short way and back again. Oran rubbed at his chin, his hip jutting out to one side in a rather florid pose as he watched Jaron's faltering steps with an intent look on his face.

'He needs something else to help him, I think,' he spoke to his mother. 'Has he ever had any special insoles fitted?'

'No, do you think he needs them?' Rella's voice was anxious.

'The fire damage might have shortened the muscles. His left leg walks slightly shorter than the other.'

'My leg is shorter?' Jaron looked down at his legs, dismayed. Oran's heavy hand suddenly landed on his shoulder, making him jump and scattering his thoughts.

'Only by the tiniest of margins. An untrained eye wouldn't spot it.' His smile was kind and Jaron decided he quite liked this strange Oran after all. 'I suspect your hip muscles pull a little harder on that side?'

Surprised, Jaron nodded.

'The burns on his hip make the skin tighter,' his mother smiled at her son. *Did everyone know about his past here?* 'Can you do anything, Oran?' she asked.

'Dear lady, do not fret. A simple wedge fitted within the boot will help him.' He held up two fingers spread a tiny width apart. 'You only need this much and you will be amazed at the difference it will make. Does your hip get tired when you walk, Jaron?'

'Yes, it always has done since… since the attack.'

Oran pointed a finger theatrically into the air. 'I will get on it straightaway,' he turned to Rella. 'I will need an old pair of his boots please. Ones that have been worn with use.'

'I brought a pair with me. We're heading back to Jaron's

room now anyway, come back with us, Oran.'

Jaron was glad to hear it. As he trekked back he leaned more heavily on his walking stick, exhausted. Yet it was Oran who offered his arm and, not wanting to appear rude, he accepted it. It wasn't long before Oran was barking out instructions.

'Do not lean so heavily! Keep your chin up, UP!' Two boys coming in the opposite direction flattened themselves against the rough cavern wall as the entourage passed by. Jaron could feel their eyes on him. 'You twist your body if you lean too hard on the stick. This will not help. Shoulders further back, that's good. NO! *Don't* look down, up, always up.'

When they at last turned into the short tunnel and emerged into Jaron's cave he nearly fell onto the bed. He lay flat out on his back, the sweat on his body drying quickly as the wound in his thigh throbbed. Oran pulled off one of his boots, and he raised his head off the pillow with a jolt. The carpenter had hold of his leg and was rubbing it, avoiding the bandage. Jaron hurriedly tried to sit up. 'I'm fine,' he muttered. But Oran continued to give his leg a pummelling.

'Did the healer not tell you this? Rub your muscles! Hard. Like this.'

The boy winced as long strong fingers dug into his screaming hip muscles through his thin woollen leggings. Oran was frowning in concentration as he worked and Rella sat down on the bed to watch. Jaron felt Oran's fingers working inexorably into his ridged skin. 'The scar tissue needs to be broken down, after exercise is best when the muscles are warm. Always do this after you have walked, you will see how much better it feels.'

Not now, it doesn't. Jaron threw a pleading look at his mother and she placed a hand on Oran's arm. 'Perhaps that's enough for now, Oran. It is the first time he has been out of his room, after all.'

'Very well.' Oran patted Jaron's knee and stood up, stooping to pick up a pair of old boots that Rella had brought out. 'I will leave you now to rest.' As he said this he turned the soles up and was examining them with interest. 'Hmm, every boot tells a story. Good evening to you, lovely Rella.' He bowed low and with a swirl of cloak was gone.

Jaron let out a breath and his mother laughed. 'You'll like him when you get to know him.'

'I think I already do. Is he a healer as well as a carpenter?'

Rella shook her head. 'No, but he has a *feel* for things; when he carves it's like he's working with the natural qualities of the wood. His work is wonderful – the sculpture of the firedrake in the hall is his.'

'Really?' Jaron asked in wonder.

'Yes, and I think his innate artistry carries over into other living tissues as well.' She looked down at Jaron. 'Your leg, he can feel the wrongness,' she put out a hand in apology at the word. 'The *tension* in the leg, something you may not even notice yourself. When he works he's trying to get it to remember how nature designed it to work.'

Jaron stared up at the rock ceiling, watching the glow from the fire lamps dance across the ridged stone. 'It's too late.'

'Don't be so defeatist,' his mother's voice was sharp. 'Only eighteen months since the fire, Jaron, and if Oran sees room for improvement then believe me there's room, he's that good. His mother was blessed with the same gift and she was the best healer we ever had. Oran chose carpentry and art rather than healing.'

Jaron propped himself up on an elbow. 'Have you always missed it, Mum? Rakenar?'

She smiled but her eyes were sad.

'Then why did you leave?' Jaron asked. 'You never did tell me.'

His mother brushed his fringe back, her eyes soft. 'It's a

long story, for another time.' Jaron made to protest but she stood up. 'You must rest now. I'll get you some water while you undress.'

Jaron watched her pull back the curtain to pass into the small washroom beyond and listened to her soft humming. He realised he had never asked her about her life before Teel. As a child his questions had been only about the firedrake. Now he wondered why that was as he laid back onto the soft bed. Tired, he closed his eyes and for a moment the rippling Plains of Wake were before him as he watched from his vantage point on Caliber's broad back. He wondered if the kelpra had been found. He thought of Liam and Sanra and realised how much he missed them both. His mother seemed like a different person to him here and it bothered him, this other life she had before him.

Mulling over his thoughts his eyelids drooped of their own accord. He was already asleep when his mother returned to his bedside with a tankard of water.

11

To Jaron's mind the sooner he was better the sooner he could leave this place. So, the next morning he stood at the tunnel end, hidden from view as he peered out to check the walkway was empty. His hand tightened around his stick as he stepped out. A further glance up and down the walkway proved there was nobody there to stare at one scarred, injured boy. Edging over to the railing he looked down. The hall below was quiet apart from a few servants clearing up what must be the remains of breakfast.

Satisfied, Jaron started walking. Fewer torches were lit this morning yet it was lighter on the walkway, which came as a surprise, considering it was built inside a mountain. Jaron looked around for the source of light and far above and behind him he saw another entrance, a massive hole cut into the side of the mountain through which blue sky could be seen. He turned to stare up at it, aware this was potentially another entrance for the firedrake as well as a light source. However, there was nothing he could do about that so he shrugged and turned back to continue on, keeping Oran's instructions in mind to remain upright and straight. The carpenter (although that description didn't seem to go far enough to portray the talented Oran) had proved true to his word and when Jaron pulled on his boots he had found a small wedge inserted into the sole of one. With it, his hip felt lighter and his stiff muscles seemed to be able to push off better. He shook his head in disbelief – one small adjustment and it made so much difference. Proof then, that he really did have one leg now shorter than the other. At this thought he frowned. The result was what mattered, he told himself.

His mother had already been in with his breakfast, so once back in his cave Jaron was left to his own devices for the rest of the morning. He tried to rest but after tossing and turning on the bed sat up and looked across to the view the open double doors afforded him. The sky was a brilliant blue above the mountains and the morning sun threw sharp, hard shadows across their craggy facades. Jaron got to his feet and, without his stick, limped gingerly across the cave in his socks. At the door frame, he peered out cautiously. The cloudless blue sky was empty.

On the wide ledge sat a leather-coated chair and a stool. It had been brought out here for him days ago, although he had not yet dared to come out and use it. Jaron hesitated, but he felt starved of the sunlight and it was now over a fortnight since he had arrived. After another check on the sky he made his way towards the chair and eased himself into its sumptuous embrace. There was a blanket thrown thoughtfully across the arm rest.

Looking around, Jaron saw that his mountain face curved away, and he took comfort that he couldn't be seen by any close neighbours. He looked up to see another ledge hanging a little way above his head so he assumed there was another cave up there, but there was no firedrake head peering down at him. Shaking out the blanket he put his feet on the stool, covering his legs. Then he sat back and took in the view.

From here he could get his first decent look at the verdant green valley basin with the wide glistening ribbon of river cutting across the valley, which widened out into a central lake. As before, he could see the tiny figures of people walking, and for the first time he noticed a road that ran along the base of the mountains rimming the valley. A few carts were trundling along it and they looked heavily laden. As he watched, one followed a split in the road and travelled off towards a large entrance that was carved into a mountain at ground level. He saw all the mountains had the same and supposed they were like his, with large caverns for eating and socialising. The scale was daunting and he wondered how long the Raken people had been living here. The work of digging into the rock and creating such a network of tunnels and caverns was amazing to him and he didn't doubt firedrake brawn had made it possible. Rella had never spoken of her people's history to him as he was growing up, perhaps because by the time he was old enough the attack he had suffered had made his mother think he wouldn't be interested. Jaron shook his head. Of course, he wasn't, not really, but who wouldn't be impressed by a place such as this?

A mountain breeze ruffled his hair and Jaron filled his lungs with the clear air. It felt good to be out of his cave. He spied two green firedrake on the valley floor, and a small group of people by the river close by where it widened into the lake. The firedrakes' wings were furled and they were so far below him he found he could relax. One of the firedrake lumbered into the lake and flapped its wings as it bathed until it was joined by the other. The people sat on the bank to watch them.

Just then, he caught sight of more firedrake flying in from between the mountain peaks with their riders. Hurriedly throwing aside the blanket he stood up and limped inside.

Another week went by. Now his thigh was so much better, Jaron even started to feel a little bored. One afternoon, he managed to get all the way round the walkway before he stopped to rest and leant on the railing.

'Hello.' The voice made him jump and he looked both ways along the walkway but there was no one around. There came a giggle, a girl's giggle. 'Up here,' the voice called. He looked up – and gasped.

A firedrake was hovering in the air above him, its green head cocked to one side. Jaron registered this and had taken a step back before he caught sight of a girl's face with a cloud of red hair wafting in the breeze of its wings. She was looking over its shoulder at him. As he stared she grinned and waved. When he didn't return it, the girl cocked her head much like her firedrake had done and her smile faded a little. Next moment the beast suddenly dipped down, far too close for comfort, its wings flapping heavily.

Terrified fear overrode everything else and instinct kicked in. Jaron hurriedly turned, his hip couldn't keep up and he stumbled and fell with a cry, banging knees on rock. His stick skittered away and frantically he tried to grab it, his outstretched fingers just missing. Panting, he flipped over and shot a terrified look up at the firedrake.

Who now had its foreclaws hooked on the railing, its enormous wings flapping close and hemming him in. He stifled a scream as the luminous reptilian eyes fixed on him. The beast cocked its head again and rumbled.

'Oh, scorching scales! I'm so sorry!' The girl was sliding down the beast's shoulder, she stepped onto her firedrake's foreleg and, with complete disregard for the long drop directly below her, swung herself easily over the railing.

The firedrake rumbled again, peeled away, and flew upwards. Jaron tore his eyes away from the beast to find the girl was now crouched directly in front of him, studying him with wide violet eyes, her face a patchwork of freckles.

'We didn't mean to startle you,' she said, and put out a helping hand.

He didn't take it, too caught up with trying to still his hammering heart. 'My stick,' he panted.

She cast about, saw it laying behind her, and reached over to retrieve it. Jaron silently took it from her, his face hot now with embarrassment and shame. With one hand on the wall and the other pressing on his stick for leverage, he managed to get to his feet, ignoring again her outstretched hand. He cast a wary look up and saw the firedrake above, hanging like an enormous bat from a rocky ledge. When he lowered his gaze, it was to see the girl standing directly in front of him.

She was a bit taller than him and wore a sleeveless tunic that revealed tanned and surprisingly well-muscled arms. He stared at her, his anger dribbling away at the worried frown on her face. Her gaze shifted slightly in a way he was well-practiced with and he felt his cheeks flush even hotter, glad he had his neck scarf on at least. She unexpectedly grinned, revealing dimples amongst her freckles. 'I'm Marla,' she said.

'Jaron.'

Her look turned sheepish. 'Sorry about that.'

'I just fell,' he lied.

'My fault.' She stuck out her hand again, and this time he took it, noticing the roughness of her palm and strong grip. She pulled her hand away a bit too soon. 'Jaron,' she tried his name out and glanced down at his stick. 'You must be the boy who was nearly killed by the mountain men.'

Jaron nodded, surprised. 'You heard about that?' he asked.

'Everyone has, our Lord Carna rescued you. You're the rider of the carnivorous horses.'

'Yes, a race rider.' Jaron was distracted by her comment: *everyone knew of him.* 'And they're called kelpra.'

'Unpredictable beasts, my father said.'

Jaron stared at her. 'Much like your firedrake, then.'

'At least they're loyal,' Marla shot back.

'The kelpra I was riding, Caliber, he saved my life, I would say that's being pretty loyal.'

'Where is he now?' she asked and he shook his head. 'I don't know.' He glanced anxiously up at the firedrake again and when he looked back her rather direct stare made him peer down at his boots.

'I'm sure he'll just go wild,' he heard her say. 'I'll walk with you, if you like. It must be pretty boring on your own like this.'

They started to walk and although she was two strides in front straight away she soon slowed her walk to match his. She was on his scar side, he realised – but although she glanced at his cheek once more she kept her eyes forward after that.

'I suppose Rakenar is quite different from the south?' she asked after a moment.

Jaron nodded. 'Tiara is an old trading city.'

'Tiara,' she tried out the name. 'Sounds like a jewel.'

'I suppose it is, it's known as the jewel of the Corelands for its trading. They produce beef and grain there.'

'Oh, they're farmers then.'

The way she said it annoyed him a little, as if she thought less of them for it. 'I believe Rakenar has benefited from their grain.'

She shrugged and gave him a sideways look. 'Quite a change for you here, then.'

Jaron sought to divert her. 'What did you say your firedrake's name was?'

'Channon, but she's not mine. I'm not really supposed to be flying out alone yet.'

'Oh?'

'No, new riders attend flying school then choose their firedrake.'

Despite himself, Jaron found this snippet of information interesting. Nobody had really divulged much about Rakenar life to him. 'Is everybody in Rakenar a flyer?' he asked.

Marla shook her thick hair. 'The riders live in the mountains once they win their own firedrake, but they can have close family in with them. It's difficult moving around

FIRE RIDER

here if you don't fly so some families choose to stay where
they are, in villages just behind here. The workers for
Rakenar live there as well.'

Jaron thought it sounded a bit harsh. 'It must be hard for
the families to be separated.'

Marla looked at him in surprise. 'No, it's a great honour
to become a flyer, every family is proud.'

'So, you're living here? In the mountain?' he asked.

She shook her head. 'Just exploring. I'm in training so
I'm at Mount Treen.' Her face cracked into a wide smile.
'I've been flying two weeks, and it's brilliant! I've even
done a Rickral manoeuvre.' To his puzzled look she stopped
and turned to face him, putting her hands up level with her
face. 'You go up high,' she soared with her flattened hand,
'then Channon folds her wings in and you drop!' She swept
her hand down fast in front of Jaron's face, who blinked.
'She spins, and you have to hold on really tight and keep
your head to pull out of it.' She dropped her hands and stood
smiling at him. 'Parl, he's the instructor, said I did it
brilliantly, I'm the only one so far out of the group he's
trusted to try it.' She lifted her chin proudly.

'Err, great, well done,' Jaron said, and resumed walking.

She fell into step beside him again. 'It was over the lake,
of course, in case I lost her, but still. You've ridden a
firedrake too, haven't you?'

Jaron looked at her in disbelief. 'I haven't.'

'Yes, you have, and Lord Carna's Madrag too. What an
honour that must have been,' her eyes went dreamy. 'To ride
the red beast…'

'I was unconscious most of the time. I don't really
remember it.' He reached his tunnel entrance and paused,
relieved to have made it without asking Marla to stop and
wait for him. 'This is me.'

'Oh, right! Well, nice to meet you,' she grinned at him,
showing those dimples again, and he found himself smiling

102

back. 'If I'm around I'll come and see you, would that be alright?'

For a moment, he hesitated. But he hadn't spoken to anybody his own age since coming here. 'I would like that very much.'

'Alright then,' she said, and brought her fingers to her mouth. Her high-pitched whistle was answered by a snort and suddenly there was the green beast, sweeping down towards them.

Jaron hurriedly backed into his entrance. 'Bye then,' his words came out in a rush and by the time she had turned back to him he had been swallowed up into the blessed darkness of the tunnel. He didn't immediately turn away to go through to his cave, but watched, hidden, as Channon hovered before the girl, claws gripping the railing.

'Clever girl, beautiful girl,' he heard Marla say and saw her step forward and reach up to rub her hand down the long scaly nose. The firedrake's luminous eyes softened as she nudged the girl gently with her nose and breathed over her, causing her heavy mane of hair to lift.

Jaron turned away. The way the firedrake had nudged at her reminded him of Caliber when he was enjoying a stroke. Marla must think him a coward. Sudden, angry tears of shame filled his eyes. For the first time, Jaron regretted his fear of these beasts. He rubbed at his eyes as he moved along the short tunnel. Pulling the curtain aside, he froze.

His mother and the Raken lord stood close together in his room, framed by the light of the open double doors as they faced each other.

Something about the way they were looking at each other, engrossed even, disturbed Jaron and he chewed his bottom lip as he stared. At the same moment, both became aware of his presence and took a hurried step back.

'Jaron,' Rella said as she turned to him with a bright smile. It immediately faded on seeing his face. 'Are you alright, son?' But Jaron had seen the flushed look on her face, the shining eyes just a moment before – and sudden jealous anger fired in his chest.

'I want to leave,' he stated in a flat tone.

'Leave?'

'Yes, back to Tiara, I'm well enough.'

'I'm not ready to leave yet, Jaron.' She shot a worried frown over to Carna.

'I'm not asking you to come with me.' Jaron swallowed as the anger he had felt but a moment before drained away. 'I know you're happy here.' He wondered if she knew how much that had cost him.

She did. In three strides, her arms went around him, pressing his face to her chest. He sagged against her, his anger dribbling away. 'Mum,' he whispered. 'I can't stay here.'

He felt her chin against his hair. 'You belong here, Jaron. As do I.' Her voice was strained.

'I don't, Mum. I'm sorry, but I can't get past it.'

Carna spoke then. 'Do you want to? Get past it, Jaron?' The lord stepped closer.

Jaron wished he would go away, this was between his mother and him. Yet the question made him hesitate.

His mother's eyes were shining with tears. 'I won't let you go back alone, but I won't lie to you either. Rakenar is my home and I don't want to leave it again,' she took a deep breath. 'It could be your home too, Jaron.'

He saw the hope in her eyes. It was turning out as he had feared. Either way, he had asked her to make a sacrifice.

Carna came to stand beside his mother. 'Do you want to get past this fear?' he repeated. 'We will help you, Jaron, but you have to want to do it.' His voice was clear and determined, but Jaron saw his mother's fingers lightly touch the lord's arm, seeking comfort.

He turned away and gazed out onto the mountains as he

considered. He wanted to stay where his mother was, he knew that much. The loss of Teel had kept mother and son close and since his stepfather's death all her concentration had been on getting him better. He knew it would make her happiness complete if he would only take this last step in shaking off the past. He remembered her words back at the lake. *It was one rogue firedrake, Jaron.* The firedrake had saved him from the Ernots and saved Caliber. He wouldn't be here otherwise and they had spared Rella a lifetime of pain. It occurred to him that he hadn't had one nightmare concerning the firedrake since he had been here. Yet he doubted his ability to get past his fears. *Coward,* he berated himself and remembered how he had felt on the walkway, the shame. He turned back to his mother.

'I don't belong here.'

Her reply was fierce. 'You do, you have Raken blood. You know that.'

Jaron spread his hands. 'From you, Mum, yes, but you never told me who *he* was.'

'You never asked. I thought with Teel you didn't feel a need to know.'

'I'm asking now.'

He saw her body tense and she shot a look at Carna beside her. The lord nodded. Suddenly, Jaron thought he knew the answer and felt sick. It was so obvious really, only he had denied facing it. He swallowed. 'Are you saying...?' He couldn't finish.

But she was shaking her head no. Jaron felt such relief wash over him he nearly had to sit down. Of course not, he was a lord. How stupid.

'He's your uncle, Jaron.'

'I'm sorry?'

Carna stepped closer and his eyes were shining with something Jaron couldn't read. 'I'm your uncle, Jaron. Torrit was my elder brother, and you are his son.'

Then Jaron did sit down on his bed. His mother was beside him in an instant. She took his cold hand in both of hers and clasped it tight. The cave was quiet as they gave him time to digest this news. *Torrit,* he had a name. His father was Torrit. And Carna, lord of all Rakenar, was his uncle.

'What was he like? My... father?' The word sounded strange on his lips.

It was Carna who answered. 'Very much like me, same build. The elder by three years. We – I miss him.' Deep sorrow etched into the Raken lord's face.

Rella stroked Jaron's fringe back with gentle fingers. 'We will talk more of him later.'

For a fleeting moment Jaron wondered why she didn't use his name, Torrit – *my father* – but she was still talking and he tried to focus.

'Now, I want you to answer Carna's question. Will you stay, Jaron, and do as your uncle asked, will you try to conquer your fear, give the firedrake a chance? For me?'

Her son stared at her then at Carna. *Uncle.* The question didn't seem as important as it had five minutes ago and he wondered at his mother asking it again now. Dumbly, he nodded. Her face burst into a radiant smile. 'Thank you,' she whispered and kissed his cheek as she stood.

Carna was smiling, a rare sight. It made him look younger. 'There is nothing to fear from our firedrake,' he said. 'I will help you in this.'

Jaron stared up at him uncomprehendingly. He couldn't get his head round him being his uncle. He looked down at his hands, wishing Carna would leave. When he lifted his head, it was to find he had got his wish – only his mother had left too, and while there were still questions forming on his lips.

12

As the shadows across the mountains lengthened, and the summer afternoon sun sank lower in the sky, it was not his mother who came but Carna, and not by the usual method either.

'Jaron?'

Looking up, the boy saw the huge red hovering just beyond his ledge. The firedrake's red scales took on a phoenix fire in the setting sun, which served to make the yellow eyes even more brilliant as they locked on to him. Jaron swallowed from where he sat on the edge of his bed, his fingers pulling the blanket up into his clenched fists. His pride kept him rooted; he would not allow Carna to witness his fear. *My uncle.*

'May we land?' Carna called. Jaron thought he had misheard him. *What was Carna thinking of?* But in the next instant he knew exactly; his 'help' was about to begin.

He stood up and gave a short nod. That was enough for Carna's sharp eyes and Jaron watched as the beast lifted up and turned his massive body sideways to descend, hovering, onto the ledge. Jaron's hair lifted as the throbbing wind from the red's wings rushed into the cave.

The firedrake touched down with no room to spare and his rider threw a leg over and slid down his shoulder to his raised leg. The huge red furled his wings on the ledge and found the space to swing his head round on its long neck to watch as his rider walked into the cave and across to where Jaron stood. The boy wondered if Lord Carna could see the fear that must show in his eyes.

'Well met, Jaron,' the lord said. Jaron gave a slight bow, his gaze never leaving the firedrake.

'Have you seen my mother?'

'She is resting. Your mother needs some time as well, Jaron.' Carna pulled off his riding gloves as he spoke then slapped his gloves against his thigh, making Jaron jump. 'I thought you would like to spend a little time with Madrag here, and I'll answer any questions you might have.'

'About my father?'

A look of pain crossed the lord's face. 'No, Jaron, I meant about the firedrake.'

'Oh, right.' Jaron hesitated and cast an apprehensive look at the huge beast, who rumbled from deep within his bright blue chest.

'That,' Carna said, 'is how they say hello; a firedrake will often greet his rider this way. Sometimes they will rumble at the rider's close friends or family, those who it knows and likes. It is very unusual for them to greet a stranger this way, as Madrag just did to you.'

'Lucky me,' Jaron replied.

'Now, come a little closer.' The lord stepped towards Madrag and held out a hand to Jaron, who hesitated.

'Isn't lesson one moving a little bit fast here?' he muttered. To his surprise, Carna laughed, a deep rolling sound. His hand beckoned but Jaron stood rooted. 'Perhaps I need a green one, you know, a bit smaller?'

'Jaron,' the lord tried to look stern but there was a twinkle of mirth remaining in his eyes. When the boy still didn't move Carna turned serious. 'I know this is difficult for you, but you must trust me and Madrag.'

The sincerity of his words threw Jaron. He had said to his mother he would try. Summoning up his courage, he stepped forward and felt Carna's hand close about his upper arm. Probably afraid he was going to bolt at any moment, Jaron supposed. Yet it was a comfort, to feel that touch as Carna escorted him closer to Madrag. The firedrake watched them coming and began to stretch out his neck towards them. Jaron stopped short and saw Carna raise a hand to Madrag, palm out. The beast froze, his eyes on his rider.

'To put out a palm, fingers close together, means to be still and wait for my next command,' Carna explained. 'So now we'll go closer...' He walked on and a reluctant Jaron was forced to go with him or else embarrass himself by pulling back. Carna didn't take him to the head, however, but moved towards the firedrake's furled wing. Below it, Jaron could see the rise and fall of the massive belly and hear the beast's breath – it reminded him of the blacksmith's bellows in the forge back in his village. He had never been so aware of an animal in his life before.

'Their wings are just like a bat's, you see this claw here?' Carna pointed at the long, hooked talon at the foremost fold of the wing where it folded against Madrag's scaled side. 'They use this to hang onto a vertical surface.' Jaron eyed the ridged talon warily for it was bigger than his hand. 'So, if there is nowhere to land you could aim your firedrake to a sheer gradient and as long as there is something to grip onto they can hang quite comfortably for a long period of time. The wing membranes are the most vulnerable part of a firedrake as they obviously have no scales for protection.' He moved closer to Madrag's head, still as a statue as it stretched towards the cave. 'You see these pockets on the side of the neck here?' Carna cupped the mound that was just below the jawbone. 'These are fire sacs.'

'Fire sacs?'

'Feel them.'

Jaron stared. 'You want me to touch him?'

'Yes.' Carna dropped his hand away from Jaron's arm and stood impassively, like he was not asking anything much at all.

Jaron hesitated, stepped forward and cast a quick check

at Madrag's head. A big yellow eye was watching him, but the red firedrake might have been made from stone. Slowly, he stepped within the fold of the firedrake's neck. After a moment he reached out and touched the sac with one finger. 'Hmm, yes,' he said.

'Squeeze it,' Carna said.

'Won't it upset him?'

'Not at all.'

Jaron bit his lip and did as he was told, gently folding his fingers over the raised pocket of skin. 'It's soft, and... it feels like there's fluid in there.' His interest was piqued and he forgot to be afraid. 'What is it? Water?'

'No, it's an inflammable liquid we call *Flagra*. When a firedrake dies we harvest that. Spark it and up it goes. Good for starting fires and used for blasts.'

'Blasts?'

'When we cut into rock; if we need to expand in the future we'll use our stores.'

So that was how the Raken had managed to cut so deep into the mountains, Jaron thought.

'The scales cover the body as protection, apart from the ears and... here.' Carna tapped Madrag's leg and the firedrake obediently lifted it forward. Jaron was now so interested he forgot to flinch. 'You see this spot in the armpit here?' Carna was pointing to a blue patch of skin. 'Here is where a firedrake is vulnerable to something other than another firedrake, also the eyes, nostrils or the mouth.'

'If it's not breathing fire.'

'Yes, if it's not breathing fire. But even a firedrake must take a breath before it blasts. It can't fire then.'

He tapped Madrag's leg again and the firedrake put it back down. Carna ran his hand along the ridges of the neck scales. 'A firedrake's skin needs very little looking after. The scales grow along with the firedrake. Oiling them serves to enhance the rider and beast relationship, and it shows a beast is well cared for by its rider.' While he had been talking Carna had moved further up the neck until they now stood next to the head. He clicked with his tongue and the firedrake flicked an ear back at him. 'Their hearing is acute,' he ran his hand along the long ears. 'See how the skin is black here? No scales and it feels like tough leather.' He took a surprised Jaron's hand and Madrag dipped his head a little lower so before he knew it, the long, thick ear was clasped in his hand.

'It feels warm,' Jaron said in surprise.

'Yes, no scales, as I said. Madrag likes nothing better than to have his ears rubbed.' He paused and eyed Jaron, like he was daring him to do it.

Jaron hesitated then slowly he began to run his hand up and down the soft ear. It felt spongy in his hand and Madrag gave a low moan that reverberated along his long neck, causing Jaron to jump back.

'It's alright, that's his pleasure moan, he loves it, don't you Madrag?' Carna murmured softly to his firedrake and took over where Jaron had left off, rubbing the ear. His firedrake closed his eyes in ecstasy and nudged him. Jaron stared in wonder.

'Well,' Carna stepped away from his firedrake, who seemed disappointed he had stopped caressing him. 'I think that's enough for today. I'll walk you back in.' He let Jaron go first. By the time Jaron had reached the middle of his cave and turned, the Raken lord had already gone back to Madrag and was standing at the massive beast's shoulder.

'You did very well,' he said.

'Thank you,' Jaron said, and meant it.

Carna turned to Madrag, who obediently lifted his foreleg. Stepping up, the lord took hold of a raised scale and swung himself up with one fluid practiced movement. 'Good evening, Jaron.' He clicked at Madrag and the beast turned, his tail sweeping back into the cave and causing

Jaron to step aside in alarm. Madrag dropped off the ledge out of sight. After a moment he rose into view, gliding across the valley with his massive wings outstretched.

Jaron moved to the entrance and watched; the sun was now setting and the red beast did indeed look like a phoenix of fire. The firedrake flapped his wings to gain more height and soared over the lip of a mountain, his long tail rippling behind him. A firedrake cry, long and keening, reached Jaron's ears and he felt something inside him give at the sound.

For a long time afterwards, he stood at the cave entrance, staring out across the valley.

13

It wasn't until the sun was just setting behind the mountains and painting the sky in ripples of orange and purple that she emerged from the tunnel, softly padding across his room with a tray laden with food. Jaron was sitting out on the ledge but looking out for her. He came in to help.

There were two plates. 'I thought we might eat together?' Rella asked, and her son was pleased she was staying. 'How about outside? It's such a lovely evening.'

'Alright.' Jaron dragged the bedside chair out for her and Rella the little table. She fetched the tray and the tantalising smell of chicken rose from the plates. She seemed preoccupied and didn't meet his eyes. Jaron waited until she sat, but still didn't touch his food. 'Mum…' he began.

She looked down at her plate. 'After we've eaten, we'll talk then.' Her voice sounded strained and in the fading light her son could see her face was drawn and tired. Apprehension stole through him.

The chicken tasted delicious, it peeled away from the bone easily as Jaron bit into the leg and the vegetables were crunchy and fresh. They sat in companionable silence as they enjoyed the food. After dinner, they eased back in their chairs and gazed at the view.

The valley haze had lifted as night took hold and was now dotted with fires. White and blue lanterns had been lit around the lake and at intervals along the river. To Jaron it seemed like a picture from a child's book and not real at all. Rella rose to light the torches that were set in the outside wall and the ledge became bathed in a warm glow.

'I've always loved this view,' his mother's voice was soft. Jaron didn't reply, wanting her to tell him now. She sat down, perched on the front of her chair. 'Carna said you did very well with Madrag today.' She pushed the plates away and put her elbows on the table. 'Thank you, Jaron, for trying. I know it must have been hard for you.'

He nodded but he didn't want to talk about the firedrake tonight and she saw the questions in his eyes and sighed, bringing up a hand to tuck her hair behind her ears.

'I was born in one of the villages behind the mountains,' she began. 'My father was a flyer and my mother worked as head cook in the kitchens in the bowls of Mount Scarf, this very mountain. It is the home of the council and where the leaders of Rakenar live.'

'Just like you back in Tiara,' Jaron said and his mother nodded but her brown eyes were far away.

'As soon as I was old enough I worked at her side. She taught me everything I know about cooking and I loved it. Not just the work but the whole atmosphere of a large kitchen, the smells, the noise and chatter. A good working kitchen is a village in itself, where everyone looks out for each other.' Rella sat back and gazed over the valley with its winking lights. 'I thought I would always be here, working at my mother's side, becoming head cook one day just like her,' she paused and Jaron waited, she had never told him anything of her life here before and he didn't want to speak for fear of stopping her now. 'My father was made captain of High Lord Mandra's flight and my mother and I came to live in the mountain; we were afforded that honour with my father's position.' Her eyes flicked across to Jaron and away again.

'I was seventeen and out on an errand for my mother when a red firedrake landed in the valley and its rider dismounted and walked towards me.' In the firelight Jaron saw her slow smile. 'He was not much older than me, lanky as a young colt, and with a shock of thick hair that fell below his shoulders and eyes that pierced me to my core. '*That looks too heavy a bundle for you to carry,*' he said and before I knew what had happened he had taken my load from me and was asking where I was going with it. When I told him, he said he would fly me to the village if I wanted to,' her eyes were shining as she remembered. 'Of course, I said yes! A great red firedrake and a handsome young rider. I had seen him from afar but never so close. I put my shyness to one side and he flew me to my errand.' Rella laughed and Jaron could see that excited young girl. 'I had been on my father's firedrake, of course, but to be on the great red...' she sighed, lost in her memories. 'After that he seemed to appear whenever I was out of the kitchens. I never in my wildest dreams imagined that the son of our lord would be interested in me. People started to notice but when I asked him if he minded, him a lord and me a kitchen girl, he laughed then berated me. '*He was the lucky one,*' he always said.' Rella paused and seemed to be considering something more before meeting Jaron's gaze.

'And that was how Lord Carna and I met.'

Jaron was jolted out of his reverie. 'Lord Carna?'

'Yes.'

'Not... Torrit, my father?' Jaron's voice was a whisper.

Rella shook her thick hair. 'Carna was my first love.'

Jaron digested this news and she waited, silent, until he looked up. 'But... why didn't you stay with him then? What about Torrit?' He frowned. 'I don't understand.'

Rella smiled sadly. She turned away from him again as she stared into the night. 'Carna had one brother, Lord Torrit, older by three years. Both boys were loved by their father but Torrit, being the eldest, would inherit his father's mantle and become High Lord so it was natural he would be the most revered by the council and his father. From the first moment he saw me and his brother together Torrit wanted me. I knew it. I sensed it. Carna told me that in childhood Torrit always took from his younger brother. As a young man it was no different, it was like some terrible game to him. He was jealous of what his younger brother and I had. Eventually, Torrit went to his father and announced he wanted to make me his.'

Jaron shook his head, hardly believing what he was hearing. 'But,' he whispered, 'surely the oldest son of a high lord…'

Rella's smile was bitter. 'Couldn't set up with a lowly cook? This isn't Tiara, Jaron. There are no rules to say otherwise. Whoever he chose was his, and he chose me, despite Carna's strenuous protests. High Lord Mandra thought Carna too young to know his own mind,' she sighed. 'He gave Torrit his blessing and there was nothing to be done, not by Carna and not by me. I was to feel honoured by such an offer.' Her voice was fading. When she spoke again it was a mere whisper, 'Carna wanted to take me and leave but I couldn't let him do it. He was next in line. I couldn't take him away from the place he loved and a firedrake flyer belongs here in Rakenar.' She sighed. 'Lord Mandra came to see me. He wanted me to stop the feud between his sons. I had no choice but to accept Torrit.' She bowed her head into shadow again. 'Every day I saw the hurt and rage in Carna's eyes and it didn't diminish.' She raised her head and her eyes were shining with unshed tears. 'I knew I couldn't stay and it broke my heart.' Jaron saw a tear slide down her cheek. He pushed his hand out towards where hers lay, but she didn't take it.

'The only person I told of my intention to leave was my friend Oran. I trusted him and he made the arrangements. With Oran's help, I left and travelled south to live amongst the villages where my mother's relations lived. Torrit was looking for me and I moved whenever one of the villagers heard he was close. In time, the sightings got less and less. I was pregnant and at last I finally managed to settle enough for you to be born,' she smiled across at him and lifted a hand to brush his fringe away. 'You were the light in my life, Jaron, and I never regretted my decision, never.'

Jaron stared as he digested her words. 'But... I thought you left because your mother died. To live with your aunt.'

His mother shook her head. 'She died years later. And I was not at her side.' Tears glistened in her eyes. She took a moment to compose herself, took a deep breath and continued. 'We were living in Harnt when seven years later I met Teel, your stepfather, and I loved him, he was a good man and a good father to you.' she sighed. 'For many years I was content – until that terrible night.'

She was silent while Jaron digested all that she had told him. He couldn't help feeling there was something more she wasn't revealing. His mind began to race like a trapped bird. 'It was all because of me,' he whispered.

'No,' her reply was immediate. She shifted in her chair to face him properly. 'I left because I couldn't bear to stay. Jaron, you are the best thing that's ever happened to me. I feel blessed to have you. I wouldn't change a thing if it meant I wouldn't have you in my life.' Despite her words, her eyes slid away from him. There was something she still wasn't telling him, he felt it. *And where was Torrit now?*

'Is Torrit dead?' he asked in a tight voice. He had to be, now Carna was lord. Jaron found he hoped he was after what the man had done to his mother.

'No.' She dashed his hopes with one word. 'He was banished.'

'Banished? But... wasn't he high lord by then?' Jaron couldn't believe it could get any worse. 'It must have been something been really bad for Rakenar's leader to be banished.'

'It was.' She swallowed and lifted her eyes to meet his. They were wide, fearful. His heart began to hammer in his chest. He knew what she was waiting for. It was the reason she had told him more than a mother might have done. It had all led to this. His hands started to shake and Rella reached out and clasped them tight.

'It was him, wasn't it?' he asked in a small voice.

'Yes,' she still held onto him like a drowning woman.

'Torrit, my father, it was he who razed the village that night. He was after you.'

His mother bowed her head, her hair falling across her face. 'Yes,' she whispered.

Jaron went cold. 'There *was* a rider, it was him – and you knew it!' He pulled his hands free and stood up, scraping his chair back. Rella quickly rose with him, her eyes wide with fear.

'I didn't know, Jaron – not until I met Carna again.' She came around the table but he took a step back out of reach. His father was a killer. His father had razed a whole village to the ground. His father had taken Rella by force – and *he* was the result.

'Jaron–' She was in front of him, her arms going around him.

'Get off!' he shouted into her shocked face and threw off her arms. 'Leave me alone!' He stumbled into the cave and fell onto the bed.

'Oh, Jaron,' her voice was full of fear and hurt and he could hear she was crying. 'Jaron, I'm so sorry, please listen. Torrit didn't know you existed; had he known I'm sure he wouldn't have burnt you.'

'No! I don't want to hear anymore.' He buried his head in the soft embrace of the pillow, balling it up into his fists. A sob racked his body. He couldn't take it in, all he could do was lay there and quietly rage against what she had told him. He heard his mother's light steps cross the cave. When he at last raised his tear-streaked face from the damp pillow the room was empty.

His hands clenched and released until Jaron gave the pillow a hefty punch. Torrit, his father, murderer of all those villagers, of Teel... He flipped over onto his back and wiped at his wet face. She had kept this from him. Had treated him like a child. Well, he would show her he could be a man and make his own decisions.

He sat up and stared out into the night through the open doors, at the dark shapes of the mountains reaching up into the starred sky, at the lighted caves he could see running like fairy lights across the walls of the mountains. All he could think of was the power of the beasts that slept out on their ledges, the destruction they could wreak.

Another tear ran down his cheek and he angrily dashed at it. His jaw set and he knew what he had to do. He would leave here, first thing tomorrow, no matter what they said, Carna nor his mother. He wanted to be no part of Rakenar. Not anymore.

Mind made up, he lay back down. Yes, it was the best option. Return to Tiara and take up where he left off. He could make a good career as a race rider. He would forget all about who his father was. He got up to close the doors and collected together a few clothes and his old boots, wrapping them up in the bedside chair blanket. His leg had healed well – there was no need to stay any longer.

14

Jaron woke and took a moment to let the image of Teel fade from his dreams. He wiped at his wet face and turned over onto his side. He shifted automatically to make his leg more comfortable, absently noting his wound wasn't sore anymore, sniffed, and opened his eyes.

Oran was sitting by his bed. Jaron blinked, and sat up with a start.

The master carpenter sat languidly in the bedside chair, the ankle of one tasselled velvet boot balancing on his knee. His hands were steepled and above them his black-lined rich brown eyes watched Jaron intently. 'Good morning,' he said, raising his head and placing his chin on his fingers. He wore a rather bright satin blue shirt with voluminous sleeves.

'Is it?' Jaron muttered. Adjusting his pillows, he lay back against them and waited for the carpenter to say something. When he didn't but continued to stare at Jaron, his lips in a concentrated pout, the boy shifted uneasily under his silent scrutiny; he felt uncomfortable that Oran had been watching him while he slept. Clearing his throat, he asked, 'How long have you been sitting there?'

'Not long.' Oran reached to one side and plucked a tankard off the table beside him, lifting the lid. 'Here, it's still warm.'

Jaron accepted the tankard and eyed the green liquid suspiciously. It smelt of damp dead leaves in autumn and warm soil. 'What is it?'

'It's brewed leaves from the Tapala tree; a stunted tree that grows at the base of the mountains, very invigorating.'

Jaron took a sip. The taste was as earthy as it smelt and the consistency more like soup than tea but as it slipped down he realised he quite liked the bitter taste and felt his body thrum in response. He took another sip. Oran was right, it did indeed invigorate. Now fully awake, he peered at the master carpenter over the tankard rim.

Oran smiled. 'You are wondering why I am here.'

'Well, yes, did my mother send you?'

'No, she does not know.'

His response made Jaron even more uneasy.

'Then why–'

But Oran raised a hand to cut off further questions. Jaron was already beginning to feel irritated with this strange dramatic man. Oran unfolded himself from the chair, leaned forward and placed his elbows on his knees. 'I am here because Rella is too upset to see you this morning.'

'Too upset?' Jaron felt a flush of shame colour his cheeks but he felt anger too and raised his chin a little, only to drop it again when he realised Oran would be getting a good view of his scarred neck. 'Well, I've been a little upset myself,' he muttered.

Oran looked pointedly down at the bulging bundle left on the floor. 'I can see. Going somewhere?' His painted eyebrows arched. Jaron set his jaw and glared down into the tankard. He heard Oran sigh. 'Ah, so you have judged your mother and found her guilty. It is all too easy to blame when one feels powerless, young Jaron, all too easy to judge in hindsight.'

Jaron sat up straighter, angry now. 'Do you know what she told me? About my...' He couldn't say the word and looked down again at the tankard clasped tightly in his hands.

'Your father. Yes.' Oran stood up with deceptive grace for one so tall and began to pace around the cave, shirt sleeves billowing, and looking at the floor with a slight frown pulling at his smooth features. Jaron watched him, grimly silent. At last, Oran stopped and faced him. 'Do you realise what it cost her to tell you? She worried and fretted until Carna pointed out it was more dangerous to *not* tell you. Better you heard it from her lips than some well-meaning stranger.' He continued his pacing. 'And you would have heard it, my dear boy, here in Rakenar – an innocent mention of Torrit, how he was, what he became–'

'A murderer.' Jaron heard his voice break on the word. *My father.*

Oran came to stand at the foot of Jaron's bed, his face grave. 'As it turned out, yes. But nobody had any idea of what he was truly capable of. Rella knew he might come after her so she planned her escape well, but not even she, who suffered him the most, knew he would bear such hatred so many years later, nor go so far.' He sighed. 'Your mother sacrificed all that she could have become, her life here, her love, leaving her own mother behind – to protect you.'

'Only it didn't work, did it?'

'She saved you from being brought up by him.'

'But Teel and the villagers weren't saved. They all died.'

'I know, she told me. But you would have suffered Torrit's cruelty all your growing life, Jaron. Your mother endured it for herself, but she vowed never to allow him to do it to her child.'

'I suffer it anyway,' Jaron countered. 'I will bear the scars from his firedrake's fire for as long as I live.' He wedged the tankard between his knees, staring moodily into the cooling dark liquid. 'None of this would have happened if I hadn't existed,' he mumbled.

Oran sucked in a sharp breath. 'Don't you *ever* say that again! Especially not to your mother!' He spoke with such force it startled Jaron. 'That is a coward's way of talking, Jaron, and I don't think you are that.' The man scowled for a bit longer then his shoulders drooped and he appeared deflated. The bed dipped as he sat on its edge. 'She was afraid of this,' Oran muttered, half to himself. 'I know you suffer still, Jaron.' He reached out and patted his knee. 'I heard your anguish while you slept.'

Jaron bit his lip and looked away.

'It is not of your doing, dear boy, none of it,' Oran said softly, 'not your mother leaving Rakenar, nor the village being attacked. But did you really need to hear me say this? No, *look* at me.' Jaron felt his throat tighten as he did as he was bid. Oran smiled but his eyes were sad. 'Your mother came to me for help before her pregnancy started to show. She was trying to do what was best, the only way she knew how, yet every day she bears the guilt of your injury and what happened to your village and stepfather. A man she also loved.' He paused. 'She blames herself for all of it.'

'No,' Jaron whispered.

'Yes.' Oran's face hardened. 'And now *you* are trying to do the same – when your father didn't even know of your existence. It is *Torrit* at fault. I tell your mother this, as I now tell you; over and over I say it, but I cannot banish her guilt. Do not blame your mother for doing what she could to protect you – she already blames herself more than you ever could.'

'I don't blame her,' Jaron said in a small voice. 'It was a shock, that she hated my father, that he was a…' He trailed off but found he couldn't voice the word again. He put the tankard on his bedside table and clasped his hands tightly together.

'You are your father's son, it is a fact,' Oran said softly. Jaron stared miserably at him. The carpenter placed his own large heavy hand on both of his where they lay in Jaron's lap. 'But you are your mother's also and have the blood of the Rakenar lords in your veins, many of whom were adored by the people. From what I have heard from your mother and Carna and seen for myself – you are a gentle boy and far

removed from what Torrit was like at your age.' Oran
sighed. 'A cruel boy, always, cruel and a bully. Carna was
the quiet one, the sensitive one, and I think you take more
after your uncle, young Jaron.'

Jaron shook his head. 'I think you are seeing things.'

Oran laughed and his smile was kind. 'It was a shock for
you. I can also see you and your mother have something
special. Will you let Torrit ruin that too? After all Rella's
efforts to protect you?'

Jaron felt a sudden rush of shame and bowed his head.
'No.'

'Good,' Oran whispered and, bending forward, lifted his
hand to grip Jaron's shoulder. He gave him a little shake.
'Now, we move on with our lives, yes?' Jaron nodded. 'And
we go to see your mother now?' Jaron swallowed and
nodded again. Oran released him and stood. 'I will be
outside.'

Jaron rose and dressed quickly. Oran was waiting at the
tunnel end and indicated they were to turn left along the
walkway. Jaron could feel his eyes on him, studying his
walk, and he tried to remember to look up and keep himself
straight.

'The wedge in your boot helps?' Oran asked.

'Yes, thank you, it feels much better.'

Oran appraised him and nodded in satisfaction. 'I can see
it does, very good.'

It wasn't long before the carpenter stopped at a tunnel
much larger than Jaron's own and with a heavy door set in
the entrance. 'She's here?' Jaron was surprised she was his
neighbour.

'This is Carna's cave, so yes, she is here.' Oran knocked
twice and stood back. Jaron was still coming to terms with
the fact his mother lived with Carna when they heard
footsteps and the lord himself pulled open the door. He was
dressed in his usual riding clothes but stood in socked feet.

He stared at them with tired eyes.

'Oran,' he greeted the carpenter and opened the door wide for them to enter.

The cave beyond was at least four times the size of Jaron's; a tapestry hung on one wall depicting a red firedrake flying amongst a flock of greens. He recognized the valley that was outside his own cave woven into the fabric at the bottom of the tapestry. Walking further in Jaron looked around the room. It was furnished with matching dark polished wood, the legs engraved with intricate designs of firedrakes. A huge table graced the middle of the room, which Jaron guessed was for meetings, and a long, padded seat sat under a window that had been cut into the rock and served to throw some light into the room. A pair of worn boots stood by the wall and a leather tunic was thrown over a stone firedrake statue that reared up in one corner, obscuring the head.

'She's through here, Jaron.' Carna walked past him and led the way to a large curtain at the other end. He pulled it aside and waved him through.

The room faced out onto a ledge much like Jaron's did, but again was much larger. There Carna's red firedrake lay, his massive stomach rising like bellows as he slept, head turned away and tucked under a folded wing. He fitted comfortably on the large ledge with room to spare for two more. Jaron didn't look twice at Madrag but went straight over to the bed and the mound of blankets that was Rella.

'Mum?' She didn't respond and he sat on the bed. 'Mum. It's me.' Slowly, the covers stirred and Rella's face emerged. Her son was shocked at her appearance. Her eyes were red-rimmed with grey shadows underneath; her hair, usually so sleek, was dishevelled from the sleepless night she must have had. Jaron felt a rush of guilt. *I caused this.*

'Jaron,' she croaked but she didn't smile and her eyes were large in her drawn face.

'I'm sorry,' he said and the words came out in a rush. 'I didn't mean it. I didn't know what I was saying. I'm sorry I shouted at you – I just needed time.' He looked down, avoiding her gaze. Her hand found its way out from under the covers. Jaron took it and clutched it tight. 'I'm sorry,' he whispered again.

Rella seemed to come to life then; she shoved back the blankets and sat up. 'It's me who should be sorry,' her voice was strained. 'It was too much for you to hear, but I was left with no choice, not if I wanted you to stay in Rakenar. You had to know, all of it, and as it was I'd left it too long.' She scooted forward and put her arms around him. Jaron, pressed against her chest and with his arms around her waist, breathed in her familiar jasmine scent and thought how light her body felt, so delicate, like a bird. He forgot that, he realised, how small she was; her spirit served to make her larger than life and he had callously broken it with his hurt and anger. He pulled back a little and looked at her worn beautiful face.

'It was the shock. I couldn't take it all in.'

'And now?' she asked, her voice barely more than a whisper.

'Oran talked to me. I just want us to be alright, to move on.'

She smiled and stroked his fringe back from his face. 'Don't be silly, we will always be alright.'

Jaron nodded, relieved.

Oran sniffed loudly then and they both looked at him. The master carpenter was dabbing at his eyes, a lace-trimmed handkerchief coming away with dark smudges. 'I'm sorry,' he said. Rella smiled and beckoned him over. She reached up to stroke his cheek.

'My very good friend,' she said. 'Dear Oran, still looking out for me after all these years.'

Oran leant his head into her hand then engulfed it into his

own and kissed it. 'I will always be here for you, my lady.'

Jaron noticed Carna standing apart while he observed the little group. He had forgotten the Raken lord was even in the room. His arm was looped around Madrag's neck, who was now wide awake and watching the three of them. But it was not the red firedrake who Jaron was looking at now, it was the rare wide smile etched onto the Raken lord's face.

15

Long ago, the Raken people lived in caves in the Arkenara mountain range that marked the Northern Lands. Their villages had been burned to the ground by the flying beasts that preyed on them. Forced to live in the caves like animals and enduring daily attacks by the fire-breathing dragons, the people were at constant war and losses were high. These were dark days for our people…

Jaron stared at the ink drawing of a firedrake breathing fire into a cave whilst another flew with a dead man clutched bleeding in his talons. The book had been given to him by Carna. 'Time you learned about your people, Jaron,' he had said.

Jaron had taken the large but slim leather-bound book eagerly and flicked through the pages. There were short passages with ink drawings dotted throughout. He had looked up at his uncle, disappointed. 'But it's a child's book.'

Carna had shrugged. 'You've got some catching up to do and this is the quickest version.'

Jaron turned over the page and began to read.

A child was born to Ayla, wife of Chief Leon, head of the Raken tribe. He was named Rillion son of Leon. As he grew he was expected to take his place by his father's side and fight the dragons.

But Rillion felt only wonder at the beasts. Still more boy than man, Rillion began to observe the dragons. One day, whilst out on his first hunting party with his father, they were attacked. Leon felled the dragon with a well-aimed spear at its wing. It crashed to the ground and the men ran in to kill it. But Rillion could see the bulging belly of the female and couldn't bring himself to join in. When the men at last stepped back he moved forward and, taking his knife, sliced the belly open to extract a single, gleaming white egg.

Jaron stared at the picture of a boy kneeling at the shoulder of the dead firedrake and holding up the egg while the men looked on. He turned the page but there came a knock on the door at the back of the cave before he could read on.

'Come in,' he called, looking up. The curtain was already drawn back and as the door opened a red-haired girl of about his own age peered round it at him. He remembered her, the girl who flew the green.

'Hello,' she said. 'Not disturbing you, am I?'

'Not at all… Marla,' Jaron said, remembering her name and closing the book. Marla sauntered into the room, her wavy red hair cascading over her hunched shoulders and with her hands stuffed deep into her tunic pockets. She wore the soft leather trousers and boots that all the riders wore.

'Nice,' she said, looking around. 'The students' rooms are cupboards with a bunk bed and not much else.'

'Where is that?' Jaron asked, waving her to the chair. She sat carefully and ran her hand over the soft leather arm before settling back and crossing her legs.

'In Mount Treen,' she puckered her lips. 'But the lower level on the east side, it's where all the students stay.' Her eyes flicked to the book now closed on his bed. 'I recognise that book.'

Jaron held it up. 'I'm to learn about the history of the Raken people.'

'I read it when I was seven,' her violet eyes appraised him.

Jaron shifted uncomfortably. 'Carna gave me the quick version to catch up.' He put the book down, surreptitiously pushing it half under his pillow.

'Don't you mean *Lord* Carna?'

'Um, yes, of course.' Jaron felt on the back foot already and this strange girl had only been in here a short time. She got up and wandered round the room again. He watched her move to the open doors and lean against the doorway as she stared out at the view. He wanted to go over and join her but, unsure of himself, stayed sitting on the bed, glad he had thought to put on his scarf that morning.

'Nice,' he heard her say again before she turned back to look at him. 'Are you feeling better?'

'Yes, thank you. The bandage is off.' He put a hand to his thigh and his fingers trailed over the scar left under his trousers. Another scar that he would bear for the rest of his life. 'It itches sometimes but doesn't hurt. And I've been doing the exercises the healer prescribed…' He trailed off, aware he was babbling, and watched as Marla pushed off from the doorway and returned to her seat.

'That's good,' she said. For a moment she stared at him then put her elbows on her knees. 'It's strange you being here.'

'What do you mean?' He would die if everyone knew of his fears.

'I mean here, in Mount Scarf and on this level, right next door to where Lord Carna lives. Only our lord and the council leaders live up here,' she looked him in the eye. 'Are you someone?'

Jaron swallowed. 'Someone? I'm not sure if I know what you mean.'

She waved a hand in his direction. 'People are talking, wondering about you. Our lord rescued you and brought you here and he seems to be taking quite an interest in your wellbeing.' She rested her chin on her hand and looked at him from under her long lashes.

Jaron stared. 'Um, well yes, he did rescue me but Mum

used to know him and they are good, err, friends,' he swallowed under her shrewd gaze. 'That's probably it.'

She nodded but it didn't put her off. 'So why–'

'How's it going in firedrake school?' he interrupted.

It worked. Her face broke into a broad grin, showing those dimples. 'Great, I'm top of the class so Parl says. Of course, Tench is furious.'

'Tench?'

'He's son of Thorel Rand, chief advisor to our Lord Carna,' she added, on seeing his questioning look. 'Tench thinks he's better than anyone else so he's really put out. Channon, the school firedrake?' Jaron nodded. 'She doesn't like him, I can tell. She allows him on her back but she's not quite so quick for him.' Marla laughed, a surprisingly deep sound, Jaron thought.

'So, when do you get your own firedrake?' he asked, intent on keeping the conversation safely on the subject of flying school.

'When the firedrake mothers return,' she tucked her thick wavy hair behind one ear. It immediately sprang free again. 'They fly off to lay their eggs at the nesting mountains and the scouts follow then keep an eye on them with their riders, who camp by the nests to help protect them. They incubate the eggs for four weeks until they hatch and it's another six months of training before the drakel are strong enough to take a rider.'

'Drakel?'

'Young firedrake.' Marla sat back, her eyes shining. 'I can't wait for mine! Scouts' word is they should be here in about three weeks' time.'

Jaron found himself envying her and his feelings surprised him. 'You choose your firedrake?'

'And they choose us, well, the drakel chooses really. If a rider is rejected by the firedrake she or he picks, then nothing for it but to move on to the next one.' She stopped talking and dimpled at Jaron, who couldn't help but smile back. 'So, if you're joining us there's not much time.'

Jaron's smile froze. 'I'm sorry?'

Marla's grin became fixed in turn at the look on his face. She spoke carefully. 'I mean, I was as surprised as anybody when Parl said we would be getting a new student so late in the course…' She trailed off as Jaron stood up.

'I think there must be some kind of mistake,' he said, and despite himself he heard his words rasp.

Marla stood as well and Jaron had forgotten she was slightly taller than him. 'No, I don't think so,' she said, looking down at him and arching her ginger eyebrows.

'Your teacher must have been talking about somebody else, I mean, did he mention me by name?'

'No.'

'Well then,' Jaron said, relieved.

'Parl said the injured boy who had been flown in on Madrag four weeks ago.'

Jaron's shoulders slumped and he sat down on his bed with a heavy thud.

'Look, is there a problem here?' Marla asked. 'I mean, don't you *want* to come to flying school?' This last was said in absolute disbelief.

Before Jaron could reply there came another knock and the door at the back of the cave opened to reveal Flick. 'Marla! What are you doing up here?' The girl gave a guilty start and a flush spread over her face as Flick strode over and stopped in front of them, putting his hands on his hips. 'Students aren't allowed up here, you know that, Marla. Have you been stealing Channon again? I wondered what she was doing perched on the walkway inside.'

'She came to see me,' Jaron said, standing up again to face Flick. He felt the need to protect his new friend. 'I invited her.'

Flick frowned. 'Well, I suppose it'll be okay – this time.

You wouldn't know, Jaron, but students aren't allowed up on this level.' His blue eyes narrowed. 'Marla, you'd best get Channon back where she belongs. You know she's old and it's enough for her to be working with the students, let alone you flying her about out of classes. A good rider always thinks of her firedrake first.'

Marla lowered her head further in shame, thick red hair falling like a rippled curtain across her face. 'Yes, Lord Flick,' she said and ducked past them both to the door. Behind Flick's back her face broke into a cheeky grin. 'Bye Jaron,' and with a wink and a wave she was gone.

'She wasn't doing any harm,' Jaron said.

Flick was unrepentant. 'She's too cheeky by far that one. She took advantage of you, Jaron.'

'Well, there's not many people my own age I know round here.' He folded his arms and eyed Flick. 'Although I hear all that's about to change.'

The young man looked confused. 'What do you mean?'

'Apparently I'm to be enrolled in flying school?'

'Ah, Parl must have told them.' Flick's tanned face broke into a grin. 'Great, isn't it? You'll get the chance to make some new friends.'

Jaron's lips tightened. 'I take it Lord Carna arranged it?'

'Your uncle wanted to tell you himself, but that little madam got in first. Had we known you'd met her he wouldn't have left anything to chance and told you sooner.'

Jaron stared. 'You know?'

'What? Oh, about you being Lord Carna's nephew? Of course!' Flick grinned. 'I can't tell you how pleased I am, Jaron. You're of Raken blood. I think I knew it from the first moment I saw you.'

Jaron slumped down onto the bed. Flick sat down next to him. 'Look, Jaron,' he said. 'I know it's hard for you. Oh yes,' he said, as the boy looked up in surprise. 'Lord Carna and your mother told me what happened to you at the village. Your mother thought I should know, us being friends and all.'

Friends. Jaron thought about it. Back in Tiara this personable young man had been a firedrake rider to avoid. Now, he realised how much he looked forward to his visits. He met Flick's steady gaze.

'I don't mind you knowing, Flick. It's just…'

'What?'

Jaron pushed himself off the bed and limped over to the open doors. He spoke looking out over the valley. 'I feel ashamed, Flick.'

'Of what?' Flick was at his shoulder in an instant. 'There's nothing for you to be ashamed about.' His voice was fierce.

'I'm terrified of the beasts,' he admitted in a hoarse whisper. 'I'm scared of them, Flick, the firedrake. How can I make a life for myself here and stay with my mother when every time a firedrake flies over I feel like dropping to the floor and rolling into a ball?'

'I'm not surprised, given the circumstances.' Flick laid a hand on his shoulder. 'You need to cut yourself a little slack, Jaron. No doubt I would be the same if I'd gone through what you went through.'

'No, I don't believe you would,' Jaron said. Then a thought occurred to him and he turned to face the rider. 'But you knew already how I felt, didn't you?' Flick nodded and Jaron sighed. 'And I thought I'd covered it up pretty well.'

Flick smiled. 'I guessed. We're kind of used to that reaction from anyone who doesn't know the firedrake,' he paused. 'And Tarp and I heard you, one night… on watch.'

He means the screaming. Embarrassed, Jaron looked away.

'But the important thing is that you're going to try. That's right, isn't it?'

Jaron hesitated and at last nodded. 'Yes, yes I am.'

'Well then,' Flick stepped back, rubbing his hands together in a brisk fashion. 'We'd best get started.'

'Started with what?'

'Your first ride.'

Jaron felt his chest constrict. 'You don't mean…'

Flick's smile was sympathetic. 'Yes, I do, Jaron. Lord Carna wanted to do it himself but Rella thought it would be too much for you to fly a red just yet. He is the same colour as Brane, after all.'

'Brane?'

'Torrit's firedrake.' Flick was watching him carefully.

Jaron stared. So Torrit's red firedrake was called Brane. The beast who had razed the village and killed his stepfather. His scarred chest burned against his shirt.

'Jaron?' Flick asked, his gaze concerned.

'I'm alright,' Jaron breathed.

'With Tarp being smaller they thought it might be easier for you.' Flick waited while Jaron digested all this and thought it through. 'And I thought we could go looking for your kelpra.'

'Caliber?' Not a day had gone by without Jaron wondering about him. He chewed his lip. Caliber had saved him from the Ernots, had fought for him. He had to know what had happened to him. At last he looked up at a watching Flick and nodded yes.

Flick grinned. 'Alright then! I'll go and get Tarp.' Flick strode out the room but was immediately back again, carrying a fleece-lined leather jacket. 'Here,' he handed it to Jaron. 'It can get cold in the air. I brought this for you.' In a daze, Jaron took it. The jacket was heavy. 'Won't be long,' Flick said.

Left alone, Jaron stared down at the jacket. No doubt Flick had put it in the tunnel on his way in. First hearing about flying school and now this, he felt manipulated; a pawn. Jaron threw the jacket on the bed and clenched and unclenched his fists. His palms started to sweat and he took a deep breath. He couldn't back out, not now. His pride wouldn't allow it and he owed it to Caliber to do this. He squared his shoulders. It was time for lesson two.

16

Jaron pulled on his boots and put on the jacket. Then he took it off again because he felt too hot. He was sweating and not only from wearing the heavy fleece-lined coat. He limped back and forth, slapping his thigh to centre himself. It occurred to him that Flick was leaving him time to get prepared, for he could have just whistled for Tarp from Jaron's ledge. The more he thought about what he was about to do, the more he found he couldn't breathe. He stopped and bent over to put his hands on his knees, forcing himself to take deep juddering breaths. *Think of lesson one, you touched him, remember? Touched a firedrake, a big flaming beast of a red firedrake. And you have flown before.* But Jaron knew he was kidding himself. When Lord Carna had rescued him and forced him onto Madrag it was only a short time before he passed out. No, this would be his first flight. The one that counted. If he could do it.

'Jaron?' Flick's voice caused Jaron to jump and he hurriedly straightened from his bent position. Tarp was hovering just outside, long neck turned and green eyes watching him. Sitting behind the young rider was Lord Carna and even from here Jaron could see his etched frown. The boy noticed Flick was also looking at him with some concern and he forced a smile and moved closer to the entrance even though his legs were shaking.

'I'll get Tarp to land,' Flick warned him and the firedrake swung closer to the ledge. Jaron glimpsed the brown underbelly just before Tarp landed. The firedrake furled his wings and swung his head so it was on the threshold of

Jaron's room. A rumbling came from his chest as the eyes fixed unblinking on his.

'Good morning, Jaron,' Lord Carna said as he slid off. Jaron gave a short bow from where he now stood further back in his room. Flick had dismounted and gone to turn Tarp's head. He grinned over at Jaron. 'Tarp said hello,' he called.

'Uh, hello Tarp,' Jaron's voice sounded unnaturally high to his own ears. Carna had stepped into his room and was now waiting for him, a riding helmet dangling from one hand. As Jaron forced his legs to move closer he caught the grim set of the Raken lord's face. It made him feel even more uneasy; was what he was going to do that dangerous?

'I'm sorry, Jaron,' Carna said as he approached. 'You were told I had made arrangements for you to start flying school.' The boy caught the flash of the other's eyes and realised the Raken lord was fuming. 'I would have liked to have given you more time and it should have come from me or your mother.'

'Well, it did come as a bit of a shock.'

Carna's jaw muscles tensed. 'I will have words with Parl and see the girl is punished for her indiscretion.'

'Oh, no please,' Jaron held up his hands in denial. 'There's been no real harm done, I would have only been told of it later.' The last thing he wanted to do was to get Marla into trouble.

But Carna was not to be put off. 'No one is allowed at this level without permission, least of all a student.'

'I was glad to have her company.' Jaron swallowed under the lord's scrutiny. 'And it will help to know at least one person when I start.'

'So you agree?'

Jaron was perplexed. 'Agree – I don't understand.'

Carna crossed his arms. 'To enter flying school?'

'Err, I suppose so.' He saw Carna's hard-flinted gaze

soften and found he didn't feel quite so well disposed towards Marla now that he had lost his chance to get out of it. He looked across at the waiting Tarp. The firedrake was rubbing his head against Flick's shoulder, causing the young man to stagger then brace himself against his green to stay on his feet.

Carna held out the helmet. Reluctantly Jaron took it, surprised at its lightness. It lacked the leather plume that the riders often wore but leather bands were braided all over its surface. Jaron ran his fingers over the woven leather and felt the hard skull of the helmet beneath. At the front, just above the eye level, was a ridge of hard clear material; he supposed to keep the wind out of his eyes.

He put it on and Carna stepped forward to do up the chin strap as if he were a child and pulled out a pair of thick sheepskin gloves from where they had been tucked into his belt. He handed them to Jaron. 'Ready?' he asked. *Hardly,* Jaron thought, but he pulled on the gloves and managed to nod. Carna wasted no more time. Taking Jaron's arm, he marched him the last few yards to Tarp's side, who yawned, stretching his maw wide. Jaron made to pull back but the lord's hand on his upper arm prevented him.

'We've put a double saddle on for you,' Carna was saying and Jaron forced his eyes away from Tarp's fearsome looking teeth. 'See the straps there? You will be quite safe.' Jaron stared at the leather straps with hooks on their ends attached to the empty seat. Flick handed Carna a wide belt Jaron hadn't noticed he was holding and before he had time to think anymore Carna had bent down and was buckling him into it. It jangled a little and, looking down, Jaron saw metal rings were attached to the leather. He cast a wary eye at the firedrake who was again rubbing his head up and down Flick's back, nearly knocking the rider over.

'Flick!' Carna's voice rapped out directly below Jaron's chin, making him jump. 'Keep Tarp still.'

Flick looked shamefaced and whipped round to raise a hand palm out towards the firedrake, who instantly became statue-like. The young rider vaulted on to the firedrake's back, settled himself and looked down at Jaron with a broad grin. Jaron couldn't return it. Next moment he was being led to the firedrake's side, the massive belly rising and falling. Distracted by the nearness of the beast, Jaron jumped as Carna put his hands on his waist, obviously with the intention of putting him on. Tarp lifted a foreleg, his huge wing helpfully moving further back out of the way. The boy eyed the seat on the saddle destined for him. A sudden wave of panic threatened to choke him. 'No, wait,' he squeaked and tried to prise Carna's hands from his waist. 'I need more time.'

'The time is now,' Carna's voice came into his ear just before he lifted him like he was no weight at all and, with Jaron trapped in his arms, stepped up onto Tarp's leg. Jaron had no time to register the scales filling his sight before Carna boosted him up. He landed chest first over the saddle and the air went out of his lungs in a whoosh. A glimpse of the green membrane of the wing folded just below – then Carna was pushing at his legs and before he knew it he was forced to grab hold of the saddle and awkwardly swing a leg over in the cramped space to settle behind Flick. A small squeak come out of his throat. He saw Carna was standing at his knee while balancing on Tarp's raised leg, his hands busily clipping Jaron's belt to the straps. Before he knew what he was about, Jaron clutched at the lord's forearm. Carna looked up and gave him a rare reassuring smile. 'Rella and I will be here when you return,' he said. The lord prised Jaron's hand free, stepped down from Tarp's raised foreleg, and gave a nod to Flick.

Tarp half unfurled his wings and Carna's face was obscured by the membrane as it stretched out. Jaron could see the long bones that ran just under the skin extending like huge skeletal fingers. The boy took a firm hold of Flick's jacket as the firedrake started to waddle round in a turn on the ledge with wings still half-raised.

The basin floor spread out before them, hemmed in by the mountain range. From Tarp's back, it looked even further down. Jaron gulped then leaned forward to wind his arms tight around Flick's waist. There Jaron crouched, eyes now tight closed as he waited for the inevitable boost up into the air. He felt Tarp's body beneath him dip slightly. Despite himself, he opened his eyes – just as Tarp stepped off the ledge, and dropped.

'Ah!' Jaron's stomach lurched up. A sound like a bed sheet catching the wind and his belly slumped back. The boy turned his face to press it against Flick's back and wondered if the young rider could feel his heart hammering.

After a moment, the unexpected lack of movement made Jaron lift his head despite his fear. The wing membrane beside him was stretched fully out as it rode the wind, making slight adjustments in the air. Jaron could see the mauves and blues that ran along the green wing from the midday sun, the veins ridged along its surface. Jaron shifted to look down over the firedrake's shoulder. Far below, he could see the green of the mountain valley and the mirror of the sun's light as it caught the river that ran along its length. He swallowed.

'Alright?' Flick had half-turned his face towards him.

'We're not moving,' Jaron tried to keep the panic from his voice. 'Why aren't we falling?'

'The wind and air pressure rising up the mountainside is keeping us here. Tarp just has to make minor adjustments to stay up. Best to take it slowly, I thought,' he grinned. 'So now we fly.' Flick faced front and leaned slightly forward. The firedrake's wings flapped once as he glided away from the mountain. Jaron hunkered down further as the wing rose right next to him, fearful lest it come further across and knock him off; he didn't trust the straps entirely.

They soared across the valley, Tarp's wings now fully outstretched and only occasionally giving a half-flap. The predominant sound was the breeze and after a moment Jaron sat up a little and peered over Flick's shoulder. He could see a wagon far below trundling down the valley road that rimmed the base of the mountains. It reminded him of the toy carriage he had played with as a young child, it seemed so tiny. They passed firedrake nesting on ledges in front of their rider's caves. Some curled up asleep, others stretched out; some with riders sitting out next to their firedrake as they watched them fly by. Apart from the breeze, Jaron felt an underlying quiet. It was quite peaceful even, he realised in surprise. They flew over the lake in the centre of the valley and the sun flashing off its surface momentarily blinded him. He twisted a little in the saddle, making sure he had a good hold of Flick's jacket as he risked a look behind him. Tarp's long tail snaked away into the air. Now and then it moved from side to side, making tiny adjustments. Beyond it Jaron could see his cave entrance a level down from the top of the huge mountain where the tiny figure of Carna stood watching them. The scale of it was an awesome sight.

'Still with me?' Flick said over his shoulder. 'How are you feeling?'

'Alright,' Jaron said, and the surprise in his voice made Flick chuckle.

'We're going to rise up and fly over the mountains, it will be a bit windier but I'll dip down as soon as I can.'

Jaron shifted forward and tucked his arms around Flick's waist again, apprehension rising anew. Tarp's long neck rose up in front of them, ears rippling in the breeze. His wings beat more strongly now and beneath the saddle Jaron could feel the muscles working harder. As the firedrake's body angled upwards Jaron felt the pull of gravity on his thighs and it seemed as though his stomach was travelling towards his backbone. Fear rose in his throat and he tightened his arms even further around Flick's waist, knotting his gloved fingers together whilst bringing his knees up into his customary race position out of habit. He peered over Flick's shoulder at the mountain top getting closer and closer, the harsh noon sun etching the ridges and crags. A flock of crows flew up in alarm at the firedrake's coming and their caws filled the air as they scattered. The mountainside fell away as they rose with dizzying speed. At last they were over its lip and a strong wind hit Jaron's face. The firedrake's body dropped a wing suddenly and Jaron gasped as he was thrown first to one side, then the other, thankful his arms were still knotted around Flick's waist.

'Sorry about that,' Flick's voice rushed past his ears. 'Always get a buffeting here.'

Tarp's front dipped sharply and now Jaron slipped forward until he was being pushed into Flick's back. At last, the wind eased and it was with some relief Jaron felt Tarp levelling out.

'This is the Arkenara,' Flick called back.

He risked a look over Flick's shoulder. A mountain range was laid out before them. Snow capped the higher peaks, jutting out of a blanket of downy cloud as far as the eye could see. It was so beautiful it took Jaron's breath away. They flew on and where the cloud thinned it rolled across the mountains like a silk sheet, the crags and canyons jagged dark tears. Jaron took a deep breath and dragged the sharp clear air into his lungs. As he let it out his tension eased a little.

As Tarp passed over the range the land opened out more into a different wilderness, full of rock and scrub with deep valleys. Jaron marvelled how quickly the land swept past below them. A canopy of forest came into view up ahead and Tarp flew lower over the trees. A flock of bright blue and pink birds cried out in alarm and tumbled into the air.

FIRE RIDER

The cries they made were unlike any bird he had heard, almost like a human's whistle.

'What are they?' he asked in Flick's ear.

'Myrads. Devilishly noisy birds, a real bane if you're trying to hunt – their calls travel far and alert everything. By the way, this forest we call Kenara.'

It was much steadier flying now and Jaron felt safe enough to look around and wonder at how quiet it was up here, the only sound the pushing of the wind. Flick didn't talk for a long while, letting him settle and get used to the flight. After roughly an hour had passed, the firedrake angled his right wing and Jaron felt them change direction slightly. He tightened his hold as Tarp's body slanted.

Flick pointed up ahead. 'There's the Notresia Mountains.'

Jaron stared at them. Far away in the distance they rose in a grey ridge of rotten teeth. He remembered when he had last seen them. He had only had the race on his mind back then, completely unaware of how his life was about to change.

The mountains drew ever closer and larger until they filled Jaron's sight. He shifted uneasily in the saddle, wondering when Tarp was going to rise to fly over them. Instead, the firedrake's body went into a roll.

'Flick!' Jaron shouted in alarm, his gloved fingers digging in as his whole world tilted.

'It's alright, Tarp's angling himself for the pass.'

Jaron peered over his shoulder. A dark slit between the mountains was fast approaching and Jaron eyed it warily, sure it was too narrow for such a big beast. He gripped even tighter as they flew sideways into the darkened pass. A sudden shocking wave of cold air made him gasp and he risked a look up to see sheer rock flashing by in a blur. There was a roaring sound in his ears and turning his head Jaron saw a river broiling far below, churning along the narrow crag floor. Feeling sick and uncomfortably hemmed in Jaron hunkered down, glad of the straps, yet he instinctively felt it was the pressure in the air that kept him miraculously in place.

Flick must have realised his discomfort. 'We'll be out in the open soon,' he called back to him.

At last, Tarp came out of the pass and the sun hit them again as they levelled out over thick green forest. Swallowing the acrid taste in his mouth, Jaron looked down over the Rotarn Forest. He stared at the green canopy as images of the attack and his own pain and near-death resurfaced in his mind. Tarp was following the path of the River Not as it widened and calmed its pace, partly obscured by trees. Jaron made himself look away.

In a short space of time, the borders of the Plains of Wake came into view, the vast plains spreading out to cover the land. Jaron gasped at how beautiful it was from the air. As Tarp moved into a silent glide, he could see brown blobs dotted over the landscape: the Tiarian cattle grazing, who did not even look up as they flew over. The golden grass turned into the bare stubble of the harvested fields and slowly the white-stone walls of Tiara rose out of the distant haze like a ghost city.

It surprised Jaron how much his heart leapt on seeing it. He thought of Liam and Sanra and realised how much he wanted to see them.

'Can we drop in on Tiara?' he asked Flick. When there was no response he tried again, shouting into the rider's ear with cupped hand. 'I said–'

'That wasn't in Lord Carna's instructions, and I thought you wanted to look for your kelpra?'

From the flat tone of Flick's voice there was no way he was going to be allowed to go to Tiara. Pushing down his irritation, as it wasn't Flick's fault, Jaron contented himself with enjoying the space of the plains after his cave and the dark tunnels of Mount Scarf.

Not long after, Tarp's wings back-flapped. Next moment, the firedrake's neck rose and he seemed to rear up in the air. Jaron, finally relaxed while he took in the view, would have tumbled backward if it hadn't been for the straps holding him to the saddle.

'Sorry,' Flick said, as Tarp hovered in the air and Jaron clutched at his jacket in alarm. 'Should have warned you.' Jaron could see his sheepish grin as he half-turned back to him.

It was uncomfortable hovering. Tarp's wings were held high and Jaron didn't like the flapping membrane hemming him in on both sides.

'This is where I dropped your yowling beast off,' Flick said, and right away Jaron forgot his discomfort.

'Which way did he go?'

'East,' Flick pointed and turned Tarp. With one powerful beat the firedrake increased his speed. Jaron looked back at the distant towers of Tiara fast disappearing behind him.

It took a while before the rippling dried grass turned into rough scrubland. Jaron had never realised how far the Wake extended beyond the city in this direction. Flick pointed down and Jaron leaned over to look, making sure his gloved fingers had a good hold of Flick's jacket.

A herd of deer were running and leaping below them. Tarp twisted his neck to look down and Jaron felt the saddle vibrate as he rumbled. Flick laughed. 'I know, boy, maybe later.'

'Is he hungry?'

'Not really, but that doesn't mean to say he wouldn't like a go.'

'Oh. Do you stay on his back when…?'

'He hunts? Some riders don't, but I like to be on Tarp's back so I'm right there with him.' He grinned over his shoulder, showing his teeth. 'It feels like I'm the one doing the hunting – it's quite a rush actually.'

Jaron tried to imagine how he would feel if Tarp was sweeping down on those deer, grabbing one up in his jaws. He shivered, and noticed the bushy scrubland below now had a few trees. They went by in a blur and soon there was nothing *but* trees below them. Tarp raised his level to fly over the top of the dense forest and the force of the wind picked up.

'The Camorian Forest,' Flick shouted back to him.

Jaron nodded and looked down but his eyes couldn't penetrate the canopy at all. It looked to be much thicker than even the Rotarn Forest and his hopes dropped to another level even as Tarp flapped his wings to fly higher still over a huge cedar. *It's impossible, I'll never find Caliber if he's down there.*

Flick must have sensed his disappointment. 'Don't worry, I know a gorge where it's more open.' He banked Tarp to the left.

As they flew on, still not wanting to give up, Jaron leant over Tarp's side as far as he dared and searched below for any breaks in the canopy. When he raised his head again he was surprised to see white stone walls rising out of the forest. Tarp headed straight for them. As they rose up to fly over the cliffs, Jaron gasped. A river broiled down one side into a cascading waterfall, water mist rising up from its depths. Below, there was a large flat valley with huge herds of grazing deer and antelope. He had never seen so many grazing animals in one place before. Tarp cocked his head and another low rumble shook the saddle.

'Shhh, Tarp, stay quiet.' Flick turned his head to speak to Jaron. 'A good place for a predator to hunt, we'll need to stay high enough so as not to spook them.'

They soared high above the herds, who were oblivious to the firedrake up above as they grazed undisturbed. Reaching the other side, Flick directed Tarp to land on one of the cliff tops. The green firedrake angled himself and Jaron clutched onto Flick's jacket again as he felt himself tipping back. He eyed the bare rock plateau getting closer. The firedrake did one backward flap as his head rose higher. Jaron felt a slight jolt as the firedrake's back legs came down before Tarp fell forward onto all fours, causing Jaron to nearly bump his nose on Flick's back.

'This is as good a vantage place as any,' Flick said as Tarp furled his wings. 'If you see anything start to run, look for what's frightened it. Perhaps it'll be kelpra.'

Jaron nodded and eagerly scanned the valley below. Tarp's ears were pricked in interest as he watched the herds. From the other side of the valley, the river rumbled in the background as it swept over the cliffs. The white of the plateau stone where they had landed seemed to radiate heat and the warmth was quite pleasant.

After a long while Tarp sighed and lowered his body as he settled into a more comfortable crouch. He turned his long neck and sniffed at the ground to one side. Whatever it was seemed to consume his attention and he rubbed his chin in it with relish.

'Hey, Tarp, stop that!' Flick slapped his neck. 'He'll stink now,' he said, sighing.

'I can't smell anything,' Jaron began, then gasped and put his hand over his nose as the pungent aroma reached his nostrils and hit the back of his throat.

The afternoon wore on and still nothing disturbed the grazing herds. The flies droned faintly around Tarp's head and Jaron opened his jacket. His head was hot under the helmet and he tried not to let the warmth and peace affect his attention, but gradually the tiredness of his first flight caught up with him and his eyelids began to droop.

'Jaron?' He started. Flick was looking at him, half turned in the saddle. He must have nodded off. Mortified, the boy sat up to pay attention. 'Nice to see you're relaxed, not too bad so far, eh?' Flick's smooth tanned face was smiling.

Jaron thought about it. 'No, not too bad,' he said in surprise.

Flick laughed, showing even white teeth. Jaron felt a prickle of annoyance and it must have shown on his face for the young Raken's eyes were suddenly serious. 'I know how difficult it was for you to get on Tarp, Jaron.'

'Sometimes I don't think I'm going to ever feel as comfortable as the Raken riders do.'

Flick hitched a leg over Tarp's wither so he was sitting sideways. 'You will, I promise you; after all, each firedrake you've come into contact with seems to like you and that's very unusual.'

'Is it?'

'Oh yes, they're one-man beasts normally.'

Tarp let out another large sigh, his sides lifting their legs. Flick laughed. 'We'd better head back, it's getting too hot for anything to hunt this afternoon. Don't want you out too long for your first flight.'

'I'm fine,' Jaron mumbled.

'Well, let's not overcook it.' Flick turned and swung his leg back over Tarp's wither. 'Anyway, there are wild firedrake here and its best we don't run into them.'

Jaron was instantly fully alert. 'What? Where?'

Flick pointed to a now squashed brown mess forward of the firedrake's head. 'I'm afraid that's what we can smell.'

'Would they attack us?' Jaron cast fearful looks all about.

'It's unusual.'

'*Unusual?* You mean it has happened?'

'The wild blues are rare now, and those left would rather avoid their tame brethren.' Flick clicked at Tarp and Jaron hunkered forward to hang on tight as the firedrake opened his wings. 'Ready?'

Jaron barely had time to answer before Tarp dropped off the ledge and Jaron's stomach lurched up into his ribcage as the green swept down at dizzying speed. He levelled out low across the valley, causing the grazing beasts to look up with a start. A stag hollered a warning and the herds began to run. Flick whooped in delight and Jaron closed his eyes as the firedrake flew over the pounding haunches and brown backs of the galloping, leaping herds before arcing steeply up and over the valley rim. Tarp settled into a glide with outstretched wings over the forest, Flick complaining loudly at the whiff that radiated back towards them from Tarp's head.

Behind them, unseen and directly below their former landing place, two purple eyes emerged from the darkness of a large crag in the cliff wall and looked out. Silver claws scraped on stone as the blue firedrake emerged from hiding. For a moment, it hung on the cliff side, craning its neck to stare after the departing green until the stranger was lost from sight. It sniffed the air and a low whine came from its throat. With a sudden lash of its tail it pushed itself off the stone and twisted mid-air, opening its wings. The firedrake darted across the valley, an iridescent blue streak against the verdant green of the valley floor. It alighted on the far side and raised its neck to sniff the air. Again, it whined, a high-pitched sound from deep in its throat. Suddenly it boosted straight up, wings folded tight against its body as it spun. High up in the air, it snapped them out to stop. Hovering, it looked behind it at the valley then in the direction the stranger had taken. It did this a couple of times until, with a squawk, it darted lower, hovered again while it sniffed the air once more, then moved forward over the trees, flying slower this time as it followed the flight path the green firedrake had taken.

17

Jaron's relief at getting his first flight over with was short-lived – for that evening Carna paid him an unexpected visit.

'Flying school,' the lord announced, ignoring Jaron's open-mouthed stare. 'Don't be late, I'll be here when the sun reaches into the valley tomorrow morning.'

'But...' Jaron spluttered, 'so soon? Can't I–'

'You'll need a lift down to the lake,' Carna cut smoothly across his protest in a voice that brooked no argument, then ducked into the tunnel and was gone. Jaron had wondered if he should go and plead his case to his mother, but soon dismissed that thought. Earlier, she had been waiting out on his ledge when he had returned on Tarp, fussing over him so much he had felt embarrassed in front of the men, but she hadn't come to his cave with the lord which suggested she was siding with Carna over this. And he *had* agreed.

And so, the next morning, before the rising sun had lifted free of the mountains, he waited nervously on his ledge. On the one hand, he was glad to meet youngsters his own age, yet on the other the prospect made him feel sick. Jaron rubbed at the healed thigh wound, free at last of its bandage, then fingered the scarf at his neck to reassure himself it was still there. However, he couldn't cover his facial scar and dreaded the stares he would get. He breathed in the sharp mountain air and it occurred to him he was worried more about the class than he was the flight down.

Madrag appeared round the side of the mountain, silently gliding in on massive wings. His scales were a rich wine red in the flat early morning light. Jaron picked up his helmet and took a deep breath to steady himself. The firedrake dipped a wing and wheeled round to face the cave, rearing up and showing his brilliant blue chest as he hovered. Lord Carna's face peered around the long neck at Jaron who backed away from the beating air as Madrag dipped down, hooking onto the ledge with his sharp claws and angling himself to lumber sideways onto what was, for him, the cramped space on the ledge.

'Good morning, Jaron,' Carna called.

'M-morning,' Jaron nodded, his eyes on the massive wedge-shaped head that swung towards him, rumbling. Carna did not dismount, however, but waved him closer. Jaron took a deep breath; it was another test and he was not to be led like a child this time. Aware of Carna watching him, he forced his legs to move. Slowly, he crossed the space towards Madrag's head. His eyes flicked up to Carna who looked away over the valley, apparently not even bothering to watch his progress, but Jaron saw his knee nudge the firedrake who moved his head away from Jaron. It helped, and Jaron made it towards Madrag's shoulder. A red foreleg lifted directly in front of him.

'You need to step up,' Carna had bent down towards him, 'onto Madrag's leg.'

'Right.' Jaron eyed it. He took another shaky breath and tried to step up but his small stature meant he couldn't angle his leg high enough without touching the huge firedrake for balance. Carna said nothing but sat patiently waiting for him to figure it out. Flushing, this time Jaron jammed the helmet on to his head and, putting any misgivings aside, bent forward and placed both gloves on the scaly leg to boost himself up. He was aware of Madrag turning his head towards him. 'Sorry,' he apologised, and wondered at himself as he pushed himself higher and managed to scramble onto the firedrake's leg. Carna's hand appeared in front of his face and he grabbed it. The Raken lord pulled him up with no effort and settled him in front. From his high vantage point, Jaron gaped at the drop below and the mountainside falling away before them at this end of the ledge. His head started to swim; Madrag was so much bigger than Tarp.

'I thought you might like to fly Madrag down to the lake.'

'Uh huh,' Jaron said, trying to quell the rising panic at the back of his throat. The lessons were running into each other far too fast for his liking. His feet scrabbled for stirrups that were non-existent for this wasn't a double saddle, and he became acutely aware that sitting on the front he wasn't even strapped in. He hurriedly did up his helmet, fumbling with gloved fingers, before clutching at what little remained of the saddle that was visible between his legs.

'When you want Madrag to fly off the ledge, give a nudge of your heels, just like riding a horse – and he will step off. In the air, flying is all about weight and balance. We lean forward to go faster; sit back to slow – and lean to whichever side we wish to turn.'

'Just like that?' Jaron asked, surprised. 'Wouldn't I use my leg to turn him?'

'You're thinking of riding. On the ground if you wanted to turn your firedrake you can nudge with the inside heel, like this… I nudge to turn him so we are in position to step off.' Madrag turned, lumbering round Carna's pushing inside leg until he was facing out towards the valley. As he did so the long tail swept back into Jaron's room and something went over with a crash behind them. Carna ignored it. 'But in flight, the firedrake will be very sensitive to your weight. Indeed, it is most natural for him to want to fill the gap your disturbed balance will create. There is more to it for special manoeuvres but to start with…'

'Right,' Jaron reached out for reins that weren't there. 'Err, how do I hold on?'

'It helps to hold onto the front scale ridge when learning.

Balance will come although I trust you didn't use the reins for balance when riding on the ground. There is no metal bit in the mouth,' Carna said with some derision. 'Our firedrake are willing partners.'

Jaron ran his gaze along Madrag's long neck. At the end of it, the head seemed so far away. He clutched onto the nearest ridge scale. It still seemed odd not to have reins to hold and he realised what a sense of security they gave even if he didn't use them to balance.

'And use your heels when you're ready.'

All Jaron's senses were screaming at him not to. The valley basin spread out before them seemed so far down. He was aware of Carna waiting patiently while, stomach clenched, he still sat frozen in place. Madrag turned his head to look back at him with a quizzical look. The red firedrake's flanks heaved out and in with a massive sigh, obviously wondering what on earth the delay was. It was enough for Jaron to muster his courage and give a nudge with his heels. The firedrake immediately opened his huge wings and stepped off the ledge, flapping heavily. Jaron held on for grim life and instinctively crouched lower. Madrag mirrored him and lowered his neck, tilted his body – and went into a dive with wings folded close.

'Arrrgghhhh!' The side of the mountain rushed past, the track far below getting wider with alarming speed. Jaron caught sight of a horse and wagon trundling out of the entrance; the driver looked up and blanched in horror.

'Lean back!' Carna shouted into his ear then and when Jaron still didn't move yanked him back by the shoulders. The wings opened then rose and fell as Madrag mercifully levelled out and flew higher. 'Now, put your weight into your left knee,' the lord's voice sounded completely unfazed. Jaron, head still spinning from the dive, marshalled his faculties. Acutely aware he had no stirrups, Jaron tightened his hold on Madrag's raised scale and pushed his weight into his knee by leaning over a little. The red beast shifted the left wing back to glide into a turn that took them round the mountain. Jaron caught sight of a huge forest beyond. He had never seen what lay beyond Mount Scarf and without thinking straightened up to take a better look. Madrag obediently mirrored him and flew straight. Carna's voice came back into his ear. 'Good, good, now the other side, turn… that's it, now straighten.'

It was a small measure of control but it made Jaron feel better and he dared to stay sitting more upright as they winged out over the valley basin. Out in front the force of the wind pressed against his chest. The valley was rushing past below them, split in half by the ribbon of water. Madrag was gliding more than flapping, the vast blue-veined wings stretched out fully. It felt incredible to Jaron that such a massive beast would allow a mere human to direct him by such slight shifts in weight; *our firedrake are willing partners.* The boy looked up between Madrag's rippling ears to the mountains that were fast approaching on the other side of the valley. The red giant was covering the basin floor so much more quickly than Tarp had. 'Err, shall I turn him?' he asked.

'Wait please, I want a steeper turn this time.'

Jaron waited, tensing as the mountain came closer. At last Carna spoke, 'Instead of shifting your weight into your knees, lean your whole body to the left.'

'What?' Jaron shouted, the wind whipping his words back, his senses filled by the massive stone bulk before them. 'But I haven't any stirrups!'

'Go with me,' Carna put his arms around him and leaned his upper body to the left, taking Jaron with him. Madrag flapped once, then fully outstretched his wings as he tilted his body in answer.

'We're going to fall!' Jaron's panicked glance saw the valley floor rising up to meet him. Yet still Madrag tilted and soon they were gliding across the mountain face, the rugged stone flashing past beneath them, some dynamic force keeping them in the saddle.

'Now back,' Carna took Jaron with him as they straightened and Madrag levelled out again as they began another sweep of the valley. Jaron breathed a sigh of relief yet there was no respite as Carna was issuing instructions again. 'See the lake?' The lord's arm pointed past him. Forward from Madrag's shoulder Jaron could see the glass surface of the lake. A green firedrake stood in the shallows and in a semi-circle around it he made out a small group of figures. They were all looking up at them, some shielding their eyes against the sun, now high enough to just peek free of the mountains. 'That's where you're landing.'

'Right,' Jaron tried to still his hammering heart. 'But I don't know how,' he shouted, panic rising yet again.

'You'll need to be thinking about slowing him six firedrake lengths away. You'll want him lower so lean forward slightly, keeping the weight *off* your knees, or you'll go faster, keep your seat in the saddle, just fold from your waist – that's it.'

Jaron listened hard, with Carna's hands on his arms, guiding him. 'Now straighten up, weight back – see how the wings spill the air, lowering us?' Jaron shot a look at the tilting wings, but he didn't want to take his eyes off the group on the ground lest he mow them down. 'Lean back more.' Madrag's body angled underneath him as the neck rose. 'Go with him, Jaron – now fold your body forward to match the angle, that's it.' Jaron caught sight of the faces on the ground staring up at them, some stepping back as they neared. Then Madrag's body reared up in the air, blocking his view, massive wings buffeting the air beside him. Carna continued calmly talking regardless. 'Back legs down, feel them touch the ground?'

Next moment, Jaron nearly fell over the shoulder as the

firedrake's front came down, Carna's hand grabbing at his jacket just in time. 'And landed. There.'

Breathing hard, Jaron stayed where he was, half-collapsed over the neck. Madrag furled his wings and cocked his head back at him. Grateful beyond measure to be on the ground, Jaron patted the hard scales, wondering if the beast would even feel it.

He heard a firedrake's call and looked over towards the lake. The green firedrake was holding her wings up as she waddled through the water towards Madrag. Jaron sat up and noticed the group standing below silently watching them. Marla's red hair fanned out in the breeze, the look on her freckled face one of astonishment. Next to her stood another girl, smaller and thinner with lank blonde hair falling over her eyes and skin the palest he'd seen. Behind them were four boys of about his own age standing in a line, and one aged man who walked stiffly forward.

'My lord,' he bowed when he reached Madrag's side, flipping a hand back at the row of students as he did so. They closed their mouths and bowed as one. The old man's face looked up at Carna. It was heavily lined with pale eyes and a broad nose.

'Parl,' Carna acknowledged him. 'I've got a new student for you.'

'Ah yes,' the narrowed pale eyes shifted to Jaron. 'Welcome, my young Lord Jaron, to our class.'

Lord? Jaron found his voice. 'Oh, but I'm not–'

'You dismount by nudging with your left foot,' Carna's voice in his ear cut him off.

Jaron recovered himself and did so. Madrag's foreleg lifted obligingly. 'Swing your leg over his neck and slide down,' Carna's voice was low enough so the others couldn't hear. Jaron forced his muscles to move and swung his leg over. He sat looking down; it seemed like a long drop. Avoiding Carna's gaze he awkwardly managed to turn his body so he was facing inwards. He levered himself off and slid down to land on Madrag's leg, clutching at the girth strap for balance. Conscious of the watching eyes, he turned carefully round before straightening his left leg and crouching with the other to lower himself onto the ground, staggering slightly as he let go. A careful dismount but at least he hadn't fallen flat on his face.

He looked up to see Carna's nod of approval. The lord clicked at Madrag who unfurled his wings while Parl put his hand on Jaron's shoulder to steer him out of the way. With legs like jelly Jaron stumbled towards the others who all still stared at him. He was aware of his limp more than ever. Marla grinned at him and, grateful, he smiled back. There came a sudden rush of wind behind him and a collective gasp from the onlookers, who were now shielding their faces as they looked up. Jaron turned in time to see Madrag shooting straight up into the air like a red comet, spreading his wings to a sudden stop high above them and gliding away across the valley until he disappeared over a mountain. Jaron couldn't quite take in that he had been aboard *that* just a short while ago.

When he turned back Parl was smiling kindly at him, revealing a gap where one front tooth should be. 'Welcome to flying school, my lord. Allow me to introduce you to your fellow students.'

'Jaron,' Jaron muttered. 'Just call me Jaron please.' He stared at the six youngsters before him and steeled himself as their glances took in him and his scarred face. Marla was grinning at him but apart from her only a blond youth, slim but broad-shouldered, would look him in the eye – and not in a friendly way, Jaron noticed.

'Well, if you wish it.' Parl was obviously a bit put out.

'Yes, I would please.' It occurred to Jaron that Carna had contrived this flight on Madrag to let them know he was connected to the Raken lord from the start. Jaron felt like an imposter to have such a title uttered.

Marla stepped forward. 'We've met,' she said in a loud voice and nodded to Jaron. 'Great to see you here, Jaron.' Parl sniffed but didn't berate her. 'This is Haley,' Marla smoothly took over the introductions and turned to beckon the slight, blonde girl forward. Haley's large blue eyes widened on looking at Jaron before she dropped her gaze and put her hands behind her back.

'Hello Haley,' Jaron sought to put her at ease. Her skin was so white it was almost translucent and she looked like a breath of air would blow her over.

'Hello,' she whispered, but still wouldn't look up.

Marla stepped forward and indicated the four youths standing in a row. 'Tench,' she said. The broad-shouldered fair-haired youth curled his lip up in a half-smile but said nothing, his open stare on Jaron's scar. 'And Wolf, well we call him Wolf, what's your real name?' The lank-haired boy didn't deign to reply but gave a thin smile at Jaron from under his long fringe. His eyes were almost coal black in the olive-skinned face and the smile didn't seem to stretch to the eyes. It was unnerving but Jaron swallowed and smiled back. 'He never tells,' Marla said in a low voice. 'Racker,' she continued and a thin, curly-haired youth grinned from ear to ear and bounced forward.

'What's it like?' he asked, his voice high and excited.

'Err...' Jaron was at a loss.

'To ride the great red. Wow, I would love to do that, is he difficult to fly? Those massive wings, how many times have you been on him? Do you think you could get me a ride?' His face turned dreamy. Jaron stared at him and was suddenly reminded of Tucker. Marla took the opportunity to jump back in.

'Better known as Racket, you can hear why.' The boy didn't seem to take any offense at her words and grinned. 'And this is Hodge,' Marla turned and a tall, big- shouldered youth stepped up. Jaron almost took a step back despite himself. Hodge was nearly as tall as Carna and twice as wide. The leather tunic he wore was bare of sleeves, despite the cold morning, and his brown arms were tightly bunched muscle. The grey eyes studied Jaron and he gave the barest of nods.

'Thank you, Marla,' Parl's gravel voice cut between them. 'For taking it upon yourself to do the introductions, even if I didn't ask you to. Now, perhaps we could get on, do you think…'

'Very good Tench, keep her level while you hover, don't let her back go down so much.'

From the back of the group, Jaron watched Tench as he hovered Channon backwards over the lake. His smooth face was grinning as he directed the school firedrake and even from here Jaron could see the glint of his white-toothed smile. Jaron had already noticed how often Tench glanced at Marla, who stood next to Jaron as the students watched by the lake. Jaron copied Tench's stance and stood more upright, holding his hands out as he would with reins, pushing his legs in as he would have done with Caliber and moving his shoulders forward just slightly. He noticed Channon had shaken her head more than once; she was not altogether happy.

'There's no need to dominate her, Tench,' Parl called. 'Don't clench your legs around her, just close them, and put your shoulders a fraction forward… good, that's it.'

Jaron moved a little way from the group as Marla, the last to go, waited for her turn to fly Channon. Watching the students perform aerial lessons Jaron had realised just how far behind the group he was in the flying stakes. He felt tired, considering how much had happened these last couple of days. Limping over to a rocky outcrop he sat down to rest. To his relief Parl had asked him just to watch today.

Especially as he doubted his own ability to even fly forwards on his own. Listening to the teacher through the morning he had found he could understand Parl's instructions very well and had learnt quite a bit just by observing. But he supposed it was a case of doing, as Sprague had always said. He felt a twinge in his thigh and rubbed it hard.

'Does it hurt?'

Jaron looked up to find Haley had followed him. She bobbed her head at him and two hot spots of colour formed on her cheeks.

'Not too bad,' he shuffled over to make room for her. She gave a small smile and perched her tiny frame on the rock beside him.

'I heard you were injured.' Her voice was so soft he had to strain to hear her.

'I'm much better now, thank you.'

For a while they sat there in silence while Jaron tried to think of something to break it. Her head was tilted forward so her hair obscured her face. Jaron cleared his throat. 'How long have you been at flying school?'

'About three weeks,' she still didn't look up.

'Oh, not very long.'

'The others started a week beforehand, it's normally the time needed.'

'Before…?'

'The drakel, the young firedrake, fly in.'

Jaron took a moment to digest this. Her fingers were constantly moving, rubbing and flicking like she was strumming to a tune only she could hear. He tried again. 'Do you enjoy it, the flying?'

'Not really.'

Jaron stared at her. 'Oh? I thought…'

She tucked her fine hair behind an ear and flicked a sideways look at him. 'That being a Raken it would come easily? Not to everyone.'

'But you're not afraid of them?'

She shook her head and her light blue eyes lifted to meet his gaze at last. 'Not on the ground, I just can't seem to get the confidence when I'm on one. Marla says I should be more determined, more commanding.' They both looked up to watch Marla eagerly taking her turn and springing up onto Channon's back.

'Well, it's easier said than done, I would imagine,' Jaron sought to make this strange girl feel better and this time she did smile.

'My mother is a firedrake rider, and a member of the council; she doesn't pressure me but it would make her so proud if I can win a firedrake for myself.' She stared at him. 'I don't think you will have any trouble.'

'Me?' Jaron stared at her. 'Oh, I might have flown in on Madrag, but C– Lord Carna was telling me what to do. I was terrified most of the time,' he admitted. To his surprise a small white hand came to rest on his.

'You have great heart,' she looked directly into his eyes so he found he couldn't look away. 'And you're brave to face your fears, the firedrake for you will see this.' Jaron stared at her and Haley dropped her hand and stood up. 'I've said too much, you'll think me strange. Like *they* all do,' she nodded to the group watching Marla flying.

Jaron stood too. 'Oh no,' he said, anxious to relieve her discomfort. 'I was just surprised, that's all.'

Haley smiled at him. 'You are kind. I'll leave you in peace.' With that she turned and ran over to re-join the group. Jaron stared after her. So, you had to win your firedrake. Well, he wasn't sure he wanted one anyhow so at least it sounded like he could make his own decision in this. It had been bothering him Carna could somehow force him to accept a firedrake as his own just as he had left him no real choice in attending flying school.

'Marla, not too fast, remember what I said about slowing

down a bit,' Parl's call caused Jaron to look up in time to see Channon flapping madly as she tried to regain her balance. Next moment she had reared up in the air and dislodged her rider. Marla, arms flailing, rolled over Channon's rump and went out the back door. Jaron gasped and stood up. There was a huge splash as she fell into the lake. Jaron hurried over to the group, his tiredness forgotten. To his relief Marla resurfaced, blowing out a plume of water.

Tench was roaring with laughter. 'Serves you right for showing off!' he called to her.

'And of course, that's something you never do,' Wolf was standing right behind Tench who whipped round and frowned at him. 'Shut up, Dog!' Wolf leered at him and Tench squared his shoulders and took a threatening step towards the lean dark-haired boy. They were the same height nose to nose but Tench was by far the stronger looking. Jaron looked over at Parl but the teacher was busy berating Marla as she trudged, sodden, out of the lake, her face so red it matched the long tendrils of dripping hair that fell over her shoulders from beneath her helmet. 'Marla, how often have I told you to always clip yourself to the saddle?' Jaron eyed the two posturing boys warily.

Racker came to stand beside Jaron as Channon landed by the lake. 'There they go again.'

'They often do this?'

Racker smiled happily. 'Oh yes, they hate each other, something to do with Wolf's sister, I believe.'

Wolf's lips were moving. Jaron couldn't hear what was said but it was enough for Tench to let out a roar of anger, step back and swung a punch at the other boy.

Wolf's reflexes were incredibly fast as he jumped aside. Tench's punch, devoid of its target and going full swing, unbalanced the bigger boy who nearly fell over. Wolf howled with laughter. Tench's face turned puce with rage and he turned and launched himself at the lank-haired youth, fingers reaching. Haley squealed but again Wolf sidestepped the charge and Tench went barrelling past him towards Hodge, who moved forward with a speed that belied his size in time to catch Tench by the back of his jacket as the youth turned to attack again.

'Lemme go, Hodge!' Tench was flailing and kicking to get free. 'Let me get him, the slimy little…'

'Boys!' Parl had seen what was happening at last. 'Stop that at once! I will not have fighting in my classes. Tench, Wolf, any more of that and you'll both be suspended.' He fixed the boys with a hard stare. Tench glowered at Wolf who crossed his arms and smiled back, apparently unfazed by the whole episode. 'Marla, go and get dried off. I've had enough of you all, class is dismissed for today.'

Relieved, Jaron turned to leave with the others, then hesitated, his eyes on where Mount Scarf rose up at the far end of the valley. He thought he could just see his cave in the second from top row.

'Jaron,' Parl called. 'I can give you a lift back up.'

Marla turned, excited on hearing this. 'Let me, sir, please sir.'

But the old teacher shook his head. 'You know you can't do that, Marla. Students are not allowed to fly alone and especially not be in charge of a passenger's safety.' Shoulders slumped again, Marla turned and squelched after the departing group. Parl turned to Jaron. 'Now, Jaron, I want you to do some mounting and dismounting for me. We might take this opportunity to give you a little bit of extra tuition to catch up.'

With a sigh of resignation Jaron tried to ignore his heart as it juddered in his chest and followed Parl. His limp was worse now he was so tired and he felt grateful the other students had left. Reluctantly he made his way over to Channon who was drinking at the edge of the lake. She lifted a dripping snout and turned her head towards him as he approached. Jaron dropped his eyes on reflex, wishing he could get up the courage to send a mental wave of reassurance to the great beast as he used to with Caliber. When he raised his eyes again it was to see Parl nod in approval before gesturing him closer.

Channon was smaller than Madrag but Jaron eyed the big beast warily. When he was standing at Parl's shoulder the teacher tapped the firedrake's leg. She lifted it. He made Jaron tap her behind the knee to lower it. And another tap on its side to lift back up. 'Now, step on to her leg, hold on to her shoulder, there at the ridge, and pull yourself up.'

Parl was not standing at Channon's head but after daring to give her a quick pat to warn her Jaron stepped up and put his fingers in the scaly ridge that ran from the neck to the shoulder and used it to pull himself higher. He swung his leg over much as he would have when mounting Caliber and settled himself slowly down into the double-seated saddle, relieved to have stirrups this time.

An eye looked back at him. 'Good girl,' he muttered. To his relief, Parl swung himself up behind him.

'Where's your safety belt?'

'Uh, I don't have one, sir.'

Parl sighed. 'Trust Lord Carna, it wouldn't have occurred to him, of course.'

Jaron looked back at the teacher. 'Did you teach him, sir?'

'Yes, reckless young thing he was, too brave for his own good sometimes. Still, turned out very well, easier than–' he stopped, coughed. 'Well, off you go.' The old man sat back.

'Um, I haven't flown from the ground before, sir.'

'Nudge with your heels and she'll jump.'

Jump? Not liking the sound of that, Jaron tentatively nudged. In answer, Channon crouched, neck rising before him. Then, she leapt straight up and his flailing hands missed the front of the saddle as the force drove him back against

Parl. He felt the teacher's hand on his back, pushing him forward again. 'Tsk! Preparation is the key, young man.' Channon levelled out and Jaron, gasping, looked over her shoulder at the lake below. 'We'll do that again, take her back down,' Parl ordered.

Breathing hard, Jaron tried to regain his faculties and remember what Carna had told him. *Lean forward slightly, keep the weight off your knees.*

'No, no, line her up first. Swing her around and keep your eye on where you want to land.' Jaron bit his lip and remembered to use his weight to fly her round. 'Good, now straighten her up, always look where you want to go, your body will follow. The tiniest of differences will be felt by the firedrake.' Jaron listened intently; he was already learning a lot more from Parl in the short time the teacher had been with him. He bent his upper body forward and looked down at the lake from over Channon's shoulder. She flapped her wings back to slow then began her descent. Jaron concentrated hard, keeping his eyes on the lake. Parl was back in his ear. 'Don't bend forward too much. It is better to keep her level as you come down; if you were in strange territory you would want to be keeping an eye out so raise your chin and lean back a little.'

When Channon touched down in the shallows of the lake with open wings it was so gentle Jaron had to bend over to check they weren't still in the air.

'Very good, Jaron,' said Parl, pleased. 'Now, up we go again and this time I'm going to sit here and let you do it all.'

To Jaron's amazement he managed to get Channon to take off and steer her up to his cave without any help. The only time Parl spoke was as he was lining her up to land on his ledge. 'She'll need to lift more at the front if you come at it head on so be prepared for that.' The noise of Channon's wings flapping madly as she lifted her neck unsettled Jaron and he threw an anxious look at the huge membrane closing him in and especially at the wickedly hooked wing claw sticking out of the foremost wing joint. He felt Parl's hand on his shoulder. 'Relax, Jaron, trust your firedrake to sort it out.' Easier said than done but he sat tight and gripped a neck plate as Channon landed, her long neck dipping into his cave. She furled her wings and waddled round to stand sideways on the ledge. Jaron let out an explosive breath of relieved air.

'Very good, now nudge her with your left foot and she'll lift her foreleg for you.'

Jaron hesitated, then dismounted by hefting his leg over her wither. As before on Madrag, he managed to turn his body to carefully slide down her side to her leg, then stepped down, immensely grateful to be on solid ground again. He turned and without giving himself time to think too much, reached up with a hesitant hand and stroked Channon's neck. 'Thank you,' he whispered to the firedrake. She batted her eyelids at him and blew out through her nose.

'I know it has been difficult for you, Jaron,' Parl's voice said. Jaron looked up at him in surprise. The teacher smiled through his short grey beard. 'Lord Carna has been keeping me informed of your progress.' Parl unbuttoned his tunic and shirt to reveal a hideous deep scar that ran from one shoulder down across his chest to his stomach.

Jaron gaped. 'Firedrake,' he murmured.

'Yes, my fault. I was young and so was he. I thought my firedrake wouldn't hurt me, but I was trying to stop him fighting with a rival male and got in the way. He didn't mean it, of course. It was stupid of me.'

He wanted to ask Parl where his firedrake was but thinking it had somehow died he bit the question back. 'This one meant it,' Jaron said, pointing at his cheek scar. 'He was intent on wiping out the whole village.'

Parl nodded, buttoning his clothes back up. 'I know. The

rider and his firedrake were banished.'

Jaron stared. 'The firedrake was banished as well?'

Parl eyed him. 'Yes, and a firedrake is only as good as the partner it has. Even wild firedrakes will not attack a whole village. Now, I'll see you tomorrow morning, young Jaron, don't be late this time.' Parl raised a finger. 'And read that book I gave Carna for you. I don't think the other students will thank you if they have to hear the history of the Raken yet again when they could be flying.' Parl nodded down at him and Channon started to turn. Jaron quickly hobbled out of the way, his hip feeling stiff after the flying. Looking back, he saw the green firedrake open her wings. She stepped off, and they dropped away below the level of his ledge.

Jaron went into his cave and when he reached his bed he let himself fall onto his back, exhausted. He should have felt immense relief but instead all he could think of were Parl's words: *The rider, and his firedrake, were banished.* Frowning, Jaron sat up and stared unseeing into the cave. He had assumed his father's firedrake had been put to death for razing the village, and Torrit exiled. Bitter anger flared up in his chest. *Still alive.* He wondered if his mother knew, but quickly decided if not before she must now.

The least they could have done was kill the firedrake if they only exiled the rider. Jaron's hands balled into fists. *All because he was a lord.* And it must have fallen to Carna to decide his brother's punishment – and that of his beast.

18

'Jaron?' Jaron looked up from his book and frowned. Carna's head was poking round the curtain. 'Your mother and I thought you would like to come down to dinner with us.'

'I'm fine, thank you. I'll take it in my room. Please tell Mum not to worry about me.' Jaron tried to keep the disappointment from his voice. His mother had been bringing his meal to him in the evening most nights and then stayed to eat with him. Jaron had been looking forward to seeing her tonight so he could tell her about his first day at flying school and ask her more about Torrit's firedrake. Rella always seemed to be busy during the day and the evening was catching up time for mother and son. The lord didn't reply further but instead stepped into the cave and fixed him with his flint eyes. Jaron glared back at him and saw Carna's eyebrows raise a little.

'I'll whistle Madrag and take you down.' It was as though Jaron hadn't spoken. Carna stalked towards the cave doors and pulled them open. By the set of Carna's shoulders it was useless to argue. Jaron muttered an oath under his breath. The last thing he felt like was being sociable and flying *again*. He supposed this was the whole idea; get him on the firedrake at every opportunity in the hope he would end up being quite *blasé* about flying. Jaron didn't think that would ever happen. His thoughts were interrupted by Carna's piercing whistle. The red firedrake lowered into view, dwarfing the tall lord's silhouette. The cave's lanterns reflected in the luminous eyes.

Jaron shielded his eyes from the buffeting wind and didn't think he would ever fail to get used to such an amazing sight. He suddenly noticed a hand waving from behind Madrag's head in the semi-darkness. He stood up to see better and there was his mother sitting demurely sideways in the saddle, with her long thick hair fanning out behind her. She looked so tiny on the back of the huge red beast.

His heart in his throat, Jaron started towards them. He slowed when Madrag's eyes locked on to him and moved to the side to give Madrag room as the beast hitched on to the ledge and pulled himself over. The head swung towards Jaron and a loud welcoming rumble came from deep within the broad blue chest. Carna looked over at his beast in surprise but Jaron hardly noticed, so caught up was he in the sight of his mother sitting on the firedrake.

'Mum,' he called, his voice high to his own ears.

'Jaron,' she nodded down at him. 'Joining us for dinner?'

She spoke as though she were sitting in a comfy chair rather than on the back of the huge red. She smiled down at her son and Jaron found himself relaxing a little; that smile said she knew what he was going through, that she appreciated him coming so close for her.

'Don't think I've got much choice,' he grumbled, shooting a glance at Lord Carna who was smiling up at Rella.

'New dress? Very nice,' the lord had come to stand at his firedrake's head, rubbing the long nose as he admired Jaron's mother. She smoothed down the front of the plush velvet.

'Glad you've noticed at last. I thought the dark green goes very well with Madrag's red.'

'It goes very well on you.'

She tossed her heavy hair as she laughed. 'You are saying all the right things tonight, my lord.'

'Not difficult with you, my lady.'

Jaron sighed. He was almost willing to get going on Madrag rather than hear all this mush going on.

His mother was appraising him with a look he knew well. 'Is that shirt clean?'

'Yes, Mother,' he said, and saw her narrow her eyes.

'Best change to the white one, and wear your tunic in the dark leather, with the wide belt.'

Jaron trudged past Madrag's nose and Carna's quizzical look back into his room. His mother's voice called after him. 'And wear the clean boots, and…'

'Wash my face,' Jaron muttered.

'Wash your face,' his mother finished.

It was a bit of a squeeze on Madrag. Carna sat in the saddle with Rella sitting sideways in the middle on account of her long dress, and Jaron astride in front of her.

'Can he take all of us?' Jaron was clutching onto a large ridged scale in front of him more than was necessary. He seemed destined to have no stirrups.

'Of course,' Carna replied. He clicked at Madrag and the beast waddled round in the cramped space of the ledge. Rella's arms were tight around Jaron's waist and his mother's nearness and the smell of her familiar perfume was calming; like a summer wood after a shower of rain. Madrag stepped off and into the darkness. Jaron was expecting his stomach to lurch, but it must have known by now what to expect and stayed more or less in place. All the same, Jaron found flying at night very disorientating. He couldn't see the lake tonight but caught a flash of the lights from the many caves shining out from the surrounding mountains. The dark slab of Madrag's raised wing sliced across his vision as the big red turned in the night sky. It was easier to get his bearings when they were heading back towards Mount Scarf.

As the firedrake spiralled down beside the mountain

Jaron stared at rows upon rows of caves lifting past, some with the shadowy bulks of firedrake crouched on the ledges and back-lit by the cave torches. Another firedrake appeared out of the shadows in front of them, side-lit by the lights and flapping down as they were. The rider looked over his shoulder, saluted and moved his firedrake aside to make room for the big red. As it did so the huge cave entrance at the base of Mount Scarf was revealed. Light streaming from the inside lit up two statues of rearing firedrake carved in stone both sides of the entrance. Each held an enormous flaming torch in their front paws.

As they drew nearer Jaron saw more firedrake flying in. *Would there be room for all of them? Supposing they collided with another firedrake coming out?* Rella's arms gave him an extra squeeze. He looked back at her and she smiled and winked. Facing forward again Jaron felt Madrag lining up to enter. He stared up to the top of the huge cave and saw there was ample room for another two firedrake to fly above them. Then they were in a huge tunnel and Jaron cringed as other firedrake, now without their riders, flapped out as Madrag passed under the archway. Jaron held his breath whenever one looked to be too close but at the last minute the firedrake seemed to be able to avoid any collision. A short way ahead and the tunnel opened up into a massive cavern. It was the hall Jaron had so often looked down upon from up high when on his walks.

Firedrake were depositing their riders in the large open area before the tables and flying back out again, some hardly bothering to land; instead hovering just above the ground whilst waiting for their riders to climb off. Jaron watched, thinking he wouldn't be able to do that without falling flat on his face. Thankfully, Madrag landed smoothly and furled his wings. Carna jumped off and helped Rella down. He stood back and let Jaron dismount on his own. Madrag helpfully raised his foreleg and Jaron managed to get off and stay on his feet.

Rella took his arm, her other resting on Carna's and the three walked slowly into the massive hall. 'How was school today?' she asked.

'Fine,' he muttered, distracted as the babble of voices ahead stilled. There was none of the formality that Tiara's Lord Bell would have demanded, but all paused politely in their chatter and some of the older ones nodded as Carna passed, their eyes coming to rest on Jaron. He managed to resist the urge to duck his head and look down at his feet.

'Well, I want to hear all about it later,' his mother said in his ear.

He nodded, and saw they were heading toward a round table at the end of the hall set slightly further apart from the others. It seemed an age before they reached it, walking past all those tables. Jaron was thankful for Oran's insole – it certainly helped him to walk more smoothly even if it didn't eliminate his limp completely.

Dominating the hall was the master carpenter's handiwork – the large sculpture of a big red he had seen from up on the walkway. Jaron could see now why it shimmered so. Polished stones of various reds and blues formed the scales on the entire body, and set in the head, nearest to the floor as the beast made to climb down from its pillar, were two clear yellow stones that caught the luminosity of the firedrake's eyes perfectly.

'Good evening, Lady Tarla, Lady Leraine, gentlemen,' Carna said as they neared. The people at this table stood up, six men and one woman, while a white-haired lady in an elaborate jewelled dress remained sitting. There was a ripple of answering greetings to Carna and Rella. The lord pulled out a chair for Rella and sat her down. She smiled and nodded to those standing while Jaron stood uncertainly by her side, bearing the weight of stares from those at the table and feeling the eyes of the hall at his back. His scar burned.

Carna came and stood behind him, his hands resting heavy on his shoulders.

'This boy is my nephew, Jaron, son of Lady Rella.'

Nephew. It felt odd to be called so and Jaron wondered about the lord using it here.

Carna was guiding him towards the chair one along from his mother and the man standing nearest pulled it out for him.

'Val,' Jaron said, and smiled in relief; at least there was one other person at the table he had met before, although it seemed an eon ago since the race dinner back in Tiara.

Val nodded down at him, smiling. 'Good evening, Lord Jaron.'

'Oh, but I'm not–' he stopped. Val's head had done the smallest of shakes and his eyes spoke a warning that froze the words on Jaron's lips. The rider sat then, looking away from him across the table and toying with his tankard. Jaron felt Carna's hand on his shoulder pressing him down into the seat next to him. Jaron stole a look around the table as the diners all sat. A lady sitting across from him with short-cropped blonde hair smiled kindly.

'I'll introduce you to them,' Carna said, standing again. He dipped his head in a respectful way at the white-haired lady who sat next to his mother. 'Lady Tarla.' She didn't acknowledge Carna at all but stared at Jaron with vacant pale eyes until he wondered if she were blind. Just then, the eyes seemed to swim into focus, proving him wrong in his first assumption. It was a strange thing to witness, like she had been somewhere else and was now back. Her eyes widened as she seemed to notice Jaron for the first time. Her skin was so thin and wrinkled it reminded Jaron of scrunched parchment.

Rella leaned towards her and placed a hand on her sleeve. 'Tarla dear, did you hear? This is Jaron, my son.' Lady Tarla looked at Rella as if she was coming out of a dream. Carna extended his hand across the table towards the other woman who had smiled at Jaron. 'Leraine Manta, Wing Commander of Mount Konraka.' The lady smiled again and nodded at him. Jaron managed a tight smile back before feeling himself blush yet *again*. 'Thorel Rand, chief advisor of the council,' a muscular, broad-shouldered man with a thick head of blond hair and beard nodded whilst his sharp deep-set eyes bored into Jaron. He remembered what Marla had said; this was Tench's father. Carna indicated a thin, lank-haired man who lounged in his chair next to Thorel. 'Minderman Burech,' the man's dark eyes appraised Jaron and his thin lips twisted into a sardonic smile. Carna moved on to the next man seated. 'Korel Baine, Wing Commander of Mount Rill and his brother Parel, Commander of Mount Makra.' The two looked as though they were twins and nodded as one with serious faces. In their forties, both with short-cropped hair and wearing sleeveless leather tunics with bare muscular arms, they had the hard look of warriors about them. 'Nave Edelle, Scarf Wing Commander.' Nave nodded and turned back to his tankard. He seemed familiar to Jaron but he couldn't remember just now, feeling a little under siege with all the new introductions. 'And Val Gin you have already met, Scarf's Wing Second.' Val winked at him.

The lord sat down and Jaron noticed Rella's hand slide across to hold Carna's where it lay on his lap below the level of the table. Their fingers entwined. Jaron raised his eyes to find his mother watching him; she smiled encouragement and her son wished he was sitting next to her instead of Carna.

The servants seemed to know the exact time there was a lull in the proceedings and swarmed around the table, placing plates and refilling the jugs of wine and ale. The level of chat in the hall rose higher as though the whole hall had been holding back, waiting for their table to start eating.

'About time. I'm dying of starvation here,' the thin-faced man with lank black hair reached across to grab a steak as soon as the serving plate was set down.

'Minderman,' Leraine shook her blonde head and laughed. 'I envy you – how come you eat so much yet never gain a paunch?' Minderman lifted the plate so she could reach it.

'Hard work, Leraine, hard work.'

'That'll be the day,' Thorel scoffed without humour. 'Worms more like.' Minderman grinned at the bearded man but didn't rise to the barb.

'Best hurry up and tuck in, my lord,' Val said as he lifted a plate of steaming new potatoes and held it while Jaron spooned some onto his plate. Jaron thanked him while still digesting the title that he was being forced to accept. Next moment Carna was putting a slab of beef onto his plate while Rella pushed across the bowl of green beans so they were within his reach. Feeling self-conscious, he quickly spooned some on and pushed the bowl towards Val. There was silence around the table as everyone concentrated on eating. Jaron was just grateful their focus was off him but unfortunately his reprieve didn't last long.

'How are you settling in, Lord Jaron?' Leraine asked. She was being kind but of course everyone now gave him attention to hear his reply. In his haste Jaron tried to swallow and speak at the same time, which led to a choking fit until Carna slapped him hard between the shoulder blades while Val offered him a tankard of ale to wash it down.

'I-It's very different from Tiara,' was all he could think to say once he had recovered. He took another sip from the tankard, savouring the strange taste, and tried to ignore the stinging between his shoulder blades where Carna's heavy hand had landed. Rella poured some water from a jug and pushed the glass towards him, a meaningful look in her eye.

Thorel grunted. 'Your Tiara's Lord Bell is not an easy

character, is he?'

'Thorel…' Carna said the man's name as a warning. But Thorel was not to be put off. 'Well, he isn't. Why not talk about it? Your young lord should know he's refusing to send any more grain.'

'Why not?' Jaron asked. It was Minderman that answered him. 'He feels we've stolen his star race rider and head chef from Tiara, Lord Jaron.' He smiled as he glanced at Rella, who flicked her heavy hair back over her shoulder.

'I'm not surprised, I *was* the best chef they'd ever had.' In a sudden change of mood, she glared across the table at Minderman. 'And I'm not ashamed of who I was, Minderman, you will do well to remember that.'

'My lady, I meant no insult, but according to Lord Bell he cannot hope to get his finest kelpra stallion back without its rider's help, and no one to ride him if he does.' He looked at Jaron. 'I gather our young lord here is the only one the carnivorous horse will allow on its back so he is very keen that Lord Jaron return.'

Jaron looked at the Raken lord. 'He's not giving you grain? Because of me?'

'It makes no difference,' Carna said in a flat tone. 'Bell can threaten as much as he likes; neither you nor Rella will return. You were never his to begin with.'

'Oh yes? We're *yours* now, are we, my lord?' Rella's eyes flashed in warning. Carna grinned at her. 'That's right, my lady, all mine, always.'

Jaron watched in surprise as his mother seemed to almost melt. 'Oh,' she breathed and parted her lips in a slow smile. Val suddenly coughed into his tankard.

So Caliber still hadn't been found, Jaron worried. No wonder Lord Bell was mad. They all knew what the kelpra stallion could do, had seen how fast he was, the fastest they had ever bred, Sprague had said. He was a valuable animal. Of course they would need his rider to get him back.

'Maybe I should go back to help them find him,' he ventured. Rella was already shaking her head and Carna's hard look caused Jaron to quail. 'Then the Raken people would get grain,' he managed to finish.

Thorel nodded. 'Not a bad idea, the young lord could just do that and Bell use the stallion for breeding to keep him happy. Winter's not far off now. Our stores are low since the crops further north were destroyed in those storms.'

Rella's sharp intake of breath was loud. She dropped her fork onto the plate with a clatter, but Carna put his hand over hers before she could speak. 'As I said,' he ran his steel gaze around the table, coming to rest on Jaron and pinning him with his grey eyes, 'it will not happen.'

'No,' it was Lady Tarla who answered and they all looked at her. The watery eyes were focused on Jaron. 'Young lord's blood, *Rillion* blood, belongs here.' Her voice was deeper than he was expecting and it seemed to silence the whole table. *Rillion blood,* he remembered the boy in the book Carna had given him had that name. Lady Tarla looked down at the plate Rella had placed in front of her and slowly began to eat. Jaron followed her lead and sliced into his beef before he noticed that the others were all staring at him now. He looked up at Carna whose face seemed a shade paler under his usual sun and wind tan.

It was Nave who broke the silence. 'Korel and Parel, what progress on the wild blue firedrake that's been seen in the area?'

Korel answered first. 'It's still about. No matter what we do, it keeps on circling back to the valley.'

Parel nodded. 'Tasker drove it right over the Arkenara range towards the north and into an ambush, but it's so quick.'

Nave nodded. 'A bluey. I've heard of them but never seen one before. I thought they had all but died out.'

'Must be a throwback,' Carna said. 'If it doesn't get the

message we might have to kill it.'

Leraine frowned. 'Surely if we fire it a singed tail will be enough.'

'It's just a yearling, two at most,' Korel agreed.

Carna shook his head. 'It seems to be drawn here. One of the young females is coming into its cycle and she might just be silly enough to mate with it. I don't like it. The drakels' arrival is only weeks away and the students are training out there in the valley. It's a loner with no pod of its own and it's too dangerous,' he sighed then moved on to other business. 'How are the firedrake looking, Val?'

'We lost one of the greens,' Val answered. 'Gusta found the body at the base of the cliff.' He shook his head. 'Shame, but it was the weakest; one of the others might have attacked it, or the mother did.'

Rella tutted. 'Poor thing.'

Val shrugged. 'The runts never catch up enough to be able to carry a rider. The red is doing well, my lord.'

'Good.' Carna seemed pleased. 'And it's suitable?'

'Yes, my lord. And the greens are good strong beasts.' Report over, Val stabbed at the last potato left on the platter and waved it at Jaron, who shook his head. Val popped it in his mouth. Jaron was grateful for the silence that fell on the table as everyone polished off their plates. He wondered about the fresh vegetables and where they came from. The servants came to take away the dishes and one hovered near Lady Tarla's half-eaten plate. She had gone off into a daze again. Rella smiled at the servant girl and handed her the plate before leaning across Lady Tarla and chatting with Leraine.

'I thought the black velvet for the Selecting,' Jaron's mother said.

Leraine disagreed. 'No, black washes you out, Rella. Red or green, or what about the purple? It sets off your hair…'

Jaron zoned out and looked over at Val, but the taciturn

rider seemed content just to sit, turning his tankard idly in his hands. He took another sneaky sip of his ale while his mother was distracted, then felt Carna's eyes on him.

'Is there anything you want to ask me, Jaron?'

Jaron thought he ought to come up with something and frantically tried to think of a suitable question for here. 'Um, will the Raken have enough to eat over winter? If there's no grain?'

Carna nodded, seemingly pleased with the question. 'We have stores, not enough to last the whole of the winter, but our riders are very good at foraging. There are roots we can collect and store and there is good hunting to be had from a firedrake's back so there will be no shortage of meat,' he paused. 'Don't worry, Jaron, we will not starve. Anyway, I rather suspect if the Ernots stage another raid then Lord Bell will be asking for our help again.'

'But I thought you had sent more riders? Flick told me.'

'Lord Bell sent them back – I suppose he wanted to show his displeasure.'

Jaron nodded. 'What is *Rillion*?'

Carna frowned.

'Lady Tarla mentioned Rillion blood? I thought *Rillion* was the first person to train a firedrake in old times, so what did she mean?'

'I see you have been reading the book I gave you.' He hesitated then sighed as though he had made up his mind about something at last. '*Rillion* isn't only the name of the first Raken who realised we could utilise our enemy rather than being its prey. It is a gift; an ability.'

'A gift?'

'Well, an affinity if you like – it surpasses normal rider and firedrake relationship, it means becoming more like one. A *sympathy* with the firedrake. It's very rare, very precious to the Raken people.'

Carna waited, watching him digest this. Jaron thought it

didn't sound so very grand. After all, he had always been able to 'think' a feeling to animals, like to calm a nervous colt, or a barking dog, and that wasn't really so special. He had found horses and dogs were pretty good at picking up signals from people, as were the kelpra. Perhaps it was just some tiny physical signal he unknowingly gave out, although he liked to fancy it was something more mysterious. But even Teel, who worked with animals, had sometimes been awed by his stepson's ability. With a mental shrug Jaron went back to his ale while Rella and Leraine continued to talk dresses. Feeling slightly light-headed, he wondered about the event they were talking about. He supposed *Selecting* was the firedrake and rider partnering. He fervently hoped he wouldn't be asked to take part.

At last, Carna pushed his chair back and stood up. All conversation ceased at their table and chairs scraped back as all but Lady Tarla stood with him. Jaron felt the room spin a little. His head felt muzzy as well. He noticed the old lady was still staring into space.

'Rella,' Carna extended his hand and she took it. 'Goodnight to you all. Nave, we'll do a sweep tomorrow of the forest for the migrating herds.'

Nave nodded. 'Yes, my lord.'

Rella took Jaron's arm, frowning at her son's rather flushed cheeks. They walked slowly out of the hall that was now only half-full of diners still loitering over drinks as they chatted. Madrag appeared from the murky heights of the cave and wheeled down in lazy circles to pick them up.

19

Next morning, early, a loud knock made Jaron jump. 'Come in,' he looked to the curtain that covered the entrance but it didn't pull aside. The knock came again, two sharp raps now, and he realised it was on the door to the outer ledge. Apprehensive, he limped over in his socks and opened the door a crack. Parl's craggy face nodded at him.

'Morning.'

'Oh, hello sir.'

'I thought we could get a lesson in for you early so you can catch up a bit to the other students.' Channon's eye came into view behind the old teacher's shoulder, peering through the gap. A rumbling growl sounded. Parl grinned, revealing his missing front tooth. 'Channon doesn't like to be kept waiting.'

'Oh, yes – I'll just grab my things.' *Yet more flying.*

Jaron sat on the bed and pulled on his boots and gloves before grabbing his helmet and jacket off the bedside chair. He took a deep breath to steady his nerves and stepped through the door. Parl had mounted and Jaron walked over, shrugging on his jacket and surprised to find he felt no hesitation today. She grumbled and he found himself smiling. 'Good morning, Channon, sorry to keep you waiting.'

He put on his helmet and the firedrake moved her foreleg up for him to mount without Jaron having to ask. Again, the intelligence of these big beasts surprised him. Parl offered his hand and pulled him up to settle in front. Jaron looked across the valley and was surprised to see it so busy with firedrake flying; they seemed to be moving in a clockwise circle and as he watched some dipped off into their caves whilst others jumped off to join the throng. He was going out in *that?* Within his riding gloves his palms started to sweat.

Parl must have sensed his apprehension for his calm voice came over his shoulder. 'All the pupils have to get used to flying when the air is busy. We are going to do a circuit of the valley. Now, turn her and line her up. You need to look to your right to see if it's clear before you ask her to fly. Oh, and strap this on please.' His hand came over his shoulder holding a belt with hooks on, much the same as he had worn on his first flight on Tarp. Jaron put it on and reached for the strips of leather attached to the saddle with rings on their end. Once he was clipped in Parl's voice sounded again in his ear. 'Right, get her facing out.'

'Yes, sir.' Jaron nudged her into position and jumped in alarm when a red firedrake boosted off from a ledge above, tail end dipping down right in front of Channon's nose before it swept off towards the left. At first, he thought it was Madrag then realised it was smaller.

'It's always busy first thing – the first flights haven't quite finished leaving yet and the night shift is returning. When the air space is busy, use the left side of the valley to leave.' Another two greens flapped away from their ledges below him. Their riders, a man and a woman, waved to each other before separating. More firedrake flew past and he tried to get his eye in and judge the speed. A gap came up but he hesitated and missed it. Channon's sides rose and fell in a big sigh. Parl put his hand on his shoulder. 'I'll tell you when to go. Ready... wait... now!'

Jaron leant forward, remembering to keep his weight off his knees as he nudged with his heels. Channon immediately stepped off the ledge into the air. She had only flapped her wings twice when a stream of firedrake came swinging down over the mountain to their right. Jaron gasped, seeing the collision that must surely happen. He leant to the left to direct Channon away but she ignored him and kept to her flight path. Most flashed by overhead but two greens were bearing down on them and Jaron could see the riders' faces, they were getting so close. One raised his arm, fist clenched. A squeak of fear came out of Jaron's throat but at the last minute the firedrake parted, one flying underneath and the other green going right over the top of them. Jaron ducked despite himself and Channon raised her head and let out a rumbling call. Relieved, Jaron blew out his cheeks.

Parl's calm voice came over his shoulder. 'You must trust your firedrake in these situations, Jaron, collisions are very rare. The beasts have a sense of their own air space that we can never hope to match. Think of a flock of birds, and how they can fly without getting in each other's way. The rider lifted his fist, did you see that? He was telling you he would go over the top.' Jaron nodded, trying to concentrate. He asked Channon to move left and again she didn't obey. Just then another firedrake passed by on the inside. 'Tsk, look over your shoulder to check it's clear first, young man. You do have some responsibility, you know.'

So many firedrake in the air and Jaron could feel his heart beginning its crawl into his throat. He risked a glance over his shoulder and, seeing it clear, asked her to move over. This time, Channon rolled her body to the left and levelled out when they were next to the mountains. They flew past the caves, some with firedrake still crouched on ledges, others taking off. It was Rakenar at its busiest. He looked across and saw more firedrake coming in over the range and the whole valley air stirred in the whirlpool of the beasts as they followed the aerial highway. The sight was impressive yet did nothing to calm his nerves. Parl made him fly two circuits of the mountain valley and had him directing Channon up high and down low, all the time having to find his way within the mass of beating wings. The school firedrake sometimes ignored his signals and each time she proved to be keeping them safe. Gradually Jaron found he got better at judging the timing and by the time Parl asked him to land by the lake Channon had had no cause to overrule him for the last half circuit.

'Very good, Jaron. Shaky start but you got into the swing of it.' Relieved, Jaron reached down to undo the clips. 'No, stay on, I think you're ready to go it alone.'

Jaron quailed. 'But… now? When there's so many?'

Parl patted his shoulder and the saddle creaked as he dismounted. On the ground, the teacher pointed up to the sky. 'Look up, Jaron.' Jaron did so and, to his amazement, in the time that they had landed the sky above the valley had emptied. 'Day shift is out on patrol and night flyers are inside eating their breakfast. The perfect time for you to have your first solo.' He moved back a few paces to give him room and stood waiting. Jaron sat frozen. The teacher frowned. 'Or we could wait for the other students to get here if you'd like an audience.'

That did it. Jaron took a deep breath. He stroked the base of the long neck and wished it had the comforting velvet warmth of Caliber's coat instead of hard scales. 'Okay, girl,' he murmured and Channon's ear cocked back at him. He nudged with his heels and felt the haunches lower in response. As her neck came up Jaron remembered just in time to lean forward to meet it before she boosted straight up. Even so, the pressure flattened him and the drag pulled his body back until the straps keeping him to the saddle were straining. Gasping, he kept low and pulled himself forward then wrapped both his arms around her neck as far as they could reach and clung on. He opened his eyes over her shoulder to see she was virtually angled upright as the ground fell rapidly away. He squeezed them shut but the disorientation was worse; his brain couldn't keep up and his head spun. Next moment the pressure eased as Channon stopped her upward thrust and now she seemed to hang in the air. Still clutching her neck, Jaron turned his head to peer out. Channon was hovering, and he dared to sit upright. Parl was a tiny figure watching on the ground, arms folded. Jaron was very definitely on his own and a well of panic filled up in his chest until he found it difficult to breathe. 'You can do this,' Jaron muttered to himself, but right now it didn't feel like it. Channon was flying in small circles now while she waited for his direction. An eye was rolled back at him and when he still didn't do anything she bent her neck to look at him fully. *What are you waiting for?* the look said and, despite himself, Jaron laughed. He brought his legs up into his customary jockey position for a moment and immediately felt better, then dropped his legs again into the weight of the stirrups, sat up straighter and took a breath. The sky was clear of any other firedrake, the sun was peeking over the mountains and there was a slight mist rising from the valley floor as the ground warmed up. He was on his own, but he trusted Channon; if anything, the flight earlier had shown him the old firedrake was not going to let him do anything stupid. She was his Chase back in Tiara, the old kelpra they put the new riders on. He ran his hand over the neck ridge as she completed another circle and a little rumble came out of her chest. He felt some comfort in that now-familiar sound. He breathed the clear mountain air in deeply through his nose and out through his mouth, then did it again until he felt steadier. It was now or never.

'Let's fly, Channon,' he said, and moved her forward.

It took the length of the valley before Jaron had the confidence to fiddle with the stirrup leathers to make them shorter. He found that by sitting upright and using his seat much like he had riding the kelpra he could get Channon to idle in the air. As he slipped his feet into the shortened stirrups he gave a sigh. *This* was the position he felt most at home with: the racing seat. Even so, he felt the pull of his skin on the hip; the time he had spent laid up and not riding had definitely stiffened it up more. He bent forward slightly and Channon moved off. He realised they were flying close to the side of Mount Scarf and, without thinking, leant over as Carna had taught him. Channon angled sideways and winged it round the end of the valley to begin the flight path back again. The morning sun picked out the harsh crags of the mountains while the fine mist rising from the damp ground softened the valley floor. It was beautiful, and Jaron found he was quite enjoying himself. He had the belt clipped in after all so he wasn't going to fall, he reasoned. Carefully, he raised his seat, lifting it from the saddle. Channon cocked an ear back at him, lowered her head, and flew faster. He bent his knees a little more to shift his weight back and she slowed. Jaron grinned. All about weight and balance – they were familiar riding rules but magnified tenfold on the back of a flying beast. He experimented some more, unbending his knees a little bit and putting his weight more in one stirrup, then the other. Channon responded immediately, almost waggling her wings to catch his slight weight. His left thigh wasn't too bad now he had healed but he still felt the pull of the muscle. Slowly, he began to feel more confident and so they flew faster. In no time at all the far mountains were looming but this time Jaron didn't hesitate and, putting his weight into one foot, he got Channon into a steep turn. The firedrake's body angled more steeply than he anticipated and Jaron's grin was wiped off his face as he felt his weight being dragged over her side. He tried to sit back down but his backside missed the saddle and one foot left the stirrup. Terrified, he grabbed hold of a neck plate. Channon helped him by levelling out by herself. She shook her ears, not best pleased with her pupil.

'I know, sorry, girl.'

They started another circuit of the valley. Carefully,

Jaron stood up in his stirrups and practiced with his weight again, learning how to lower and raise the level of flight, how to distribute it in the turns. He kept an eye out for other flyers but the air above the valley was theirs alone. Emboldened, he flew a shaky figure of eight, and as they skimmed the rock of Mount Scarf this time he managed to control her tilt. Their shadow swooped over Lord Carna where he stood watching from his cave ledge, one arm draped over Madrag's neck as the big red lay with his head on his paws.

Seeing him there and feeling suddenly self-conscious, Jaron flew back towards the lake.

A faint whistle caused Channon to look down. Parl was waving him in. The other students stood behind him in a half-circle looking up at them. Mindful of Parl's instructions to keep his eye on the patch of level ground at the lakeside, Jaron directed Channon to land; sitting back down in the saddle he tried to forget about all the students watching and concentrated hard on landing safely.

Channon touched down on all fours smoothly. He blew out and sat there, letting it all sink in; his first solo flight. Unclipping the belt, he threw his leg over the back of the saddle, sliding down her side onto Channon's already raised leg. Jaron was careful in his dismount but his legs nearly buckled as his boots touched grass. Despite the others watching, he was forced to lean on the firedrake for support until they stopped quaking.

'Everyone feels like that after the first solo flight,' Marla came up. 'It's the adrenaline.' Not trusting himself to speak, Jaron nodded. The red-haired girl folded her arms and looked at him with her head cocked to one side.

'Where did you learn to fly like that?'

Jaron frowned. 'I didn't, I mean I haven't,' he hesitated, the others had come up with Parl. 'I expect it's the rides on Tarp and Madrag, taught me more than I realised.'

She didn't seem convinced and raised the other eyebrow.

Parl pushed through the other students. 'Well done, Lord Jaron, a bit overconfident for your first ride, but very good.'

Overconfident? 'Just Jaron, please,' he reminded, flushing.

'I think we need to work on your technique, however,' Parl shook his head. 'Never seen anyone ride quite like that before.'

Tench sniggered and Marla was quick to round on him. 'It was better than your first ride, Tench. You were shouting, a lot if I recall,' she put a finger to her chin. 'What was it? Help?'

'I was not!' A flush crept up Tench's neck. Behind him, Wolf grinned.

Jaron turned away; he didn't feel strong enough for any bickering. Channon raised her neck and tilted her head to look down at him. Lowering it slowly, one green eye blinked at him. Jaron stared up at her. 'Good girl,' he whispered, and reached out, but then stopped, uncertain, his hand hanging in mid-air. Channon moved her head towards him and before he knew it his hand was on her eye ridge. He stroked it, his fingers feeling the ridges of the scales.

'Now, follow me, all of you.'

The students moved after Parl. Jaron stepped back from Channon and followed slowly, still feeling a little shaky after his flight. Channon lumbered behind him as they all headed towards the valley where the mountainside rose up in a sheer face. The rock was coal black here and as Jaron got closer he realised it was burnt. There came a puffing sound from behind him and looking over his shoulder he was in time to see white smoke coiling from Channon's nostrils. Alarmed, Jaron whipped round to face her and felt his chest constrict as he backed away. The firedrake raised her head and three perfectly round rings floated up into the air.

'Ohhh, look, Channon's blowing smoke rings!' Racker

clapped his hands like a delighted child. The other students murmured in excitement.

'Quiet now, come and stand by me, all of you. Racker, stop jumping about and pay attention.' Parl moved them away from Channon as she waddled towards the rock. 'I know some of you wouldn't have seen a firedrake fire; no firedrake apart from old Channon here is allowed to fire within the valley without permission and any rider who gives such an order to his beast will be severely reprimanded.' His pale eyes were hard as they looked at each of them in turn, coming to rest last of all on Jaron where they softened a little. 'Fire can be a devastating weapon and only in the most extreme of circumstances will a rider call for his beast to use it. Now, all of you keep back.'

He stepped forward and raised his arm towards Channon. Smoke was rising from her nostrils in curling tendrils and the green eyes were bright as she watched the teacher. Parl brought his arm down and her sides inflated as she took a deep breath and swung her head to the rock face. She coiled her neck back and made a strange little click in her throat. As her head shot forward, a thick beam of bright orange fire erupted from her roaring mouth, slamming into the mountainside and broiling against the rock in a burning mass of flames. The students threw their arms up to cover their faces. Only Hodge stood watching with Parl, strong arms folded but with wide eyes. The roar of the fire deafened Jaron and it seemed to go on and on until Channon at last ran out of breath. She closed her mouth, coughed and shook herself before turning to amble back to the lake. The students were left staring at a large circle of glowing orange rock, its heat smarting their faces.

'Wow.' Tench's grin was huge. 'That was great!'

'Can she come back and do it again, sir?' Racker asked. Beside him, Haley stood with her hands to her face.

'That was horrible, horrible,' she murmured.

'Lighten up, Haley.' Wolf came and put an arm around her thin shoulders. He looked across and frowned. 'Err, Jaron? You alright?'

Jaron didn't answer right away. Panting, he stood rigid with fists clenched tight. Marla pushed the others out of the way. 'Jaron?'

'I'm fine, fine,' he muttered through stiff lips.

'You look white as ash.'

'I said I'm fine,' he snapped before he could stop himself. Marla hesitated and turned back to the others with a shrug.

Wolf was sniffing the air. 'Whew! That stink...'

'It is a bit strong,' Parl agreed. 'We call the liquid *Flagra.* We know of no other beast in the lands that produces this fluid. It comes out of the fire sacs at the top of the firedrake's neck and into the throat; extremely dangerous to harvest when a firedrake dies, but worth the effort as it can be very useful.'

'When can we fire our firedrake, sir?' Tench asked eagerly.

'In battle, or if orders are given for clearing scrub or woodland for expansion.'

Tench looked disappointed. 'But there are no battles, no wars, and there's no expansion planned that my father's spoken of. What's the point in flying a fire-breathing beast if it doesn't get to fire at all?'

Haley shook her head at the blond boy's words. 'There are the games, I suppose. Though why you should be so keen to inflict such hurt is beyond me.'

Parl nodded in agreement. 'Yes, just be grateful, young man, that we live in peaceful times.'

That evening, after he had washed himself at his little basin, Jaron sat down on his bed and ran his fingers over the withered flesh on the left side of his chest, feeling the ridges of thickened skin. Somehow, in all the getting to know the beasts and the excitement of flying lessons, he had – despite his personal experience – conveniently pushed to the back of his mind the devastation these beasts could wreak. It had been shocking enough to see the Ernots being fired upon, even when he had been dazed and so relieved to be rescued. Parl had said the beasts were to fire in battle. Could he really do that? Burn someone like he himself had been burnt? Like Teel had died?

The boy lay back on the bed and stared up at the rough-hewn cave ceiling. No, he could never do that. A warning perhaps, but never a direct shot.

20

The days fell into a pattern for Jaron. Parl would come and pick him up in the morning for flying school. After lunch in his room, he exercised along the walkway and in the evenings Rella and Carna picked him up for dinner in the Great Hall. Life simply went on, carrying him along with it. He found he didn't want to ask about Torrit's banishment and where he might be now, preferring instead to treat him as dead and bury the hateful, evil man's existence.

One afternoon, he had stepped out to walk beyond his cave tunnel as usual. There was no mucking out nor duties as he had been used to with the kelpra and Jaron felt staid without this exercise. His thigh had healed but he still needed to keep his scarred hip moving. As he walked past the next cave door the latch lifted and it opened. The smile that was already on his lips for his mother faded when he saw it was Lord Carna standing on the threshold.

'Good afternoon,' the lord said. 'I thought I might keep you company today.' He turned to close the door behind him. When he turned back Jaron had managed to clear the disappointment from his face.

The lord fell into step beside Jaron, shortening his normal long stride to match. 'Your leg is better?'

'Yes, healed, thank you.'

They walked on in silence, Jaron desperately thinking of something to say. Carna seemed to have been doing much the same.

'I hear your lessons are going well.'

'Yes.'

'Parl is very pleased with your progress – you have already surpassed others who have been there longer.'

Jaron stole a glance up at the lord. The smooth chiselled face was looking ahead at two riders coming the other way. They stood aside to let them pass and saluted Carna. He merely nodded in return. As they left them behind, Jaron mustered his courage; this was the perfect opportunity to talk about Tiara.

'I've been thinking about the grain situation,' he began. The lord's flint eyes switched to him and Jaron rushed on before he faltered under that sharp gaze. 'I thought I could visit Tiara, help get Caliber back, then Lord Bell might give the Raken people more food. I mean, I could just spend a week there…' Carna didn't reply and he rushed on. 'I'm well now, and I could see my friends. I'm sure they've been wondering how I am.'

'You've made new friends here,' the lord said.

'Well, I don't know if I have really.'

'I hear you get on well with the students and Flick speaks very highly of you.'

He was missing the point, deliberately of course. Jaron tried again. 'I mean, I miss my old friends. I have been here six weeks.'

'Exactly why you should give it more time.'

Jaron huffed with impatience and looked away to glance over the walkway railing. The hall far below the walkway was empty of diners but Jaron could see the staff setting out the tables for dinner.

'I suppose you haven't seen much of Flick lately,' he heard Carna muse. 'I sent him on sentry duty to Tiara a couple of days ago.'

'Flick's gone to Tiara? Why?'

'The Ernots raided the grain barns twice in as many days and Lord Bell asked for our help again.' His eyes found

Jaron's. 'It is what I have been waiting for. So much better than issuing threats.'

Jaron stopped walking. 'So, the Raken *will* have more grain?'

'Yes.' Carna turned to face him.

Yet he had let Jaron ramble on without telling him at first. He tried again. 'If Tiara is on better terms with Rakenar, surely there is even less of an obstacle in me going to see my friends?'

He saw Carna's lips press together. 'You have obligations here, Jaron.'

'I'm sure Mum won't mind me visiting Tiara.' He was aware his voice had risen a notch and noticed a slight tic start up in the lord's jaw; an indication of Carna's thinning patience.

'I didn't mean Rella. You are my nephew, I am sure you can see how that might change things.'

Jaron stared. 'Because you have no heir.' It was rude of him and he regretted it as soon as the words were out.

'Quite so.' Carna folded his arms, watching him

The mountain's weight seemed to suddenly be pressing down on Jaron's head. 'There must be someone else,' his voice came out in a whisper and when Carna slowly shook his head he found his hands were clenching into fists of their own accord. 'It's not fair,' he muttered. 'I'm grateful of course, for you saving me. But now I find I'm your *sole heir.* It's impossible!'

'Anything is possible. I count my blessings to have found you both when I thought all was lost.' Carna put a hand on his shoulder and gave him an awkward pat. He kept it there, and Jaron resisted the urge to step back out of reach.

'But what about the council?'

'What about them?' Carna's hand fell away and now he didn't bother to hide his feelings; his look was hard

'Can't the council rule?' Jaron saw the eyes flare and he

swallowed; he had gone too far, but Carna's voice was calm when he answered.

'That is a possibility, *if* I had no heir, but I have you and that is infinitely more preferable to the people. The council advise, we are their spearhead.'

'But–'

'Enough!' Carna roared. 'I see Rella has spoiled you. It is time to grow up and face your responsibilities.'

'I didn't know I had any a week ago!' Jaron shot back, lord or no. 'What do I owe the Raken? If it wasn't for them I wouldn't have–' here he flapped his hand at himself, '–all this, I would still be living in our village with Teel, the man who was a father to me, and we would still be a family.' His voice had risen of its own accord and beyond Carna he could see the two riders they had passed earlier were now turned back and staring at them. Jaron ignored them. 'I heard of Torrit's firedrake being banished,' he said in a low voice. 'Not death, as Torrit and his beast really deserved.'

A flash of pain darted across Carna's face for a fleeting moment, then the lord's face might have been made from stone. His silence only served to fuel Jaron's anger even more. 'You don't have any claim on us,' he dared to say, glaring up at the man before drawing in a shuddering breath to calm himself. 'May I be excused?'

A muscle spasmed in Carna's jaw. 'If you wish it.'

'I do.' Jaron gave a short, dismissive half-bow before taking his leave of the lord.

As he neared the two staring riders, they parted for him as he limped quickly past, avoiding their eyes with his head down and his heart still hammering from his outburst. He had been rude to a lord. Shouted at him. *Let him do his worst, I don't care.*

His dinner that evening was delivered to his room by a serving boy with Rella and Carna nowhere to be seen. Jaron suspected Lord Carna had forbidden his mother to go to him.

It didn't help his mood at all.

He slept badly that night. Tossing and turning in his crumpled bed until the early hours. At least there was no flying school, he thought as he punched his pillow into submission, for Parl had reminded all the students yesterday it was a day off.

It seemed he had hardly fallen asleep when Jaron woke with a head filled with sawdust. He squinted into the gloom of the cave, wondering what had woken him.

Suddenly, he heard an unearthly shriek from outside, a firedrake's call but unlike anything Jaron had heard before. It came again, distant but powerful enough not to lose its message; a call of distress. He threw back the blankets and hopped across the cave in his socks. Yanking open the door, Jaron looked out and scanned the sky. The light was thin in the early morning, the mountains shrouded and the sky empty. He stepped through and looked down into the valley. The sight there startled him.

Eight firedrake flew low over the floor of the valley in a ragged line, feinting now and then as though they were driving something. They rose up then down, travelling up the valley and all the time moving closer to Mount Scarf. As they drew nearer Jaron realised not one of the beasts had a rider on its back. Just then, the firedrake broke the line and seemed to wheel up into the air like a flock of angry birds before arching their backs and folding their wings. They dived in unison, an impressive sight, and flashed below his eye level. Jaron moved further out onto his ledge, wondering what on earth they were doing. The distress call came again, louder this time, tearing through the air and rising up to where he stood, instilling in him a sudden sense of urgency. He cautiously moved to the edge, and peered over.

The firedrake below were massing in a body of flapping wings and lashing tails. Snarls and roars punched the air. Riders, alerted by the noise, were now standing outside their caves and adding their own clamour as they shouted. Those with firedrake standing with them were quick to order them to stay put. If any of those standing alone were trying to call their firedrake back, the beasts took no notice. Their sinuous necks were writhing and twisting amongst the hovering wings, trying to get at something that was so far in against the mountain below him Jaron still couldn't see. Frustrated, he got down on his hands and knees and lay on his stomach to peer over the edge. A couple on the ledge below were watching the battling firedrakes just as he was. The man was urgently calling, probably trying to get his firedrake back.

Just then there came a loud squeal and a blue flash hurtled past the snapping jaws. Flying straight up, the beast hit an outcropping of rock and unbalanced, flipped in towards the face. Jaron gasped as the people on the ledge below dived back into their cave just in time as the beast fell onto it, momentum rolling it over with wings caught against its body. A pale underbelly was exposed until it scrabbled with its neck and front legs to right itself, flapping madly for balance. It looked up – and straight at Jaron who was still in his prone position, his head sticking out over the edge. For a moment they stared at each other, the blue firedrake and the boy. The firedrake's eyes were a startling purple. Beyond the beast Jaron saw the green firedrake coming at him from underneath, their heads nearly at the ledge. Jaron could see the bared teeth, the glinting green eyes fixed up at the blue.

Suddenly, he was shouting down at the blue. 'Get away!' Its eyes narrowed. 'Fly!' Jaron urgently flapped both arms then clutched at the ledge in alarm as his legs came up, threatening to unbalance him and tip him over the edge. The blue, meanwhile, had looked down just in time as a firedrake reached the ledge and lunged at him. It squealed and leapt straight up into the air, escaping the green's teeth by inches. Jaron had no time to pull back as the beast flashed past his head, one claw just missing his face. The boy rolled away from the edge and ended up prone on his back.

He froze in surprise.

From far up in the air the blue was hovering, looking down at him. Just then, the green firedrake flashed past in a dense flock, causing Jaron to throw up a protective arm against the wind and dust they generated. When he lowered it, the blue was gone.

Jaron raised himself up on his arms and twisted in time to see the blue flashing across the sky, leaving his pursuers far behind. The strange firedrake lifted over the mountain rim and was gone from sight.

Jaron let out an explosive breath and sat up, hugging his knees. He watched the green firedrake wheel back towards the valley, for they did not pursue the intruder over the mountains. Flapping down, grumbling noises emitted from their throats as they sought out their riders who waited for them on ledges. One who landed nearest to Jaron's mountain got a telling off, while others were petted and praised; either way the firedrake looked pretty pleased with themselves.

Jaron picked himself up. It must be the wild bluey the dinner talk had been about. Carna had called it a 'throwback.' He remembered the beast's eyes, a deep purple and not the normal green of the firedrake nor the yellow of Madrag. There had been intelligence in that look and as Jaron went back in he vowed to ask Carna more about it.

'I say kill it,' Thorel insisted at dinner that evening. 'It's a wild firedrake and of no use to us.'

Minderman nodded. 'Rarely am I in agreement with my friend here.' Thorel glowered at him. 'But it's unpredictable and for all we know could be a man-eater.'

'Man-eater?' the words were out before Jaron could stop them. He flushed.

'We cannot know that for sure,' Oran murmured. Sometimes he joined them at the table in the evenings and Jaron was always pleased to see him. 'It might just be looking for its pod and is a bit lost at the moment.'

Rella backed up the master carpenter. 'Yes, let's not overreact, it might well just move on in the next couple of days.' She was sitting next to Jaron and he wondered, not for the first time, how his mother so easily spoke up at the council table. She caught him looking and smiled at him.

'It's had enough chances and now it's got into the valley.' Carna was shaking his head. 'Something is drawing it in and I doubt if today will scare it off. Didn't you say you nearly singed it two days ago, Nave?'

The wing commander nodded. 'Ratch surprised it coming over the mountain range. We came up from underneath. It did a lot of squealing and shouting when Ratch went for it.'

'Yet still it comes.' Carna frowned while the table watched him. 'All morning we searched for it immediately after it was driven from the valley. No sighting. It travels too fast.' He sighed. 'We are going to have to hunt and kill it.'

Jaron started at these words, remembering the intelligence in its gaze. It felt wrong.

'Did you want to say something, Jaron?' The grey eyes were challenging him.

The boy swallowed. 'Maybe it's lonely and just needs to find a home.'

'But not here. I know it seems harsh but I have the Raken people to think about. Supposing it starts to eat the animals or burn the crops? Or, even worse, the villages?'

Jaron frowned.

Leraine put her elbows on the table. 'The young female who has come into season has been escorted away to the female pod two days ago, and the bluey hasn't followed. It doesn't seem to be her that's the attraction. She smiled at Jaron, 'I think Jaron's right, it's just a loner and wanting to find its place.'

'Let us all remember that a bluey is a rare creature these days,' Oran said. 'Do we have the right to take the life of our firedrake ancestor? One of whom our whole way of life was built on?' A murmur of agreement went around the table.

Nave was frowning into his tankard. 'The drakel will be here in two days. We will want it out of the area by then. Flick is stationed in Tiara and takes Tarp to hunt in the Nidera Pass.' Jaron started at the city's name and cast a sneaky glance at Carna, but the lord was listening and didn't look at him. 'He's seen it taking off twice from the valley,' Nave continued, 'and thinks it uses that as its base. It's proving predictable and mostly tries to get into our valley at dawn before the watches change over.'

'Good,' Carna nodded. He turned his tankard absently in his hands. The table watched him and kept silent. At last, he sighed. 'Nave, be ready tomorrow and if it doesn't appear here take a pod and hunt it down at first light.' Now he did look at Jaron. 'And after tomorrow I want that to be the end of it.'

Oran shook his head. 'Such a shame,' he murmured. 'I have always wanted to do a painting of a bluey and capture that translucent colour. The old tapestries and paintings have faded so much.'

Carna drained his tankard and stood up. 'Maybe after tomorrow the hunters can bring you its scales, Oran, if that helps.' The table was silent as the lord pushed back his chair, turned, and stalked out of the hall with long strides.

Rella watched him go, sighed, and stood up. 'Goodnight to you all.' There was a scraping of chairs as the men at the table stood. 'Come along, Jaron.'

'Why does he have to kill it?' Jaron asked as they walked back.

'You heard why, Jaron, it could be dangerous and he has the people's safety to think about.'

'But surely if they try hard enough it can be driven away.'
He could see Madrag waiting for them and Carna standing
with his back to their approach, stroking the big red's nose.
Jaron pressed his lips together. 'I think he's cruel.'

At these words Rella stopped and pulled him round to
face her. He was struck how he was nearly at eye level with
her now.

'Do you think he took it lightly? That he wants to kill a
rare blue? He has to do it for the good of the city, Jaron.
Tonight, he will think of nothing else; he is not the heartless
man you think he is.'

Jaron started to protest. 'I don't...' But he hesitated.
What exactly did he think of Carna?

'It's hard for you,' Rella said. 'I see that. This man comes
into our lives and everything has changed for you.' Jaron
stared at her. 'Oh yes, I heard about yesterday. He is not the
enemy, Jaron. I really wish you would give him a chance
because he happens to think a lot of you.'

Jaron frowned.

Rella's face softened as she watched him. 'We come as
a package, you and I, but I think it was more than he dared
hope that he would have an heir to the lordship.' Jaron didn't
reply. He saw then Oran had followed them, close enough
to hear.

'I see you are upset, Jaron,' Oran said as he came and
stood at Rella's shoulder. 'It does seem a harsh order to kill
the blue.'

'I was just explaining to Jaron that Carna has no choice,
Oran.' Her voice had a slight bite to it.

Oran smiled. 'Ah, lovely Rella, it is upsetting but far be
it for me to disagree with you.' His stepped closer and his
arm went around her waist. 'I am sure you are right.'

Jaron stared at Oran, surprised at his familiarity. He saw
his mother's eyebrows rise and she twisted slightly away
from the master carpenter. 'Oran...' she began but trailed

off as Carna approached them.

The lord's eyes were hard as they looked at the other man. 'Did you want something, Oran?' His voice was cold, his flint gaze aimed at the carpenter's arm still about Rella's waist.

Oran immediately uncurled his arm and stepped away. His smile was contrite. 'Forgive me, my lord,' he gave a florid bow. 'I was merely concerned that young Jaron seemed upset.'

Carna didn't deign to reply. Taking Rella's arm, he turned his back on Oran and escorted her towards Madrag. Jaron made to follow them but, looking up at the carpenter, he saw the man was staring after the lord, his painted lips pressed into a thin line. Seeing Jaron, he swiftly composed himself and, smiling broadly, gave a little bow.

'Good evening, Jaron.'

Jaron mumbled a reply and hurried after his mother.

21

The talk amongst the students at the lesson the next morning was all about the blue firedrake.

'There was nearly a fight!' Racker was excited. 'Did you see how our firedrake went for it? I thought it was a goner for sure.'

'Too quick,' Tench said. 'Pity, I've never seen a firedrake kill another.'

'Tench!' Haley gasped. 'Don't be so cruel.'

The students were sitting on the outcrop of rocks near the lake while Parl checked Channon's girth strap. Tench smirked at the blonde girl. 'They're vermin, Haley, and a danger to Rakenar,' he folded his arms. 'You know your history, they hunted us in the past.'

'Yeah, eons ago,' Marla stuck up for Haley, who had gone quiet. 'We wouldn't have the firedrake now if it wasn't for them. What do you think, Wolf?'

The lanky youth reclined amongst the rocks. Even here he sat with his legs crossed as though he were on a comfy chair. 'I say let it alone; eventually it'll realise it's not welcome and leave.' His black eyes flicked across to the blond youth. 'We're not all as bloodthirsty as you, Tench.'

'Don't be soft. I was just thinking about the safety of our people. That's what a good leader would do.'

'And we all know your aspirations there, don't we?' Wolf replied quietly. Tench clenched his jaw and threw a glance Jaron's way. He laughed then, but it sounded forced. 'Yeah, right,' Wolf muttered under his breath.

'They're rare nowadays,' Hodge said. Jaron looked up at

him where he stood at his shoulder. The large youth was smiling. 'I'm glad I had the chance to see one.'

Tench pushed off from his rock. 'Might be your last chance, my father told me they were out hunting it at first light. Carna, sorry, *Lord* Carna wants it dead.'

'No,' Haley whispered. Jaron saw her dip her head so her fine hair shielded her face.

'Don't worry,' he said quietly to her. 'It's so quick it will probably get away.'

She looked up at him and he was startled to see her blue eyes were moist. 'I didn't know about the blue, Mother didn't tell me.'

'Your mother?'

'Leraine Manta.'

Jaron remembered the short-haired blonde lady who had been so kind to him. He could see now the resemblance in the high cheekbones and blue eyes. 'I expect she didn't want you to worry.'

'That's enough talking.' Parl was walking back. 'Today, we are flying over more open land in the forest bowl beyond Mount Scarf. It will be a chance for faster flying.' He paused, eyeing the students. 'And, as the drakel are arriving tomorrow, I want to talk to you afterwards about the selection process.'

The students gasped as one. 'Yes!' Tench punched the air while Racker jumped up and down on the spot.

Jaron felt his heart drop into his boots. As the excited students gathered closer to their teacher he held back, trying to get his emotions under control.

'Jaron?' Marla was at his shoulder. 'What's up? Are you worried you won't get chosen?'

He took her misapprehension and used it. 'Well, you seem very confident.'

Marla laughed. 'I mean, come on,' she spread her arms. 'What firedrake wouldn't be able to resist?' Jaron laughed.

She looked at Jaron from under her lashes. 'I suppose it's harder for you, being Lord Carna's nephew and all.'

'Sorry?'

'Well, you'll be expected to net a red for yourself.'

Jaron stared. 'Will I?' He hadn't considered it would have to be a red.

Marla was watching him. 'Don't worry – it is the firedrake's choice after all, so nobody would blame you if a green chose you instead.'

'I thought we had a choice too.' How could he possibly tell her he wasn't even sure he wanted *any* firedrake, no matter what colour?

'We do, I suppose, but when it comes to it I think every rider worries about missing out and takes what they can get. It's the higher ups,' here she eyed Jaron, 'who have the pressure to get the reds. They're rarer and I heard there's only one this season.'

He stared at her.

'Red for the leaders, always has been that way.' She was watching him closely as she said this. When he didn't reply her lips pursed. 'Jaron, you do *want* to be chosen, don't you?' She said it as fact but Jaron became still. He could feel his cheeks getting hot under her astute look. 'Oh,' Marla whispered, staring at him like she had never really seen him before. Dropping her eyes, she left him to go over and join the other students.

The huge forest bowl beyond Mount Scarf served to make Jaron forget his fears about the selection. It was in stark contrast to the wild mountain range the other side of Rakenar. When it was his turn to fly Channon, he enjoyed being out of the confines of the valley and flew Channon fast, intrigued to see glimpses of the villages below, half-hidden by trees. His flying time was soon up, however, and he found himself regretting going back. It occurred to Jaron that here he was flying Channon out on his own and he hadn't felt any qualms about it at all. But to have a firedrake of your own was another matter. He watched as a dense flock of birds flew out of the trees in alarm at their passing. *I'm just not ready.*

Below them, the white birds below increased speed and the flock became denser. Jaron idly watched them, still musing about tomorrow's selection. It was the finality, he guessed – having his own firedrake meant he would be unable to leave Rakenar if he chose. Yet again he felt like a pawn. *Why wouldn't they let him decide his own life?*

The birds' calls of alarm increased in pitch, distracting him, and he wondered about their noise when Channon was lifting higher away from them.

A blue streak flashed by underneath from Channon's tail to head, scattering the flock. Jaron jumped in surprise. 'What?'

Channon let out a snarl that turned his blood cold. She spun in the air and the boy was thrown to one side. He clutched at the saddle in alarm, shifted his seat to a more central position and searched wildly about. There was just blue sky with scudding clouds. Perplexed, he saw Channon's long neck lifting high as she hovered and searched the sky, her nostrils flaring.

'I think it's gone, Channon,' he leant forward and patted the hard scales. 'Carna didn't manage to kill it after all, did he, girl?' Channon twisted her head back towards her rider and Jaron saw the green eyes narrow. He looked over his shoulder, and gasped. At that moment, he wished Carna had succeeded.

The blue was coming right at them, on a collision course with wings flat against its body. Channon lowered her neck and dove. Jaron, crouched in the saddle, ducked his head down, and his instinct saved him as a whoosh of air rushed over his helmet. He looked up in time to glimpse the white underbelly of the blue firedrake as it flashed over them. The long tail thrashed once and it arced higher, scorching into the air. He had never seen a firedrake move so fast. Channon sent a bellow of fury after it. The blue stopped at the highest point of its arc and angled itself, wings back against its body. It reminded Jaron of the falcons he had once seen the nobles fly back in Tiara. All wonder was snatched away as it began to fall back to them. A distant whistling filled Jaron's ears.

'Oh no,' he whispered.

Another shocking jolt to his body as Channon took evasive action and banked sharp on a wing tip. Righting himself again, Jaron risked a look over his shoulder. The blue had adjusted its flight path and was still coming at them. *So fast!* Channon dived again, steeper this time, and Jaron, carried along with her, felt his seat leave the saddle, his feet slipping out of the stirrups. He shrieked, but the straps clipping him to the saddle stretched taut and saved him. Frantically, Jaron struggled against the pressure, his fingers hanging on to the saddle front, but the rest of him was left flailing in the air against the force of her dive. He squinted at the canopy of the trees below growing larger and larger. Just as it seemed a crash was unavoidable up she came again and his body banged back down on the saddle as the air went out of his lungs in a whoosh. She rolled in the air in the nick of time for a blue blur whistled past on their left. Jaron was nothing but a passenger and had to trust the old green would get him out of this. Feet scrabbling for his stirrups, he watched in horror as the blue winged around behind them. It easily caught a snarling Channon up and slowed to fly right beside her. A purple eye looked directly at Jaron before the wedge head turned towards him. Its maw opened, displaying a double row of white teeth.

'*Channon!*'

She dropped a wing, tilting sideways in the air and taking him away from the blue. At the same time, she thrashed out with outstretched talons. Her claws must have hit home for the blue squealed and dropped away from Jaron's sight. Channon didn't linger but flew fast towards the safety of Mount Scarf, ears flat and dark smoke rising from her flared nostrils. Jaron cast frequent panicked glances back over his shoulder but there was no sign. Just as he was starting to hope they would make it the blue suddenly rose up in front of them. With a snarl Channon spilled the air from her wings.

The two firedrake faced each other, hovering in the air. Channon flapped to the left and it immediately mirrored her movement. It was a lot smaller than the green but it wasn't going to back down. Channon growled in fury at this young upstart and Jaron hunkered down lower as he peered past the base of her neck. The blue cocked its head while the purple eyes locked onto him. It keened, an odd wheedling sound. Channon's answering growl was so deep Jaron could feel it reverberate through her body. He noticed blood on the white belly of the blue and oozing between scale plates on its chest. Channon took a deep breath and the blue's gaze snapped back towards her. She exhaled, and a channel of fire roared out of her mouth. Jaron quailed in terror. The blue dove down with a loud squeal. In the next breath Channon let out a rumbling call towards Mount Scarf.

A response floated over the bowl and Jaron saw a firedrake wheel out from behind the mountain, then another. His heart lifted, only for it to drop once more when the blue appeared before them again. This time the old firedrake didn't hesitate. She tilted her wings forward, thrashed her tail, and charged, snarling. Jaron, carried along on her back, closed his eyes. He felt her roll just as something caught his shoulder and there was a sharp tug that nearly lifted him clean from the saddle. Cloth ripped as he cried out, his stomach lurching as Channon swooped down lower. He opened his eyes – half his jacket was in tatters, flapping madly across his chest. He twisted round in time to see the blue's tail whip the air as it turned to come in again. So much quicker than Channon, and the old firedrake's wings were more laboured now. Desperate, he looked ahead and saw the two greens racing towards them with their riders, too far away yet to help. Behind them more firedrake spilled from Mount Scarf. He saw the huge red in their midst: Carna was coming.

'Come *on*, Channon!' Jaron yelled.

Silver claws suddenly landed both sides of him, drawing blood from Channon's back as they dug in between the scale plates. His horrified scream mingled with her roar of pain. Green and blue wing membrane flapped against each other as the two firedrake, locked together, fell from the sky. The silver talons unhinged themselves and a cage of claws ensnared Jaron around his middle, pulling his kicking, struggling body from Channon's back. His mind froze even as he grabbed hold of the saddle; another yank and his hands lost their grip but the safety straps pulled taut and saved him from being carried away. Channon swung her head round and snapped at the blue, her teeth landing on empty air when it ducked but kept hold of its prize. The beasts tumbled through the air, their fighting screams deafening and terrible. Jaron felt himself being pulled away. '*No!*' Teeth flashed before his chest as, with a snap of the blue's jaws, one strap went. He screamed. Another flashing cut and the last straps fell away.

'No!' Jaron screamed again as his body lurched up into the air and away. He stretched his arms out towards Channon like a plea as she landed on her back on the cracking, snapping trees, leaves showering into the air at the impact. Two firedrake appeared, wheeled over her and looked up after him, their mouths opening as they roared and gave chase. Jaron felt the claws tighten, their edges digging into his rib cage as he was clasped to softer scales. A sobbing cry escaped his lips. He was boosted up into the air and the downward force pushed his chin onto his chest, cutting off his breath. The blue levelled out and Jaron, pinned against the firedrake's chest and gasping, saw the forest bowl go past in a green blur underneath him before his mind mercifully closed down.

22

Thirst woke him, his mouth like wool. He mumbled and tried to move his arms. Something prevented them and sudden fear shot through him. His eyes flew open to a clear night with a full moon.

He was lying on his side and his ribs hurt; something was cocooning him. Jaron tried his legs but could only move them the tiniest of margins. He began to struggle as panic set in. Something shifted along one side of his body and instantly the boy went still. A breath of warm air came from behind, rippling over his shoulders.

His stricken mind remembered then, being pulled from Channon and snatched up into the air. He looked down and saw the thing imprisoning him was leathery membrane, the ridged veins glowing silver in the moonlight. A keening sound came from behind him and vibrated along the length of his body. Every nerve screamed at him to get away.

He panicked then, struggling and shouting incoherently, his voice breaking and rasping. The cocoon loosened a little and Jaron frantically kicked at it. He got his arms free and tried to get leverage, his hands reaching out behind him. Hard ridges of scales pressed against his palms. Cringing away, Jaron found the room to pitch forward onto his knees. Gasping, he crawled out of his prison and turned to face his attacker.

And trembled with fear.

The beast laid against a wall of rock and the blue's whole body was rippled through with scales glowing silver in the moonlight. It was shocking to see. Luminous eyes stared down at him – shining orbs shot through with silver in the darkness.

A wing lay stretched out nearest to Jaron, who noticed his feet were still under the membrane and slowly drew them out. For a long while the boy and the firedrake stared at each other. When it still did nothing, Jaron edged just a tiny shift further away on his behind. The firedrake watched him. He did it again, then again until he had put a little distance between them. He risked a look behind him to search for his path of escape and groaned in dismay. He was on a ledge, a high ledge, with no visible way of getting off.

A slithering noise made Jaron jump. The long tail was travelling towards him. He watched in frozen horror as it slithered around, cringing as it touched his back. Then he was pushed, feet frantically scrabbling, across the ledge and back towards the silver-scaled beast. A long grey tongue licked along the ridges of pointed white teeth. Jaron whimpered and his mother's face rose up in his mind's eye. She would never get over his death, especially like this; a rabbit torn apart. The blue stood up and Jaron now lay cringing between its front legs. It brought its nose down and the boy screamed, throwing up his arms in terror.

The nose nudged him, cutting off his cries as the breath was knocked out of his lungs, making his sore ribs protest. It nosed down to his stomach. Jaron frantically wriggled, shouting something incoherent. The nose pushed and he desperately batted at it, knowing it was futile, silently begging the fates to be merciful and let him pass out before the teeth cut in. His death was always going to be by firedrake; somehow, he had known it in his bones and now here it was. He hit out in panic. The nose pulled back and the nostrils flared. Jaron squeezed his eyes tight shut against certain pain and death.

A gentle puff of air blew into his face; shocked, he opened them again. The blue did it again, and keened. Jaron

stared as it cocked its head a little and a sudden image of
Caliber came into his mind. The blue's head filled his sight,
waiting – for what? Not knowing what else to do, the boy
did what he often had with the kelpra; he blew a shaky breath
back, directly into the nostrils so close to his face. The blue
started, then came in again and a puff of air lifted Jaron's
fringe. He swallowed painfully and summoned the breath to
blow back harder this time. The blue snorted and shook its
head. It yawned, and Jaron was left staring at rows of teeth.
He lay still as a rabbit, heart pounding and mind frozen. The
firedrake lifted a paw and he shrieked in terror, but it passed
over and landed beyond his head somewhere. The white
belly filled his sight as the firedrake walked right over him
without stepping on him. The tail trailed last and he closed
his eyes and cringed as it travelled along the length of his
body, its tapered end slithering off his face.

For a moment longer Jaron lay there, unable to move
until his lungs demanded air and he was forced to draw in a
shaky breath. Slowly, he lifted his chin and saw the blue was
settled against the cliff face further along the wide ledge.

Trembling, Jaron carefully sat up. The blue looked over
at him. It unfurled a wing. Jaron stared, hardly believing
what he was seeing; it was inviting him back. The boy drew
his knees up and looked away. He heard the firedrake let out
a big sigh and eyed it again. It lowered its nose onto its front
paws and closed its brilliant eyes. *Not dinner then, or am I
breakfast?* He put a hand over his mouth to push down his
terror but an insane sounding laugh bubbled through his lips.
He was dehydrated, exhausted, terrified, had cheated death
– for now – and was losing his mind, obviously.

Not trusting to take his eyes off it, Jaron hugged his
knees, watching the silver glowing beast while it slept. It
wasn't a wild firedrake; he was certain of it, or he would
have been torn apart as soon as it had set down with him.
Someone owned it, or had, once. Would that be enough for

it not to kill him? he wondered.

The night passed on and Jaron sat out in the moonlight, arms wrapped round his torn jacket against the growing cold and fighting a burning thirst. He stared out over the land swathed in blue radiance, trying to see anything that seemed familiar. His eyes swept the distant mountainous horizon, dark silhouettes against the glow of the moon. But no firedrake flew there looking for him and the blue travelled so fast they could be anywhere. Whenever he looked back at the firedrake it breathed deeply in sleep. Jaron slid to the edge as quietly as he could and peered over. Far below he could just see the silver canopy of a forest gently moving in the faint breeze. Stretching out on his stomach and craning his neck out as far as he dared, Jaron studied just below the ledge. By the moonlight he could see it was a sheer rockface. Even if the daylight did reveal a possible way for him to climb down, he knew he couldn't do it without risk of terrible injury. He thought about casting himself over and ending it there and then. Anything was better than being torn apart. His head stuck out over the edge, he considered it seriously for a time before letting out a sigh. He had to cling to the hope that he was right; the blue was not wild and was just lonely. Maybe it had lost its rider. Maybe there was another mountain city somewhere that favoured only blues, despite what the Raken thought of them. Whatever it was, he couldn't give up. His mother would never forgive him.

It must have been in the dying hours of the night when, despite his fears and discomfort, the boy at last fell into an exhausted, fitful sleep.

It seemed no time at all before something dripping on his face woke him. His eyelids fluttered and he let out a desperate groan. Still half-asleep he raised a hand and liquid dropped onto it. *Water*. Now wide awake, Jaron sat up as quickly as his stiff, cold body and sore ribs would allow. He had difficulty focusing at first and rubbed at his eyes. When he dropped his hands, it was to cringe away. The firedrake was standing right over him and Jaron scrabbled across the rock on his backside, raising little dust clouds, desperate to put some distance between them. A silver claw hooked into his belt and yanked him forward again, lifting his body clean off the ground as it did so. Jaron cried out in fear and wriggled frantically, his hands batting weakly at the claw. The blue's mouth came closer and grunted as Jaron's boot struck the sensitive nose. The claw released him but now a heavy paw landed on the boy's chest, pinning him down. Jaron groaned in terror and pain. The firedrake eyed him then rolled its head to one side. Water dribbled out of the side of its mouth. A few trickles landed on Jaron's face and his body's need took over as he forgot his fear and eagerly opened his mouth to catch the precious liquid. Swallowing was painful at first but the more water the blue trickled into his mouth the more Jaron's throat was eased. He choked, and the blue lifted his paw.

Jaron sat up, wiping at his mouth. Beast and boy stared at each other, Jaron hardly believing what the beast had just done. It was certainly intelligent and now more than ever he had to believe it was not going to hurt him.

The sun's rays were slanting across the ledge and Jaron, desperate for warmth, risked crawling to the light. The firedrake didn't follow him but sat on its haunches, watching his progress. Once he was in the sun Jaron looked around for a possible escape route now he could see better. Sheer rock towered above, and when he moved closer to the edge to peer down it was more of the same.

Feeling hopeless, Jaron scooted away from the edge and, settling his back against the rock, undid his helmet and took it off. Turning his face to the weak early morning warmth, he studied the landscape. The forest stretched out as far as the eye could see with the mountains he had looked at last night now a purple haze in the distance. Nothing looked at all familiar.

Out of the corner of his eye, he noticed the firedrake shuffle closer. Alarmed, he half turned to look at it fully. It cocked its head at him and lowered its haunches to sit up again. Jaron watched warily, noticing the slash on the belly that Channon's claw had caused yesterday.

The blue rumbled and dropped down on all fours. It stepped over to him and Jaron started in alarm. Keeping its head low it slunk closer still and the boy got unsteadily to his feet. He tried to take a sidestep away, but in his weakness stumbled over a stone. In an instant the blue was there, thrusting its head and neck between him and the edge. Jaron's flailing hand landed on a neck scale and, regaining his balance, the boy cringed away, stepping back as he frowned at the firedrake. It had just saved him from going over the edge. He shook his head in disbelief.

The beast crouched down and rumbled at him. Jaron recognised the pose. 'I'm not getting on your back, alright?' he croaked. The blue shifted its body closer and Jaron edged away along the rock face. 'No!' he shook his head and tried to sound firm about it but now the firedrake's body was alongside him, pressing him back until cold stone dug into his shoulders. Its body remained hemming him in. There was nowhere to go with the head at one end and a raised tail at the other. Jaron sighed. How else was he going to get off this ledge? But it was best to let the blue know he wasn't completely weak and feeble, or at least try to. The blue's head lifted over its wing to look down at him.

'No,' he repeated, though his knees were quaking. He even tried making his voice deeper, as he had sometimes used with Caliber. 'I said, *NO!*' For the first time he dared to back it up with a wave of mental command.

At this, the firedrake quickly shuffled round and stood up on its hind legs, facing him. It cocked its head and huffed as the purple eyes stared into his. Its forelegs reached out for him, claws opening.

Jaron screeched and ducked out from under them, stumbling along the ledge. The blue snaked its head after him. After a moment he stopped, realising it was insane to try to get away from the firedrake here – there was nowhere to go. As he turned the blue rose up in front of him again, front paws reaching and claws open.

'Alright!' He put his hands up, admitting defeat. His ribs were sore enough without being clasped to its chest again.

The blue immediately dropped down on all fours and looked expectantly at him.

He took a reluctant step towards the beast; the way this thing flew he doubted he could stay on – and would it just let him fall? He had to trust it but even to touch it was hard. As he neared its shoulder it turned its head towards him. Slowly he raised a hand and laid it on the blue scales, watching the firedrake's reaction. Its purple eyes stared at him but it didn't move. Jaron carefully laid his other hand on the shoulder ridge and stepped closer. The beast stayed stock still as Jaron lifted a leg to get a toehold.

It was smaller than Channon and only half the size of Madrag, but without any straps to grab hold of he struggled to get on and fell back. He froze then, worried lest the blue would take fright at his sudden fall and attack him. It merely watched him, long ears pricked. He got back up, groaning, and tried again. It didn't lift its leg like the Raken firedrake did for their riders and he lost his toehold and slipped down to land in a crumpled heap on the floor, clutching at his ribs. The third time he struggled, exhausted, the blue, which still had its head turned to watch his progress, pushed him from behind with its nose. A startled cry of fear left his lips as he fell forward against its stomach. Next moment it had snaked its nose under his bottom, and Jaron gasped as he was lifted up, his hands walking up the side of the beast as his feet dangled. A sudden push forced him to swing a leg over or else flip over the other side.

Now sitting astride its back, he sat up cautiously. The blue looked at him with one eye and rumbled. Jaron thought it sounded happy.

'Take me back?' Jaron asked. 'Please?' The blue rumbled again in answer and moved to the edge. Jaron eyed the drop below. 'By all the fates,' he muttered under his breath, and grasped hold of the neck ridge as he crouched down on the beast's back.

The blue boosted straight off without even opening its wings first and Jaron gasped and hid his face from the wind, concentrating on trying to keep his grip. His scalp prickled and he realised, too late, he had forgotten his helmet. Under an armpit, he saw blue silver-laced wings flapping much quicker than Channon's did. He caught sight of the forest below flashing by in a blur, the speed of the beast preventing him from even trying to see if he recognized anything. In a short time, the force became too great. Jaron had no saddle and his body was inexorably pushed back towards the tail. His bruised ribs protested under the strain of his stretch as one by one his fingers began to lose their hold.

'Slow down!' he gasped. The wind tore his words away, but incredibly the beast immediately tilted its wings back and slowed its pace. It turned its head to look back at Jaron, who shifted himself forward and brought his knees up when he got closer to the base of the neck. The blue hovered, waiting for him, and after a moment's hesitation he carefully hooked his legs over the front of the wings. Peering down to the forest below, Jaron gulped. It was precarious but it might stop him slipping out over the back end. He heard the blue rumble. 'Good boy,' he couldn't believe he was speaking to his abductor but if he could just get the beast on his side…

The blue moved forward again, more carefully this time, and they flew over the forest at normal firedrake pace. Jaron squinted into the wind and saw they were heading for the distant mountain range, the peaks glowing white in the morning sun. He tightened his grip on the raised scale and scrabbled his dangling feet until they found the points of the blue's shoulders, which he found were handy foot rests. The long ears, longer than the Raken firedrake, rippled back towards him and he thought they looked like possible reins if he only had the courage to grab them. The fear of being thrown off kept his hands where they were. He did dare to experiment with his weight though, trying to turn the firedrake. Nothing happened. He tried to still his nerves and mentally 'push' out at the beast as he had done when riding feisty young horses, but the blue juddered its wings and shook its head. Jaron sat tight after that, realising there was nothing he could do now he was at the whim of this strange beast.

The forest eventually gave way to mountains and the blue took him over the first jagged line of the range, then dipped down and flew in a pass above a grey tumbling river that bubbled and broiled over the mountain rocks that had been flung in its path. For a long while the blue followed the water, flying sideways through the gaps where the mountains pressed close.

Jaron crouched low, his arms wrapped around the neck after the first sideways flight; although the pressure seemed to seal him in place, he didn't trust the fact he wouldn't slide off. It was terrifying to see the rock face sheet by, hemming them in. He turned to rest his cheek on the hard scales and watched the blue's wing on that side, raised up and rigid. It was a strange shape for a firedrake's wing, shorter and broader before tapering down into a narrow tip. It reminded Jaron again of a falcon. There was a sudden shift as the firedrake cornered on its wingtip and Jaron's stomach gave a sickening lurch. He peered anxiously ahead through the rippling ears.

They were rounding a bend, and Jaron gasped. Carved

into the mountain was what looked like a stone fortress. As they got nearer Jaron could see huge columns rising up against the mountain, hewed from the rock itself. The blue angled its wings to fly higher and Jaron saw an archway directly on their flight path with a dark mouth beyond. Jaron sat up, studying the stronghold. As they flew nearer, he froze.

Two firedrake were watching them, he saw, one each side of the entrance, crouched on separate stone columns. They had no riders and looked odd somehow. As the blue neared Jaron realized their scales were black and red, a colouring Jaron had never seen before. They raised their necks and bugled in unison. Apprehension rose anew in the boy's chest. As they got closer to the fortress mouth he saw it was huge, nearly as big as the entrance to Mount Scarf. He stared in fear at the two lookouts; they didn't take to the wing but returned his stare with strange glowing white eyes. He would have thought them blind if they weren't looking right at him. Jaron looked away, into the blackness. It seemed impenetrable and as the blue flew into it a cold blanket prickled the hairs on the back of his neck. He shivered and tried to peer ahead through the gloom.

The blue flew through a tunnel until Jaron saw there was light up ahead, an orange glow, and his fear grew at the sight of it. They flew around a bend and into the light, and his heart quailed.

They had entered a vast cavern, with ledges etched into the walls. It was lit by huge torches that rose from the floor on stone towers, the flames burning in iron-wrought nests. More beasts hung from the walls like bats, or crouched on the crumbling stone shelves half-hidden in shadow, heads turning as one to look at them as they passed by, orbs of white eyes shining like hard ice. Jaron, terrified, saw firedrake bodies everywhere; they covered the entire hall from the floor below to the rib-vaulted ceiling high above.

An acrid smell filled his nostrils and he recognised it as firedrake breath. A chorus of growls and roaring calls rose as the blue flew further in, deafening Jaron. It didn't sound to him like they were calls of welcome and he tried to melt into the blue's neck. They flew along the length of the huge cavern and some of the firedrake flapped over to fly beside them. He saw there were no greens nor solid reds here. They were all mottled in black and red like night and fire. Their ghostly eyes fixed on him and one snapped at the blue as it passed close, its jaws drooling, causing Jaron's mount to squeak and duck away. Jaron's intense fear kept him from crying out for he sensed he was prey here. He kept still, a rabbit once again, his heart hammering in his chest.

More of the firedrake took off and wheeled in a dizzying circle, Jaron and the blue hemmed in their midst by the flapping wings. Through his terror Jaron looked down and saw a wide stone plinth rising from the centre of the floor; the only way off by foot was one stone bridge that stretched away into darkness. The blue fluttered down to land directly in its centre. It furled its wings and crouched in a defensive position, cawing in fear up at the whirling pool of firedrake that still flew tight around them. Jaron kept low and tightened his grip on the blue's neck. He felt it trembling as much as he was and the thought came into his mind that he should have thrown himself off the ledge last night while he had the chance.

'Leave him!' a deep voice shouted. Weighted with authority, it echoed off the walls of the hall and instantly the firedrake flapped away. Returning to their perches, every glowing eye turned to fix on the plinth. Jaron sat up cautiously, looking for the source of the voice. A figure was walking along the stone bridge towards them. He wore a flying helmet and jacket much like the Raken and a small stab of hope found its way through Jaron's fear. The discontented rumbles of the firedrake were accompanied by the man's boots thudding on the stone bridge. He raised an arm and instantly all the firedrake went quiet. Jaron watched him approach. Something about the proud bearing, the way the man walked, seemed familiar.

The blue gave a reedy squeak and placed its chin on the floor as the figure neared. 'You have done well, Skite,' the man's voice was deep. 'Although I expected you last night.' Something in it, a hint of steel, made Jaron sit up even as his mount cringed lower.

'Who are you?' Jaron found his voice. 'And why am I here?'

The man came closer before answering until he stood at Jaron's knee. He looked up at him and Jaron noticed the eyes under the helmet were silver-blue. They searched his face like they were drinking it in. Jaron bore the scrutiny, refusing to look away. The chin was strong, if the cheeks a little hollow, the mouth a thin line. The eyes seemed to soften slightly as the man peeled back his lips.

'Well met, young Jaron.'

'You know who I am?' Jaron asked. 'I don't know you.'

'Of course, but we have not met before. That was not of my choosing. You were taken from me, stolen in fact.'

Jaron stared and the man hesitated for just a moment before removing his helmet. His hair was shoulder length, brown shot through with grey. The face was a startling white, and the strange silver eyes, much like his own silver-blue, gleamed from sunken dark sockets above a straight, sculpted nose and strong jaw. The man searched Jaron's face with intensity and suddenly Jaron knew who it was the man reminded him of: Lord Carna, Jaron's uncle – and this man's brother. With a sinking heart he swallowed against the horror that now clenched his throat. 'You're Torrit,' he croaked.

The thin mouth widened into a delighted smile. 'Yes, you are most welcome, Jaron.' A heavy hand landed on his knee.

Jaron cringed but the man didn't seem to notice and continued to stare up at him, smiling.

'You sent the blue to get me.' Jaron stated it as fact.

The man smiled. 'He was a little slow about it,' he cast a withering glance at the blue who squeaked nervously. 'But he is my fastest firedrake, the most intelligent, the only one who could go into Rakenar and out again without being caught.' He paused, his stare hungry. 'And now, at last, here you are, where you belong – with me.' His eyes became moist. 'My son,' he said and at the same time reached out and grasped Jaron's arm, pulling him from the blue's back to envelop him in a suffocating hug.

Jaron, stunned, sagged limply in his father's arms since they were the only thing stopping him from crumbling to the ground.

23

After a moment, Jaron managed to recover from his shock enough to squirm, and Torrit's arms fell away. Jaron stepped back. The silver eyes flared for an instant before the man smiled again.

'You need time to get to know me; we have that now, at long last. Come. You need a change of clothes and some food inside you. I expect it has been rather traumatic.' He led the way off the plinth. Jaron looked after him, then up at all the watching firedrake. The blue nudged him in the back. He staggered, and reluctantly followed. The man turned back and his eyes fell on Jaron's uneven gait. 'Skite, bring him,' he waved a hand as he turned and Jaron's knees gave way as the blue's nose pushed into the back of his legs. With a cry, he fell backwards. Suddenly he was being lifted, arms flailing, sliding backwards over the blue's head. Gasping, he found himself sitting astride the neck just behind the blue's head. The blue raised it and Jaron slid further down, his bottom bumping uncomfortably over the raised neck plates while his hands grappled for purchase. He came to a stop at the base of its neck and sat up, smacking the blue with his hand. 'I hate you,' he muttered to it. The blue cocked an ear back at him and trotted after its master along the bridge, wings half held up.

They passed into a huge cave. It seemed to be lit by daylight and Jaron craned his neck to find the source and possible escape route. There were a series of breaks in the ceiling, he saw, and light streamed in, lighting some parts of the room and leaving other areas in shadow.

The blue turned its head and dipped it, its front bobbing down. Curious, Jaron looked across – and into the flaming yellow eyes of a huge red. Half its body was in shadow but the head alone was half again the size of Madrag's. One white, gleaming canine tooth grew outside of the mouth and was twisted at an odd angle.

Jaron shrank down as the yellow eyes pinned on him. *Brane. This* was the firedrake who had killed his stepfather, the villagers, his friends – and rendered him scarred for the rest of his life. He looked ahead to Torrit as he passed through another, smaller cave entrance and a wave of hate washed over him. As the blue followed its master Jaron could feel the weighted stare of those reptilian eyes burning holes in his back until they reached the opening.

As they passed into the next cave Jaron saw it was smaller, only three times the size of his cave back in Rakenar. There was a table and chairs here, and faded rugs adorned the floor. The room was lit by narrow windows carved into the thick rock, too narrow even for him to squeeze through. His gaze lifted to cracks in the ceiling through which more shards of light broke in. Too high for escape. He saw a fire burning softly in its grate against one wall. On the other he saw a curtain pulled aside and into the small room beyond Jaron could just see the corner of a bed.

'Welcome.' Torrit was standing in the centre of the room, his arm extended. A cold chill entered Jaron's heart. He imagined spewing a channel of fire from the blue and slamming it into the man's chest. He felt his mount shudder and suddenly there were channels of thin smoke rising from the firedrake's nostrils. Torrit stepped forward, looking his prisoner directly in the eye. Jaron gulped and the smoke dissipated into the air.

The man smiled and came around to his knee and Jaron immediately threw his leg over the firedrake's withers and slid down the other side, nearly falling when his boots hit the floor. Torrit waved a dismissive hand and the blue skittered over to the side of the cave to crouch in shadow. Boy and man now faced each other across the vacated space. Torrit took a step towards him and Jaron took one back in turn. The man's smile was thin.

'No matter, this is all so new and I expect you are still in shock.' When Jaron didn't answer he turned and indicated the small room Jaron had noticed earlier. 'In there you will find a basin of water and fresh clothes while I arrange a meal for us.'

Jaron hesitated, but reasoned he could think his situation through if better prepared. He limped towards the smaller room and paused on the threshold. It was sparsely furnished. A bed and a cupboard, with a bowl of water set on top next to a folded cloth and a bar of soap. Jaron's throat was parched but the water smelt a little stale and he dared not drink it. On the bed was a brown tunic with shirt and soft riding trousers. He stared at them, went over and lifted the shirt, then threw it aside to finger the trousers. They were his own clothes from Rakenar. *Someone must have taken them from my room.* With this sick realisation came the knowledge Carna's elder brother must have his followers on the inside of the Raken city. Jaron let out a tortured breath; he couldn't think about the implications of that fact just now – he had enough to deal with.

He pulled off his gloves and tossed them on the bed. Peeling off what was left of his ripped flying jacket and shirt Jaron looked down at the bruises blooming on his ribs that the blue's claws had caused. Shivering, he washed his aching body then quickly dried himself with the cloth and got dressed. Feeling better for being clean at least, he sat on the bed and worried until the smell of cooked meat distracted him. Fear had kept the hunger away but now his body was begging him to get up and seek nourishment.

When he cautiously stuck his head out from behind the

curtain, Torrit was standing with his back to the fire, facing the little room.

'There you are at last. Now, come and eat.'

Jaron's attention was caught by the mound of sliced meat on the table together with plates of bread and vegetables. Torrit walked round the table and pulled out a chair for him. He had changed out of his flying gear and had on a long black robe. Together with his white face, tall height and broad shoulders he was a pale image of Lord Carna. The man waited for him, a small smile playing on his thin lips. Jaron's stomach was hollow from hunger but caution kept his feet planted. After a moment Torrit walked around to a high-backed chair at the far side of the table and sat down. With the table now between them, Jaron moved cautiously forward, registering the shadowy bulk of Skite still crouched in darkness on his right. He sat down on the edge of the chair and stared in surprise at the spread on offer.

'There is a village nearby, the occupants supply me.' The man was watching his face and now he spooned some vegetables onto a plate. 'And the firedrake hunt for the meat.' He added a large slice of venison and poured water from a pewter jug into his tankard.

They sat in silence while Torrit filled his own plate and picked up his knife. Jaron couldn't hold back any longer and reached for the water first. Once he had quenched his dry throat he began to eat. The knife cut easily and the venison was tender in his mouth. He felt it was some sort of weakness to eat with this man, but the first taste set his hunger alight and he couldn't help but gorge himself, his need unwinding his nervous stomach to receive the food. As Torrit tore off some bread for him it occurred to Jaron the villagers probably didn't have much choice in the matter of feeding this man. Torrit took his drained cup and poured more water. He seemed content after that to sit silently and allow his guest to satisfy his hunger. Whenever Jaron looked up he was watching him, studying his face. As his eating slowed Jaron shifted uneasily and Torrit laughed, making him jump. 'I apologise for my scrutiny, Jaron, but I cannot believe that at last you are here.'

'Am I a prisoner?'

'Strange choice of words for a son to ask of his father,' Torrit's smile played around his thin lips but it didn't reach the silver eyes. 'I would ask that you give me a chance, Jaron.'

'A chance,' Jaron repeated in disbelief. 'You tried to kill me – and my mother.'

Torrit put down his knife and wiped his hands on a cloth, taking his time and infuriating the boy all the more. 'I was not trying to kill you, Jaron. Remember, I did not even know of your existence back then.'

'Then you tried to kill my mother.'

Torrit's silver eyes were hooded. 'Rella betrayed me.'

Jaron didn't back down. 'By leaving you? She had no choice.'

Torrit bunched his hand into a fist. '*Of course* she had a choice! To stay! She would have wanted for nothing, *you* would have wanted for nothing.' He smacked his fist down on the table, making Jaron jump. 'I am a lord!' Torrit shouted. 'The rightful lord of Rakenar and she *dared* to leave me,' his voice sank to a harsh whisper. 'She deserved to die for her betrayal.'

'No!' Now Jaron was on his feet and his chair crashed back. From against the wall, Skite squeaked. 'You forced her to be with you!'

'Oh, really?' Torrit's voice was deadly low and he too rose from the table, towering over Jaron who felt his heart pounding. With the man's white face and dark robe, he looked like an evil wraith. 'It was a good match,' Torrit hissed, 'a golden opportunity for a lowly kitchen girl. You speak of choice? She had none! Was entitled to none! My brother was a lovesick fool but I didn't blame him, not back then. He was as helpless as a puppy in front of her, too young to know his own mind.' He leaned over the table towards Jaron until they were nose to nose and his voice rasped. 'I gave her the honour of being my mate.' Torrit spread his arms. 'Yet she chose to leave me, *me*! Who was to become high lord.' His face twisted. 'And I have water to drink when I should be dining on the finest wine!'

He suddenly swept an arm across the table and plates fell to the floor with a crash. Jaron jumped back as the contents spewed across the rug. 'My brother did this to me!' He turned to glare at Jaron. 'All because of *her*,' he paused, breathing heavily. 'Your mother lost her right to life when she left Rakenar.'

'And you lost your right to me when you fired our village.' Torrit went still at Jaron's words, his eyes glinting. Jaron swallowed. 'You killed a good man, Teel, my stepfather.' It was important to Jaron this murderer knew his name. 'The villagers, dead, they knew nothing of your feud with my mother,' his words were grating. 'They did not deserve to die, to have their homes fired to the ground.'

'It was unfortunate, yes. However, Rella brought it down upon them, and you, her own son. Had she remained by my side, none of this would have happened.' The man's face showed no shame nor sorrow at all. 'Yet still she lives,' his lips twisted in disgust before he turned away and went to stand by the fire.

Cold hatred fired through Jaron's heart. It turned into a white-hot strumming in his mind and almost before he knew what he was doing he had pivoted towards where the blue crouched in the shadows, watching them. 'Fire him!' Jaron's words rippled the air between them and, just as had happened once before when he stopped Caliber attacking Brill, it seemed to shimmer in front of his eyes with the heat of his command. Skite shuddered as his mouth opened. A sudden burning stream of white fire erupted in a narrow channel and lasered towards where Torrit stood. The man dived to one side as the fire slammed into the fireplace, turning blue and sending flames up the wall above it. Jaron flinched, throwing up an arm for protection. The room was cut in half by the fire beam until it juddered, its intensity fading as Skite's breath ran out.

Jaron, shocked, stared at the smoking, seared rock around the fireplace. He looked back at Skite; the blue had pressed himself back into the shadows but the end of its nose was still visible, smoke still coiling from the flared, trembling nostrils.

'Well, now,' Torrit was getting up from the floor, his eyes fixed on Jaron, who gulped and stepped back into a defensive crouch. He didn't understand what had just happened but he was certain his time was now up; Torrit was going to kill him. A huge roar sounded from outside the cave and a moment later the big red's face was at the entrance, his lips curled back in a snarl as he looked from his master to the boy. Jaron trembled, his eyes on the gleaming white tooth that stuck out, certain he was about to meet the same death as Teel.

Torrit chuckled and Jaron tore his eyes away from the red in surprise.

As the boy stared, incredulous, the lord clapped his hands together. 'Oh my, all that I hoped for, dreamed of, has come true.' He looked towards his firedrake. 'Brane, I am unharmed, go back to sleep.'

The red blinked at his master and backed his head out. Torrit was no longer laughing but was staring now at Jaron, the thin bloodless lips stretched into a cold smile. He stooped and whipped up the fallen tray of meat, wiping his sleeve across it. In two strides, he was round the table. Jaron shrank back, his hands coming up to defend himself, for surely now Torrit would kill him. But the man grabbed his arm and shook him. Jaron thrashed in panic.

'Look, boy!' He thrust the tray in front of his face.

Jaron gaped at his smeared reflection. His face, drawn and white, terrified – and his eyes! What had happened to his eyes? They stared back at him and their pupils were shining orbs of light with silver rippling in their depths. Torrit's face grinned behind him, his own silver eyes flaring bright, luminous. It was terrible to see.

'You take after me, Jaron,' Torrit's voice rasped in his ear. 'In more ways than I dared to hope. It runs in our veins, it sears our souls, the blood that binds us; the blood of the *Rillion*.'

24

Jaron sat on a hard bed in the little room. Torrit had left him to mull things over, he supposed. The exiled lord had gone through to his firedrake, ordering Skite 'to guard' and had not returned. It felt like the afternoon but there was no way of knowing in the windowless room. In his hand, he held the tray and for what must be the twentieth time he looked at his reflection in the light of the torch that burned on one wall. His eyes stared back at him with their normal silver-blue colour. *What just happened?* He needed answers and, much as he disliked the fact, it seemed only Torrit could provide them. Jaron didn't want to even think about this madman as his father.

'Some family reunion,' he muttered and threw the tray away in disgust. It landed on the floor with a tinny clatter. He got up to walk across to the curtain and pulled it aside.

He stuck his head out and looked around cautiously. The cave was empty and the table still lay on its side, food strewn across the floor. Shards of daylight were hitting the faded rugs. Jaron stepped forward and looked up, limping slowly around the floor as he studied the gaps. There was no opening big enough for him to fit through. He looked down, his eyes searching the shadows, and noticed Skite watching him from a corner. As soon as Jaron looked at him the firedrake flattened its over-long ears and dipped its head. Jaron hesitated then went over to it. The blue shuddered as he neared.

Jaron stopped and gazed at the cringing beast. Shame washed through him at how he had forced the young firedrake to do something against its will. Yes, it had taken him against *his* will, but now Jaron knew it was under Torrit's orders. How the man could get a firedrake to do his bidding after leaving his side, Jaron had no idea, but it didn't change the fact he, Jaron, had forced the animal to attack its own master.

'I'm sorry,' he whispered. 'Sorry that I made you fire, I didn't have the right to do that to you.'

The blue raised its head and stared at him. The silver shards in its purple eyes were glowing in the half-light. It studied him, the ears lifted a little and eventually it crept out of its corner towards him. Jaron almost made to step back but realised that after all that he had seen this young blue didn't hold as many terrors for him, not now. Carefully, the boy half raised his arm, fist clenched. The firedrake kept its body low as it weaved its neck to one side then the other, almost snake-like, until it stood just a little way off, neck lowered and nostrils twitching.

Jaron eyed the small space left between them and after a moment's hesitation he stepped forward and let the blue sniff his fist. Slowly, he opened his hand and when the firedrake didn't move, stroked it down the narrow face. It keened and seemed to be enjoying the caress, its eyes half-lidded. Wonderingly, the boy ran both hands along the cheek ridges and the firedrake closed its eyes. This beast was as much a victim as he was, Jaron realised, and, unbidden, the boy's eyes filled with tears.

'Poor us,' he murmured.

The blue didn't move and they stayed like that for a while, the boy stroking the firedrake, until at last Jaron stepped back and wiped at his tears.

'This won't help, will it, Skite?' He looked up at the blue and noticed its eyes were shining bright iridescent purple, brighter than he had ever noticed before. As Jaron stared, a strumming began to sound in his head, not unlike when he had ordered it to fire. Appalled, he stepped away and with an effort managed to push it back out.

The blue stepped forward at the same time, staying with him. The head came down and the eyes continued to look directly into his. It wanted something from him, Jaron realised, and he shook his head, perplexed as to what. He felt a sudden weird tug at his mind and immediately the strumming started again.

'No, no, NO!' Jaron stumbled back, raising his hands up to his head, trying to put some space between himself and the blue as he found the will to push the throbbing beat out of his head again. The beast followed him step for step and raised its wings, opening them out fully until they filled the room. Jaron put up his hands, palm out as he had seen the Raken riders do to still their beasts.

It didn't work; the blue wasn't trained the same way. 'Get back.' Jaron tried to sound firm, but his voice broke with fear and next moment his heel caught on the edge of a rug and over he went. The beast's head dropped low, keeping close, and the muzzle with its two protruding white fangs travelled across the floor towards him. Jaron scrabbled back.

'Get away from me,' he whispered but the nose lifted until it nearly sat in his lap. Jaron whimpered and was forced back while the nose travelled up to his chest until his shoulders touched the floor. Its warm ash breath was on his face, lifting his fringe, and there was nowhere left to go. He turned his head away and saw the wings were coming forward, enclosing him in their blue membrane, trapping him further.

'Leave me alone,' he whispered. 'Please leave me alone.' He squeezed his eyes tight shut and opened them again to see silver pulsating through the veins on the wing membrane. As he stared, it followed the network of blood vessels along the wing and began to glow brighter and brighter. When he dared to move his head to look above him a strangled gasp escaped his lips; the whole beast was iridescent with silver ribbons flowing through the blue body as he had seen it do in the moonlight that awful night, only now the silver pulsated in a steady rhythm. As he stared into the purple eyes laced through with shards of bright silver above him, the strumming in his head started once again. Jaron tried to push it back once more, but now found he couldn't stop it.

Was this what it felt like, when your firedrake chose you? *But I don't want a firedrake, I don't.* 'I don't want you,' he whispered out loud. 'I'm damaged. I couldn't – you wouldn't want me.' The air between them shimmered and he was caught up in a humming. It was coming from the firedrake and slowly increased in pitch. Jaron's head strummed louder in response but it felt good this time, pure, completely different from the white hate that had fuelled it when he had ordered Skite to attack. He became acutely aware of the beast's breath, the sides rising and falling, the blood pumping through its veins, the huge heart thudding until it seemed his own heart slowed and matched it beat for beat. A wave of warmth stole over him, a feeling of wellbeing, of safety, like he had never felt these last two years since Brane had fired him. He stared wonderingly at the blue and watched as it blinked then huffed, a happy sound. The silver pulsating all over its body dimmed and died until the firedrake was back to its normal blue. It settled back, folded its wings, and cocked its head at him.

'Skite,' Jaron murmured, and sat up, his arms reaching for the blue. Skite brought his head down and he stroked his nose in wonder. *Was this the Selection process that I missed back in Rakenar?* Jaron pondered, stroking the blue's nose. Neither Parl nor Carna had mentioned it would be anything like this.

Just then the firedrake looked towards the entrance and growled. Torrit was coming. Jaron started in fear. He tried to rise but found his legs were trembling; too many emotions had wrung out his body and mind in such a short time. The blue brought down its nose and Jaron caught hold of the chin horn. Skite raised his head, lifting him up onto his feet at the same time.

'Blue, hide, quick,' Jaron hissed, and watched in surprise as his firedrake instantly obeyed, cantering into the shadows; just in time Skite pulled his tail in under the cover of darkness as Torrit marched in. His presence seemed to fill the room and Jaron felt a stab of fear at the man's entrance.

'Ah, you're up. Good, we have work to do.'

Jaron stared. Torrit laughed; he seemed in high spirits, excited even and two red spots of colour were showing on the otherwise pale cheeks. 'Don't look so worried,' he touched his nose with his finger and tapped it. 'You need to know about the *Rillion*. Only your father can teach this to you.'

'You are no father to me,' Jaron stood his ground. 'Would a father do this to his son?' While he had been speaking he had unbuttoned his tunic and ripped open his shirt to reveal his scarred chest. Torrit stepped closer, his eyes on the melted skin. They flicked back up to Jaron's face. There was no remorse in those strange cold eyes, none at all.

'As I said, if you remember, I had no knowledge you existed. Had I been kept informed, had your mother not left like a skulking thief in the night, the village would never have been torched and I would not have been deposed.'

Jaron felt his jaw clench, his rage returning. 'You fired that village, you didn't have to do that.'

'Enough!' Torrit suddenly roared. 'It has happened – and mulling over the past won't change anything.' Jaron's stomach clenched but still he didn't move as he fought to get his anger and hatred under control. Torrit stepped closer. 'I see you feel hatred for me. Good, you will find it so much easier to use the *Rillion*.'

Jaron stared. That word again. The boy in the story… he remembered the reaction at dinner when Lady Tarla had said *Rillion's blood*. He had to know what this thing was – he was afraid but this man knew more than him, everybody knew more than him it seemed, and he was at too much of a disadvantage to be kept in the dark any longer.

While he considered, Torrit had watched him. The man nodded in satisfaction. 'I see you have some sense, after all. Follow me.' He turned and stalked out of the room.

Jaron reluctantly went, his stomach churning. Torrit was already through the cavern entrance when Jaron reached the first. He stared fearfully over at Brane, who was settling himself down along the far cave wall. The huge red didn't look at the quaking boy but placed his heavy head on his paws and, with a huge sigh, closed his eyes. The askew canine stuck out of the side of the beast's mouth and, as Jaron stared, drool began to gather around the base of the tooth and dribble onto the floor. Wishing he was anywhere else but here, Jaron moved as far away from the red beast as he could, keeping to the wall.

Something nudged his back and he nearly cried out. He turned. Skite was at his shoulder. After looking at him the firedrake lowered his neck and pushed his head between the boy's legs from behind, lifting him back up onto his neck just as he had done before. Jaron allowed himself to slide back and grabbed hold of the edge of a scale plate. The firedrake trotted across the room with the boy on his back. Jaron cast a surreptitious glance over at the big red to make sure he wasn't watching, then patted his thanks on the hard scales.

Torrit was standing just past the entrance. 'Ah, Skite, you brought him, very good. Set him down.' Jaron felt the firedrake tense. Torrit frowned. 'I said, set him down,' his voice was low, dangerous, but still Skite stood and stared at the man. Afraid now, Jaron touched the firedrake's neck at its base, making sure it was out of Torrit's line of vision, trying to communicate to him to do as the Raken lord ordered. Nevertheless, it surprised him when the blue immediately crouched at his touch. Jaron slid off as fast as he could and stepped over to Torrit, praying the blue would not follow him now.

The man was staring over his head at the blue and Jaron sought to divert him. 'So, what is this *Rillion*?' The light eyes in their sunken sockets shifted to look at him.

'I am glad to see you are curious, Jaron.' Torrit walked along the bridge. After a moment's hesitation, Jaron followed. Up ahead, Torrit strode onto the plinth and stood in its centre. He waited for Jaron to catch up. Jaron reached the plinth but stopped at the end of the bridge and looked up in fear at the firedrake hanging from the walls and ceiling of the massive entrance hall. White eyes stared down at their master and a chittering filled the hall. *How had Torrit managed to amass so many firedrake?* His village had been burnt only two years ago.

'Do not be afraid, Jaron,' Torrit called from the plinth. 'It is they who should be afraid of us.'

'Afraid of us?' Jaron repeated in disbelief as he stared up at all those teeth and claws covering the huge fortress hall. 'I can't see it somehow.'

Torrit laughed. 'You will, watch.' He raised his arms and turned in a circle, looking up at the firedrake. They fell silent, watching. He began to hum, a strumming sound that rose and fell, going on and on until the rock itself seemed to take on the resonance of the sound. It reverberated through Jaron's body and something in him stirred. He tried to push it down but it was as though there was a dragon beast of his own uncurling itself in his chest and scenting the air. He kept his eyes on Torrit while he fought to keep it in check. The man opened his eyes and Jaron gasped – they were glowing pure silver, even brighter than before. Torrit called out words that Jaron didn't recognise and swept one raised arm in a whirling circle.

Instantly, all the firedrake let go of the walls at the same time and swept into the air as one. Jaron gasped. Torrit's arm began to rotate, faster and faster. A whirlwind of black and red as the beasts flew round the cave, all heading in the same direction in a flurry of wings. Jaron noticed then that all the firedrake appeared to be not much bigger than Skite: they must all be youngsters and not yet fully grown. The flying whirlwind became more ragged as they knocked into each other. Jaws snapped as each tried to claim airspace from its neighbour. Jaron stared, hardly believing what he was seeing. He tore his eyes away to check on Skite. The firedrake hadn't been included, thank goodness, but the beast was crouched low near the cave entrance where Brane lay beyond, Skite's purple eyes wide as he too watched. Jaron turned back in time to see Torrit's arm dip lower. Down the firedrake went in a thick column of thrashing wings and writhing tails. Jaron felt sick, but also strangely alert. It was odd, but he felt he could sense their torture and fear under the lord's absolute control.

Torrit's arm shot back up and the screeching beasts surged towards the hall ceiling. Jaron saw one firedrake smash into the side of the plinth. Another bounced off the wall against the flailing tail of another and was smacked hard against the rock. It slid down, its neck limp, tongue lolling. As it fell, its half-open wings caused its body to spin faster and faster until it crashed onto a flight of crumbling stone steps to lay still. Jaron heard a tortuous screaming fill the fortress; the firedrake were all screeching as one.

'Oh, stop, please stop.' Jaron put his hands over his ears as he bent double. It felt as though his very soul was being torn from his body at their agony.

Torrit turned towards him with his terrible eyes. 'Look at

the power of the *Rillion*, my son,' he shouted to be heard over their tortured cries, 'look at what it can do!'

'No,' Jaron whispered.

The man suddenly dropped his arms and flicked a hand in a dismissive gesture. His shoulders slumped as his chin dropped. The flying firedrake became a shambolic mass of snapping jaws and flailing wings as they were released. They flapped heavily up to hang from their perches, sides heaving.

Torrit looked over at Jaron, and his glowing eyes flickered and died, back to silver blue. 'No one will be able to stand against us, my son. All will fear us. Together, we will take up our rightful places as lords of Rakenar.' He held out his arms to Jaron and walked towards him.

Horrified, the boy backed away. He saw the man stagger a little and lower his arms. Torrit was weakened, Jaron realised, by his use of the *Rillion* to control all those beasts. Jaron's mind raced. The firedrake were all exhausted, all but the blue and Brane, but Brane was sleeping and Skite was fast, faster than all of them, Torrit had said so. He was even quicker on the ground, he didn't waddle like the other firedrake.

The boy spun away from Torrit. 'Blue Skite!' he shouted. He hardly dared hope but the firedrake was already alert and looking directly at him from the beginning of the bridge. 'Come,' Jaron called. 'Please,' he pleaded in a whisper. His prayers were answered as Skite bounded into a gallop along the bridge towards him. Jaron broke into a hopping run to meet the blue. Torrit's roar of fury behind him caused Jaron to stumble with renewed fear. He risked a look over his shoulder and his breath caught; tired as he was, the man could move quicker on his long legs than Jaron had first thought. He was going to catch him. Gasping, Jaron whirled to face him, inadvertently stepping back as he did so into empty air. His arms flailed for balance for a split second –

then he fell from the bridge with a startled cry.

Torrit's snatching fingers missed his tunic front by inches. 'No!' the man screamed and Jaron saw a white, contorted mask receding above him as he fell. His brain seemed to slow everything down. Strangely detached, he noticed Skite, the unusually long legs stretched out, and how, mid-gallop, the blue dived off the bridge. He watched the wedge-shaped wings fold back against the body and the purple eyes fix directly on him. *He's coming for me*, Jaron thought with mild surprise. Slowly, for his arms felt weightless yet strangely heavy, he opened them wide to the firedrake.

The wind knocked out of him with rude, bruising force as Skite caught him mid-air, startling him out of his strange reverie and speeding everything up with a sickening jolt. He gasped in pain at his sore ribs. They flashed past underneath the Raken lord. 'Bring him back to me!' Jaron heard Torrit's order roar into the hall and the firedrake there stirred and started to flap heavily away from the walls.

Clutched facing Skite's chest, Jaron peered round the blue's shoulder and watched in horror as many white, ice-chipped eyes fixed on them. But then he saw his hunch was right; they were slower in their reactions, Torrit couldn't control them so quickly after putting on such a show. Fire flared in a roaring column from both sides but Skite shot straight through it. A blast of heat scorched Jaron's back and he hid his face in Skite's softer chest scales.

'Do not fire!' Torrit's voice roared, far below and behind them now. Firedrake were coming up at them from the lower levels, jaws open, and Jaron cried out in alarm as a beast lunged at them. Skite thrashed his tail and flew higher. More firedrake flapped out and were coming at them from all sides. Jaron, with a quick desperate look over his shoulder, could see the flight path of escape up ahead was narrowing as the wall of firedrake closed in.

'Skite, faster! Oh, come on!' he cried, his words torn away as the blue angled his wings back and whistled past the reaching claws and snapping jaws. Next moment, the light from the torches faded just as a sudden blanket of cold prickled the skin on his back. They had entered the tunnel and Jaron saw the chasing firedrake were now being forced into the narrower space, their wings tangling as they bumped against each other. Snapping and snarling, they turned on each other as they fought for room.

The blue cannoned along the tunnel as it bent to the right and Jaron lost sight of the pursuing firedrake. He pressed a cheek against Skite's chest and looked ahead with one eye tearing against the wind. His heart lifted when he saw blessed daylight lightening the tunnel. Skite increased his speed even more. The force pressing against Jaron's back became incredible; he felt his lungs would burst. They shot out of the fortress entrance into the open air and Jaron's stomach lurched when he saw the sentry firedrake crouched out on the plinths. They screeched, and both leapt up to cut off their escape. They hadn't even fully opened their wings when Skite flew straight past them and twisted into a side dive through the narrow pass. Jaron glimpsed the river churning around the boulders below just before the blue changed direction into another pass. With a sudden twist of his tail, Skite angled his body and flew straight up into the sky.

Thick cloud closed in all around Jaron and harsh cold seared his bones. The pressure was so intense he felt as though his body would snap in two. Just as he thought he could no longer bear it, Skite levelled out and flew slower now, with his prize clutched in his claws.

Jaron opened one eye. They were above the level of the clouds and he took gulping gasps of air. He felt light-headed and his lungs hurt. Just as he began to lose any sense of time or reality the blue reduced their height again, flying back down into the cloud bank and its searing cold embrace. When they emerged into clear air, Jaron was relieved to find he could breathe more easily.

As Skite flew on he lost track of how long it had been since escaping the fortress. The sun was setting and the thin mist rolling across the landscape below glowed in its dying light. The beauty of it all was lost on Jaron. He was exhausted and the searing pain in his ribs where the blue clutched him seemed to be the only thing preventing him from passing out. Or maybe he already had a few times; he just didn't know anymore. Skite's wings were more laboured now and Jaron painfully reached up an encouraging hand to stroke the firedrake's neck. Skite lowered his head upside down to look back at him and gave a low rumble before angling his body downwards. They dropped lower and into the thin mist. Jaron coughed as they entered the damp air, causing his ribs to painfully jar him.

It was a wild landscape of shrouded hills and valleys. Skite flew close to the ground, tendrils of mist leaking past his wing tips as he skirted the taller hills that rose up in their flightpath. Jaron watched as a small wood passed by in a soft blur. His scalp and lips felt numb, his fingers stiff. He was so tired, and the damp air would keep on making him cough.

It seemed an age before they left the hills and passed over dense forest. By now, it was almost dark, a watery moon rising. Despite his discomfort, Jaron's head was nodding on his shoulders when the blue finally dropped down to land.

25

A distant humming sound woke him. He felt warm, cosy, and a rare feeling that he had to think about for a moment to identify; safe, yes, that was it, he felt safe. Jaron opened his eyes to find a purple eye boggling down at him. The hum came again and this time he felt it vibrate throughout his body.

'Hello, Skite.' His voice sounded thick and he wondered how long he had been out. He tried to see where they were, but then realised his body was cocooned by a wing. He pushed out with the sides of his arms against the membrane. The blue unrolled him and cold stone bashed against his sore ribs. Jaron clutched at them, coughed, then levered himself up onto his knees.

Skite had landed on a ledge and for a moment Jaron thought they were back where the blue had first brought him that terrible night. Then his eyes focused more and he blinked. Spread out before him in the early morning light was a huge green valley encircled by white-stone cliffs. The distant churn of running water drew his astonished gaze to a waterfall sheeting down on one side. Jaron sat up. He recognised this place; it was the valley Flick had brought him to with Tarp on his first proper flight. His heart lifted; he knew where he was at last.

Carefully, he crawled to the edge and looked down. Below he could see the moving figures of antelope and deer grazing. Skite's claws clicked on the stone as he came to stand beside Jaron and the long ears pricked with interest as a calf trotted amongst the herd of the larger-sized antelope, bawling for its mother. Jaron watched it as well while his tired mind woke up. He ached all over, and he massaged his ribs carefully.

Suddenly, Skite dived off the ledge. Jaron flinched, arm raised at the dust kicked up. As he lowered it, he saw the blue was flying directly for the herd.

'Oh no.' Jaron watched with horror as the blue swept down with dizzying speed. As he glided low over the animals the hollering of warning calls filtered up to Jaron as the animals first scattered in fear then sought safety in numbers and came together to run shoulder to shoulder. Above all this mayhem, the firedrake flew in a lazy loop with his neck lowered and his head at a slight angle. For the first time, Jaron noticed his neck, though narrow, was shorter than the Raken firedrake even as his ears were twice the length.

With a sudden flick of his long tail Skite increased his speed. Angling on a wing tip he split a herd of the larger antelope and dived down to snatch at something in their midst without even landing. Jaron, kneeling on the ledge, put his hands up to his face. As the blue began his upward climb the antelope calf hung in his jaws, its dainty legs dangling and its neck at an odd angle.

Skite back-winged for the ledge and Jaron skittered away on his behind to give him room. The firedrake landed and dropped the inert body with a thump in front of him. Skite grumbled happily and eyed the boy.

'Uh, well done,' Jaron muttered, since Skite seemed to be expecting praise. The firedrake rumbled and bent his head, caught up the body and tossed the animal into the air. As it fell back strong jaws crunched down on the body, cutting it clean in two. Blood spurted over the ledge and dribbled down the firedrake's chest as it munched. The back half of the calf fell to the stone with a whumping squelch.

Jaron stared at the bloody mess then turned away and

crawled over to sit on the furthest point of the ledge. He gazed out over the valley and tried to ignore the slurping and crunching noises going on behind him. Good job he hadn't seen *that* when he had first been out on a ledge with the blue. He had never seen a firedrake eat before – he supposed that Carna hadn't thought him ready. This turned his thoughts to Rakenar and he unsteadily got to his feet and scanned the valley. Remarkably the herds had already returned to their grazing; Jaron supposed now the hunt was over they had nothing to fear. He searched the cliffs and took the waterfall as a marker. He thought he might be able to remember the right direction to fly back from here.

He looked back at Skite. He had a hind leg held between his front paws and was licking at it with blissful, half-closed eyes.

Jaron watched him, thinking how the blue had carried out Torrit's orders even when separated from Torrit, then turned against his former master. He remembered how, back on the ledge, Skite had dribbled water into his mouth. As a throwback to the wilder firedrake did the blues have more intelligence? Skite had understood him in a way he had never seen the Raken firedrake do with their riders. That set him thinking again of the mountain city. He had to get back, Torrit might be coming for him even now. And his mother would be frantic with worry.

Mind made up, he started to turn towards the blue when something down below caught his eye. Jaron stared for a moment and lifted his hand to shield his eyes from the morning sun. No, he hadn't been mistaken. Five horses were entering the valley from the river. The herds, who had been peacefully grazing, now had their heads raised. Some began to trot away from the group and a herd of small antelope leapt away into the scrub. They wouldn't do that with horses, it could only be – kelpra! Jaron limped stiffly along the lip of the edge, he could see they had tufted tails, definitely kelpra, but still couldn't see if one of them was Caliber. It was just too far.

He whirled and saw Skite was now laying with his head in his paws, licking his bloody chops. All that remained of the calf was its discarded tail. Jaron hesitated. He wouldn't think of approaching while the firedrake had been eating but he seemed content now and desperation overcame apprehension. Jaron walked over to him carefully; the blue had his eyes closed and was licking his lips in contentment.

'Skite?' he called. One purple eye opened and looked at him. 'Time to fly.' When the blue didn't move, he waved his arms about. 'Fly?'

The blue sighed and rolled his head to one side, closing his eye again. Daringly, Jaron took hold of an ear and tugged at it. The blue raised his head and the boy quickly stepped back.

'Time to fly, boy,' Jaron repeated, trying to keep the tremor out of his voice. The blue yawned, ignoring him. 'Skite, please,' Jaron begged and, gathering his courage, reached the blue's shoulder and tried to pull himself up, failed, then managed to jump up enough to get some leverage with his arms, a groan escaping his lips as his ribs complained. He hung there, legs kicking, not going anywhere.

'You could at least help me,' he grumbled between gasps at the blue. No sooner were the words out of his mouth than a wing moved forward and down. Jaron managed to hook a leg over its front ridge to push himself up. He was on at last. The boy shuffled into normal firedrake saddle position, then thought again and shifted forward, his legs pushing out forwards to dangle down over the shoulders until his feet found the shoulder points to rest on. Skite looked back at him and Jaron gave him a nudge with his heels. With a huge sigh, the firedrake got up and walked to the edge. Tightening his grip on a raised scale plate Jaron swallowed down his nerves.

Opening his wings, the blue stepped off and flew out over the valley. The rushing air pushed against Jaron's face and chest while his hair, with no helmet, rippled free. Wishing he had the security of a saddle, Jaron first searched the sky and was relieved to see it empty of Torrit's firedrake. He looked down past Skite's gliding, outspread wings and quickly spied the kelpra next to the river. They were standing and looking towards the herds; they hadn't noticed Skite yet.

'Alright Skite, if we can just circle round behind them.' He placed his feet on the shoulder points and leant in the direction he wanted the firedrake to go.

Nothing happened. Skite carried on flying straight and now they were losing height. If the blue carried on like this they were going to spook the kelpra before he'd got a close enough look. He asked again, and still Skite ignored him. It occurred to Jaron that it was likely the blue had never actually been ridden; maybe he was the only person that had sat on his back and that was only as a passenger. Jaron didn't want to think about the implications of that just now.

'Skite, listen to me,' this time he reached forward and dared to grab the long ears. He gently tugged on one and Skite's head turned in the direction he wanted. They soared across the valley and came in behind the kelpra. Jaron was so busy looking down, trying to see if the black there was Caliber, that he forgot to look up to see where they were going. Skite changed direction and Jaron tugged on the other ear to get him back. Skite shook his head, nearly dislodging him. Next moment there was a cliff face right in their path.

'Arrgh!' Jaron cried as the blue glanced off it. Rocks showered down to the floor below. Jaron fell forward and threw his arms around Skite's neck as the blue flapped clumsily off the rock again. He anxiously looked down, just in time to see the last kelpra's rump disappear into thick bush, tail held high. Skite levelled up and peered back at him with one baleful eye. 'I'm sorry,' Jaron apologised, patting scales. The kelpra would have to wait for now.

They were nearing the waterfall and Jaron realised just how thirsty he was. Carefully taking hold of Skite's ears again he tugged gently on one, leaning with his weight as he did so. This time the blue did as he bid. As they swept back towards the water Jaron managed to angle Skite in to fly close by leaning his weight towards it. When the sheeting water looked to be within reach Jaron sat up and put out his hand. But Skite ignored his upright position and carried on side-winging. 'Ah!' Jaron gasped as the cold water drenched him. Skite shook his head as they dived out the other end and droplets showered back onto Jaron.

'I think we need more practice, Skite,' Jaron muttered, shivering from the cold dowsing he had received. Daring to let go of the ears, he put his sleeve cuff above his mouth and wrung it out with the other hand. It was a drink, of sorts, and enough to allay his thirst. He wiped his mouth and looked down. Lush forest travelled by below them; the blue was leaving the valley and Jaron, looking around, realised they were heading in the wrong direction. He moved his weight over to turn him. When the firedrake didn't react again he reached forward, tugging on a long ear to fold the neck in that side.

Skite shook his hand off, grunting. Jaron mustered his courage. The blue had saved him, Jaron reasoned, and he knew with sudden surprising certainty Skite wasn't going hurt him. Anyway, there was no choice; he had to get back to Rakenar. Stay out here and sooner or later Torrit was going to find him.

This time, Jaron made sure his feet were planted securely on the shoulders and, determined now, took hold of both ears. Again, Skite shook his head, but Jaron grimly held on. Putting all his weight into his feet, he half-raised his seat into his familiar racing position. It was a mistake. Skite lowered his head, jerking Jaron forward. Gasping, the boy fell onto the neck. The forest canopy below tilted alarmingly but he kept hold of the ears. 'Skite, please,' Jaron begged. He sat up and, putting all his weight back, set himself against the head. In answer, Skite's body rippled in the air. It was like riding a snake, Jaron thought, as he fought to keep his balance. Skite dived sideways and Jaron cast a panicked look at the forest rising up to meet them. Keeping his head, he put all his body weight into the other foot until he was virtually riding with one knee bent to get Skite to level out. Amazingly, it worked and the blue was forced to right himself.

'Come on now,' Jaron gasped. 'Work with me here.' He mentally 'pushed out', seeking to get Skite to trust him. The blue's head turned slightly, one purple eye looking back at him. Jaron made sure his feet were placed securely, adjusting his position a little until he felt as ready as he could be. Carefully, he put his weight into a turn, using his hands at the same time to slightly bend the blue's neck. This time, Skite followed his lead; the level out was shaky with juddered wings but at least they were flying back towards the valley. Jaron steadily grew in confidence as the firedrake seemed to accept his direction more and more. Once they were over the rich grassland again Jaron had Skite fly all around the perimeter while he got his bearings until, at last, the boy pressed down with his seat. When Skite continued flying on Jaron gritted his teeth. *Stop,* he thought and repeated it over and over in his head. Skite slowed until he almost stopped mid-air and went into a hover.

'Good boy.' Jaron stroked the neck. Whatever it was, this strange connection they had, at least the blue was listening to him at last.

He stared across the Camorian forest laid out beyond the white stone cliffs. Tiara lay to the west of here and to the north, Rakenar. Hoping he was right, Jaron leant forward and gave Skite a pat.

'Time to fly, boy.' He took hold of the long ears and leant forward, nudging with his heels. Skite flapped his wings and together they flew low over the trees, a blue dart against the green, heading towards Rakenar.

They ended up flying westwards back towards Tiara because Jaron, terrified of getting lost, was forced to take what must be the longer route and thus lose precious time. Skite would have known the way but Jaron didn't know how to ask and he didn't trust the blue to guide him back when he had already been attacked by the Raken firedrakes. The boy kept on looking over his shoulder, imagining Torrit on the fearsome Brane appearing on their tail, but the sky remained empty. Jaron could only think Skite's amazing speed had given them a good start.

As they left the Camorian forest behind and flew over the Plains of Wake Jaron looked down at the rippling rich grass below them and thought how much his life had changed from living with his mother in Tiara. How terrified he had been when the Raken arrived on their beasts back then. Now, here he was flying on his own with a rare blue firedrake that was accepting his control. The irony made him chuckle. Skite rumbled and Jaron patted the blue neck.

'Just reminiscing, boy.'

The ground rose and the blue flapped higher. As they flew over the hills and scrubland that bordered the Plains of Wake Jaron looked ahead to the dense green of the Rotarn Forest that marked the end of Tiara's territory. They flew nearer and beyond the forest the Notresia mountain range rose out of the thin blue afternoon haze. Relieved, Jaron nudged Skite faster.

They winged over the forest and Jaron looked down on the River Not as it winked out from underneath the trees.

Further along, the trees opened up into a clearing and Jaron felt his throat tighten, sure this was where so many of the riders had met their deaths. He lifted his gaze and kept his eyes fixed ahead between Skite's ears, relieved when they rose up over the Notresia mountain range and left the forest behind them.

The morning was giving way to afternoon when they reached the Arkenara Mountains that bordered Rakenar. Their progress had slowed somewhat. Skite had become more and more reluctant to fly forward for him and Jaron had to concentrate on keeping him on course and moving on. Jaron understood; how could he not when Skite had already been attacked, and he had fought Channon, the respectable old school firedrake that many a rider must have a soft spot for in their hearts. Not to mention snatching her rider.

'I won't let them harm you, I won't,' he promised over and over again to the blue.

His ribs were a dull ache in his chest and his legs were trembling from the flight and pushing the reluctant firedrake on. More and more he had to rest and every time he did so Skite would slow almost to a standstill.

He judged the time as they flew over the mountains from his flight with Flick until he guessed they were nearing the outskirts of Rakenar. The wind buffeted them until Skite lowered height. Jaron sent him lower still. He didn't want to be seen until the last moment for he was certain the Raken riders would pluck him off and attack the blue. Skite's speed would be outweighed by sheer numbers as he flew directly into their territory.

The mountains rose higher, forcing them up and a harsh, buffeting wind caused the blue's wings to judder. Jaron tightened his grip on the ears. 'Nearly there, boy, you're going to have to trust me.' He looked up at a mountain whose tip was obscured by cloud and pushed with his heels; Skite's head rose and Jaron leaned forward, grateful for the long ears to hold on to. He pushed again.

Skite obeyed him and increased his speed; his wings beat stronger as he rose vertically up the side of the mountain and straight into the thick bank of cloud, hidden from any watchers from Rakenar. Jaron shivered as the damp mist touched him. He looked down over the blue's shoulder, searching. At first there were only cloud banks scudding along below them, then at last a break in the cloud and there was Rakenar far below. Jaron was surprised at how his heart leapt on seeing the familiar green valley with the ribbon of water meandering through it, the mountains surrounding it all and forming a natural protective barrier. It was strange, but it felt like coming home. He waited for the next cloud break then looked for the largest mountain, Mount Scarf. It sat at the far end of the valley and Jaron could see the huge cave at its base even from way up here before the clouds passed over again. He put the blue into a hover and stroked the scaly neck.

'I won't let them hurt you, I won't,' he promised one final time, trying to get up his own courage.

Boy and firedrake hovered in the sky as Jaron waited for the next cloud break. When it came, Jaron took a deep breath; it was now or never.

'Skite – go!'

He crouched forward, determined, praying the firedrake would trust him now. Skite did, he went with his weight and folded his wedge-shaped wings back into a dive. Jaron hoped to buy a little time coming from on high and as they neared he caught sight of a green firedrake on guard, perched on the lip of the valley with its rider. He kept his eyes on it as they scorched through the air, claiming precious seconds. It looked up, crouched in surprise, and let out a trumpeting alarm. The rider looked up and shielded his eyes. He immediately turned his firedrake to fly out over the valley. Another trumpeting call, hollow and fainter, wafted up to Jaron and the boy shifted his weight into his knees. Skite's wings pulled back and the blue dove faster, straight for the valley floor. A strange whistling reached his ears and he had to squint against the wind. With no helmet, his scalp prickled in the cold. Down below, he saw firedrake wheeling out from their ledges and searching the sky, the heads freezing as they locked onto Skite. Jaron's eyes were watering now. Fear they would surely crash into the ground caused him to lift his behind back slightly to slow the blue, but still Skite dove.

The whistling grew louder in Jaron's ears and the pressure threatened to tear him from the blue's back. Too fast! Through his tears, he saw a dense flock of firedrake fly right into their flight path. Skite saw them too and opened his wings, mercifully forced to slow down at last. He slewed to one side to avoid the flock below and Jaron, seeing a gap, pushed him on down with a shout of command to back up his drumming heels. They dropped past the snapping jaws, Jaron grateful the blue was trusting in his commands. The valley floor was coming up to meet them and Jaron desperately pulled harder on the long ears with all his strength to lift the head. Skite just managed to level out in the valley bowl, well below the whirling flocks of alarmed firedrake that now thickened the sky.

The firedrake cries of warning were deafening and Skite seemed to shrink in on himself as he looked up at the snarling beasts bearing down on them. They had shot straight through the ceiling of chasing firedrake and Jaron searched in desperation for Mount Scarf and saw it right at the far end; they had gone off course. Jaron kicked Skite with his heels and sent the blue razing across the valley length, out from underneath the firedrake now massing to attack from above. Leaning low over the neck, Jaron risked a look back to see a dense cloud of firedrake wings and lashing tails turning to give chase. Their reaction had been faster than Jaron had planned for. He felt Skite tremble beneath him as a huge red burst through the beating wings, outstripping the chasing firedrake. It was Madrag, and Jaron saw his lips lift in a snarl. Panicked, he urged Skite even faster as, desperate now, Jaron searched ahead for his cave. *Look to see where you are going and your firedrake will follow.* He spied it, a level down from the top of Mount Scarf, his chair still out on the ledge. A torch had been lit outside it even in daylight. He swallowed; his mother had put out a guiding light for his return. Jaron lifted Skite higher and levelled him out. He kept his eyes on the torch; it was coming at them with alarming speed but Skite would be torn apart if they had to come around again.

'Don't slow yet, don't slow yet,' Jaron chanted to himself.

He risked a look behind him. Madrag and a green were closest, ahead of the other chasing firedrake. He looked back and started in alarm; the open doors of the cave entrance were rushing towards them – too close! Jaron threw his weight back and pulled hard on Skite's ears. The blue shrieked as its front reared up into the air, the blue wings back-flapping to brake, tail thrashing as a rudder. Jaron kept him on course and his eyes on his cave as Parl's words came into his head: *trust your firedrake to sort it out.*

The cave mouth was upon them and Skite, still back-flapping hard, flew straight over the ledge, his front legs catching the chair outside and knocking it flying. The inner rock wall came rushing to meet them and Jaron cried out and threw up an arm to protect his face. In doing so he let go of Skite's ears and fell back over the rump. There was a loud *thwump* and the sound of wood splintering as something ripped loudly. Jaron, arms flailing, hit the deck and the wind went out of his lungs with a whoosh as his poor ribs took yet another knock.

Despite the pain, his eyes shot open. He was lying face

up and spread-eagled on his collapsed bed and a curtain ripped from its moorings had come to settle over Skite's head. The crumpled firedrake was against the wall. Laying still.

'Skite!' Jaron crawled towards him, over the blue's splayed wings and ignoring his painful ribs. 'Please be alright, please…'

A rumble came from underneath the cloth. Jaron, relieved, reached up to pull it off and the head swung down towards him, purple eyes dazed and blinking. Blood ran from the trembling nostrils.

'I'm sorry,' Jaron gasped. The firedrake's wings flapped in a feeble manner as the blue peeled himself off the wall to stand over the boy on shaking legs. Skite's nose nudged him before the blue's gaze shifted over his head. A warning growl tore from his chest and he knocked Jaron back onto the bed as he lowered into a crouch over him.

An answering snarl reverberated into the cave and Jaron forgot his ribs as he flipped over to see Madrag, eyes alight with yellow fire and revealing his teeth at this intruder. Next to him, also pressed into the cave entrance, was the head of a snarling green. Together, they filled the space. Madrag pushed closer and Skite opened his wings in warning.

'No! Madrag, it's alright!' Jaron made to crawl towards the red but Skite's claw hooked in his belt and held him back. His tail lashed out past Jaron and sent the bedside chair crashing towards Madrag. The red caught it in his mouth and snapped it into splinters in one savage bite. He spat out the leather seat and Jaron saw his fire eyes flare. *Oh no.*

The boy lifted onto his knees, his fingers fumbling as they undid the belt trapping him to Skite. Once released, he rolled away from the blue and came to his feet, staggering a little. He heard Skite squeak after him but kept his eyes on Madrag, lifting both hands up, palms out.

'Madrag, it's alright, he didn't mean any harm, he won't

hurt me–' His words faltered as he noticed Lord Carna's face, peering over Madrag's head, body bent almost double where he had wriggled into the small space there. The flint-grey eyes were locked on to the blue and a long sword was in one hand.

'He won't hurt me!' Jaron called up at him. 'He brought me back! Please don't hurt him.'

'Jaron,' Carna murmured and Jaron could hear the relief in his voice. 'Are you hurt?'

'No,' Jaron lied. 'It wasn't his fault, Torrit sent him.'

It was a mistake. 'Torrit?' Carna's eyebrows shot up and then the lips peeled back in a fierce grimace. Jaron saw the sword lift in his hand.

'No!' Jaron stumbled back to stand in front of the blue's head, shielding him. 'I told you, he got me away. I wouldn't be here if it wasn't for him.'

'Come here, Jaron.'

'No. You back off. Now.'

Carna stared at him for a long moment.

'We can't get to him,' said a calm voice and Jaron now saw it was Val's face peering over Motch's head, squeezed in next to the red. 'We have to back off.'

'No,' Carna snarled.

'It might turn on the boy if the firedrake panic it.' Val's leathery face was smooth, composed and was in stark contrast to the fury now etched into Carna's expression. After a moment, the lord's face cleared and he seemed to compose himself. He tapped Madrag's head and the red pulled back a little, eyes still fixed on the blue. Carna slid down and landed in a half-crouch, blade sweeping up. He shifted on to the balls of his feet as Val, holding a spear, dismounted. Both men, weapons at the ready, took a step forward.

'No,' Jaron pleaded as he retreated a step. Skite's head came over his shoulder, lips raised in a snarl. The boy lifted an arm and brought it over the blue's nose, pushing it back down. Carna paused, his eyes widening. He cast a quick look across at Val. Both men straightened from their protective stance at the same time.

'Could it be?' Carna muttered, half to himself. He stared at Jaron. The boy stared back, chin lifted but his heart thundering in his chest.

'Jaron!'

It was the voice he loved most and he turned. 'Mum!'

She stood in the tunnel doorway back in the corner of the room. Her hair was dishevelled and underneath the wide hazel eyes dark shadows made her face seem even paler than normal. As he stared, heart opening, he saw tears brim and spill over to run down her cheeks.

'Rella, stay back.' Carna made to step towards her, hand outstretched in a plea but she was already rushing towards Jaron, who stumbled into his mother's open arms. Skite shifted quickly across, keeping with his rider, and Madrag hissed in fury and moved closer, maintaining a low snarling growl. Enveloped in Rella's arms as she spun him round, Jaron grunted at the compression of his sore ribs. She pulled back a little and frowned down at him.

'You're hurt.'

'Just my ribs,' Jaron tried to keep the pain from his voice. He looked up at the blue. The purple eyes were anxious and he raised a hand to Skite's nose. 'It's alright, boy.'

Rella looked over her shoulder at his words and Jaron felt her body freeze. She released him and pushed her son behind her as she whirled to face the blue.

'No – Mum, it's fine.'

'It attacked you,' she rasped, pushing Jaron with her as she stepped back. The blue keened at Jaron in front of her, his eyes anxious as he stepped forward to follow. Madrag's sudden growl was deafening.

'Rella, don't move.' Carna had come two paces in and

was back into a crouch, sword held tightly. His face had gone a shade lighter under his tan.

'He won't harm us, Mum, I won't allow it,' Jaron spoke into her ear.

She turned to look down at him, her face still wet, hazel eyes wide. Jaron moved past her towards the blue and his mother stepped with him, staying at his side.

'Dammit, woman, why do you never listen to me?' Carna's eyes razed at his partner.

'Don't you *woman* me,' Rella hissed back. She looked up at the blue, her face composed. 'If Jaron says it won't hurt me, then I believe him.'

Jaron felt immense gratitude at her words and took her hand. 'His name's Skite,' he looked up at the firedrake and stroked its nose. 'Skite, meet my mother.' The purple eyes shifted from Jaron to Rella then back to Jaron. 'She's a friend, *you will not harm her*,' as he emphasised the last words they strummed when they left his lips. Skite immediately bowed his head to the boy.

Madrag's low snarling cut off and the cave went quiet. Carna lifted out of his defensive posture and the sword hand dropped to hang limply at his side. Jaron turned back to his mother and saw her staring open-mouthed at him. Her son smiled to reassure her, thinking again how drawn she looked; she must have been frantic with worry in his absence. He reached for her cold hand and lifted it onto Strike's nose. Rella tore her eyes away from Jaron and forced a smile up at the blue.

'My, what a lovely colour you are,' she whispered and daringly ran her hand up his nose. Skite blinked at her. 'And purple eyes, I've never seen the like before.'

Skite huffed at her, lifting her hair and flattening her skirt. Rella's lips widened into a genuine smile of wonder and she cooed at the blue. She turned to look at Lord Carna.

'He's quite friendly,' her lips pursed at him. 'Stop itching for a fight.'

Carna's jaw set. 'Torrit sent him to get Jaron.'

Rella's gasp of horror made Skite pull back. 'Is this true?' she demanded of her son. 'It was Torrit?'

Jaron nodded, hating the horror in her eyes. 'But I'm fine, the blue saved me, got me away.' He gazed up at Skite who was watching them. 'He turned against his master.'

Rella's hands took both of his. 'Jaron,' she looked into his eyes. 'I don't think he could have ever really accepted that man as his master or he wouldn't have done your bidding.' Her hands tightened on his. 'He's selected you, hasn't he?'

'Selected?'

'Taken you as his rider, chosen you.'

Jaron looked up at the blue. The firedrake keened and cocked its head at him. 'I suppose he has, yes.'

Her sharp intake of breath was accompanied by Carna's low groan of despair.

26

Lord Carna ordered Jaron and Skite to go and stand on the ledge so they could be seen. Outside Mount Scarf the sense of alarm was palpable in the air. Firedrake still wheeled in circles and their screeches rung in the valley.

Jaron had to tug at the blue's chin for quite a while until his young firedrake would move. Even then Skite had trembled when Madrag, hanging on the mountainside right beside the ledge, had fixed the blue with his yellow eyes. Jaron kept his hand on his firedrake's neck, terrified he might leap off the ledge to get away from the big red, only to be attacked by the Raken firedrake outside. At the other end of the ledge and hanging like a bat above it, Motch had hooked his wing claws onto the rock, his rider standing up at right angles to his hanging beast with one arm looped around the lower neck and feet planted on the saddle front arch, seemingly oblivious to the long drop below. Jaron looked up at Val and the man grinned; nothing seemed to phase the lord's second.

'Come to order!' Carna's voice rang out into the valley and the riders brought their firedrake round to hover before their lord. 'My nephew, Lord Jaron, has chosen his firedrake,' Carna's voice boomed out. 'The blue here belongs to him.' There were loud exclamations from the riders at this announcement and Carna held up his hands to quiet them. 'You know our law; no Raken attacks another's selected firedrake. The blue is not to be harmed.' Rella moved to stand next to Jaron and looped her arm through his while Carna took a deep breath. 'All is now well and you are free to return to your caves.'

The riders saluted and their firedrake turned and flapped away. A babble of voices rose as riders disembarked on other's ledges to discuss the recent events, or hung from the walls perched on their firedrakes, leaning over and chatting to those outside their caves. Jaron noticed they often looked over at him and the blue.

'They don't seem very happy,' he muttered.

Carna whirled to face him and Jaron stepped back. The lord's face was pale, his lips tight. For the first time Jaron noticed how bloodshot his eyes were. Rella's hand came up to lightly touch the lord's chest and he paused before turning away. He stalked over to where his firedrake hung and stepped off the ledge onto Madrag's saddle. Even as his rider was swinging a leg over, the big red flapped off. Carna didn't spare them a look back as he winged out over the valley.

Jaron watched them disappear over the mountain ridge. 'I seem to have upset everybody,' he muttered.

'Don't be silly, you are back here safe, that's the main thing. Everyone has been very worried.' Rella turned back to look at the collapsed bed and smashed furniture. 'You can't sleep here tonight. I'll meet you next door.'

Jaron was doubtful. 'In Carna's cave? Won't he mind?'

'He will understand that I want to spend time with my son,' her hand brushed his fringe back from his face and Jaron saw tears pool in her eyes again.

'Mum...'

'When they told me,' she swallowed, 'what had happened to you, how you were attacked on Channon...' Her eyes flicked to the blue.

'Is Channon alright?' Jaron asked. 'How she fought for me, you should have seen it – it was terrible, the noise...'

Rella put her hand on his shoulder. 'She was fine, Jaron, exhausted, a few cuts on her back, but fine.' Again, her eyes went to the blue.

'I told you, it was Torrit, not him.' It was important to Jaron she didn't blame Skite, but she only smiled.

'I'll see you next door,' she said, and turned back into the cave, picking her way back over the disarray and dabbing at her eyes with the hem of her sleeve. Jaron watched until she disappeared into the tunnel. He sighed and looked up at Skite and the blue met his gaze with wide eyes.

'It's not your fault,' he went to lean on Skite's nose and paused as he felt many eyes on them. He looked around to see all the riders on the neighbouring mountains were watching with their firedrake.

'Come on, Skite,' he made to mount up then realised he had forgotten the blue wasn't trained to raise its leg for him. Great, he was going to have to struggle to get on in front of their audience. As he stood there, looking at how high the back was, the blue crouched. Jaron smiled – yet again the firedrake had somehow understood what he wanted. He saw the blue's foreleg was flat on the ground and he took hold of the shoulder ridge and stepped onto it. From there he reached up, got a hand on Skite's backbone, and managed to crawl up, gasping as his ribs protested.

'We're getting there, aren't we, Skite?' he said between gritted teeth at the pain as he settled himself. He reached down and stroked the blue, forgetting he was being watched for a moment.

It was a short hop to Carna's cave. The ledge was designed for a red and Skite took up less than half the space. Jaron scrambled down and held out a hand, palm up. 'Stay,' he ordered and turned to join his mother. Immediately, something bumped him in the middle of his back. 'No, Skite, I said–' He stopped short.

The blue was already past him and in the cave. Rella, to her credit, raised her eyebrows but didn't flinch as Skite walked past her with his wings half held up towards the large bed. Settling himself alongside it, he put his head down to his paws and let go with a huge sigh, his sides deflating as the wings folded close.

'Knows his own mind, doesn't he?' Rella eyed him.

'I think he's a little scared to be out on the ledge on his own in case Madrag comes back.'

'Madrag won't hurt him – no Raken firedrake will now that Carna has given the order. It's our most sacred rule.'

She stepped towards him and put her arm round his shoulders. Her son rested his head against her chest and allowed his mother to take him over to a chair. Now he was safe, Jaron felt exhausted as all the horrors of the past two days finally caught up with him. His mother unbuttoned his tunic and peeled off his shirt, exclaiming when she saw the purple bruises amongst his scarred flesh all over his upper body. Jaron sat slumped in his chair and didn't protest as she rubbed thick lotion from a jar onto his chest and ribs. It smelt of peppermint and helped to revive him a little.

She pressed a steaming tankard of beef broth into his hands and he sipped at it periodically while she worked. She washed him as she had when he was a young child and he accepted it, too tired to turn aside her mothering and secretly comforted by her touch. Finally, she wrapped bandages around his body to support his ribs. Sitting back in her chair his mother pushed her long heavy hair over her shoulders. As she did so a strong breeze ruffled through the cave and Carna came striding into the room.

He stopped short when he saw the blue laid next his bed. Jaron made to stand up, muttering apologies, but his mother put her hand on his shoulder, staying him.

'Tell me,' she said, 'I want to know everything that happened.'

Jaron looked from her to Carna. Her hand reached up and her cool palm laid against his cheek, turning his face back towards her.

'Don't try to spare me anything, Jaron. Leave nothing out.'

Jaron stared at her. Her beautiful hazel eyes looked directly into his and he understood her need to know what had happened while her son had been taken from her. He put Carna out of his mind and, taking a deep breath, Jaron began to relay the terrible events of the last two days, the whole time staring at a tapestry hanging on the far wall, because if he looked at his mother's face and saw her pain he knew he would have tried to spare her.

He began with the terrible fight when Channon had defended him, the first night on the ledge with the blue – despite his promise Jaron glossed over how terrified he was for his mother's sake – Torrit's fortress, and all the terrible firedrake he had at his command. He told of how he had escaped on the blue and their subsequent journey to Rakenar. He even told how he had evaded the sentry firedrake by flying low and using the cloud cover, purely for Carna's benefit, because he knew no one should be able to sneak up on Rakenar and if he could do it, then maybe Torrit could do the same.

The only thing he left out was when he had commanded the blue to fire, and Torrit's talk of him having this terrible thing called the *Rillion*. *I'll tell them when I'm ready,* he thought to himself, when he had sorted out exactly what this thing was.

At last he slumped in his chair, exhausted. Rella sat stock-still and ramrod straight as she had throughout the whole telling. When he finally looked at her he was shocked by how white her face had gone.

'Mum,' he reached to comfort her but she spun off her chair away from him and stalked up and down the room. She looked over at Carna, who hadn't moved the whole time Jaron had been speaking. The Raken lord stood, feet apart, fists clenched tight as he stared at Jaron, a muscle twitching spasmodically in his jaw.

'Your brother!' Rella spun and pointed at Carna. 'He did this! When is that madman ever going to leave us alone? If it's not enough Teel, a good, honest man, was killed *and* a whole village razed, my son was burnt, *burnt* Carna! Now this!' Her hand flicked to Jaron. 'He wants my son, to take him from me! *My son!*'

Her voice had increased in pitch and Jaron stared at her while Skite raised his head and looked warily at this mad woman. She was incandescent with rage, her hair flying out from her face in all directions, her brown eyes flashing. Jaron looked at Carna, but the lord's face might have been made from stone for all the reaction he gave.

'You've got to kill him, Carna. You should have done it all those years ago.' At her words Carna's face contracted, like he was in pain. Rella was standing in front of the lord now, her breath coming in panting gasps. 'I don't care if he's your brother, I *don't care.* I have to live with what he's done, Carna – and I can't take any more.'

Carna stepped forward and enveloped her in his arms, holding her tight. She carried on talking, her chin tilted up on his shoulder 'If he takes my son, Carna, if he gets to him again – I won't be able to go on, do you hear me? Do you…' she collapsed in his arms, sobbing.

Jaron sat, horrified as his mother wept, her cries as frantic as a trapped animal. 'I'm sorry,' he whispered. 'Sorry.'

Hearing him, Rella broke out of Carna's arms and whirled on her son. 'Don't you dare say sorry! Do you hear me? There is nothing, *nothing* for you to apologise for.'

Jaron was at a loss to know what to say. Rella turned and walked straight towards the blue. Jaron got up quickly, seeking to pull her back, thinking she was going to hurt Skite, who might then defend himself. He saw with relief that Carna was already right behind her. The blue's ears flickered at her approach.

'Skite, it's alright,' Jaron hurriedly moved towards him. The blue's nostrils flared as next moment Rella had fallen against the blue's neck, her arms wrapped tight around it. 'Thank you,' Rella murmured, 'thank you for carrying my son home.'

Jaron came to stand beside Carna and they watched in silence as the blue rumbled from deep in his throat at this strange, distraught woman.

Later, when Rella had calmed down and was back in her chair, head nodding in her exhaustion, Jaron watched from his seat as Carna tenderly lifted her in his arms. Still half-asleep, she muttered and huddled against his chest. She looked so small, Jaron thought, like a child herself. Carna carried her around to the other side of the bed from Skite's bulk and knelt with one knee on the blankets. He laid her down gently and pulled the covers up under Rella's chin, raising a hand to stroke her cheek. Finally, he sighed and lifted off the bed, turning towards Jaron.

The boy dropped his eyes and looked away. He felt embarrassed to have witnessed such a private moment of tenderness.

'Jaron, come out to the ledge with me.'

The boy nodded and peeled himself from his chair with limbs that felt heavy as lead. He was exhausted.

Madrag raised his head at their approach. On impulse, Jaron went over to the big red and leant against the massive belly. Madrag's rumble vibrated throughout his body and it was a comfort. Jaron closed his eyes and felt the beast's whumping heartbeat against his chest, slower than his own. As he leant close against the beast he felt it quicken up, judder, and then match his own heart, beat for beat. Frowning, Jaron lifted his head to look at the beast. One eye was rolled back, watching him.

'Jaron?' The Raken lord was waiting. Reluctantly, Jaron pushed away from Madrag. His exhaustion made his limp heavy as he went over to stand before the man. Carna hooked his thumbs in his belt and appraised him for a long while until Jaron shifted uncomfortably. 'You said Torrit knew of you, that he had sources. Did he say anything else?'

Jaron considered and lowered his voice. 'He said Rella deserved to die for betraying him.' He met Carna's eyes and saw the other's flare then narrow. 'I confronted him about the villagers and Teel. He wasn't sorry for any of it, and he had some of my clothes.'

'Your clothes?' Carna frowned. 'Somebody had brought him your clothes?'

'Yes.' Jaron watched as the lord digested this.

'Do you think you could find this fortress again?'

Jaron was silent for a long while, looking down at his feet. 'I don't know. If you found it he could command all his firedrake to attack you.' He paused. 'I suppose I could try to get the blue to take us.'

'I understand your reluctance but we must find him, Jaron.'

'I know,' Jaron said in a glum voice. 'He said a village supplied him with food but didn't mention the name.'

'A village near the mountains... and a mountain fortress,' Carna mused. 'It shouldn't be hard to find. There aren't many old fortresses carved into the mountains with the columns still intact. If you think of anything else, any detail, no matter how small, you must tell me.'

Jaron nodded and, apparently satisfied, Carna turned to look out over the valley. Jaron noticed for the first time the afternoon was moving into evening. The sun had dropped behind the mountains now and dusk was settling, drawing a grainy blue half-light down over Rakenar. The caves flickered into life as torches were lit from within.

A chill took Jaron and he shivered a little. 'I still don't

know how Torrit got Skite to come and search for me,' he said, breaking the silence.

'You said he had your clothes, he might have used it to give the blue your scent and brought him close enough to latch on to you. They have a good sense of smell although I've never heard of a firedrake tracking on scent before. Torrit commands the *Rillion,* with it he can get a firedrake to do almost anything.' He paused and Jaron felt his eyes on him. 'Do you want to ask me anything, Jaron? About the *Rillion*?'

'Maybe later.' Jaron tried to sound casual but he heard again the sudden tortured firedrakes' cries as Torrit commanded them, and he found he did want to talk after all. 'What he did to them was terrible,' he whispered. 'Controlling their moves, their minds, they were in agony, I felt it.'

'You *felt* it?'

The sudden interest in Carna's voice stopped Jaron from saying anything further. He was too tired to trust himself. Carna must have sensed his reluctance for he didn't press him. For a while they stood together and watched the cave lights dotted all around the valley. A faint firedrake snore behind them made Carna look over his shoulder just as Madrag swung his head back into the cave.

'You can trust him, you know,' Jaron murmured. He felt Carna look across at him in the fading light. 'The blue, Skite.'

'We'll see.'

'He's broken away from Torrit.' Carna nodded yet Jaron felt he wasn't really agreeing with him and he was too tired to argue about it now. 'I'm very tired,' he ventured. It wasn't just an excuse, he really needed his bed now. Then he remembered it lay in smithereens next door, flattened by firedrake.

'I am glad you are back safe, Jaron.'

'Me too.' Jaron made to leave, but Carna's hand came to land on his shoulder and Jaron was turned to face him. He really wished this man would let him go to sleep. The lord's face was half in shadow, the rest lit by the flickering torches at the mouth of the cave, and Jaron was reminded of Torrit. Carna did not have the madness that lurked in his older brother's strange silver-blue eyes nor the drawn face and thin lips, but the similarities were there – the high forehead, the brooding eyes and strong jaw.

'You did well to have escaped my brother,' Carna was saying, bringing Jaron's tired mind back into focus. 'Time and time again you have had to face your fears about the firedrake.' Jaron raised his eyebrows and Carna nodded, meeting his eyes. 'Oh yes, I've watched you swallow down your fears when even to touch these beasts was unbearable to you,' he smiled. 'I think you spared Rella some things in your telling, for which I am grateful. I know your worst fears must have come true yet you managed to turn it round and escape.' He hesitated, the flint eyes looking into his. 'Tell me, was that why you chose the blue, so you could get away, because if so...'

'No,' Jaron mumbled. 'It just happened. I don't even know how. I was just looking at him and then he stepped closer and...' He paused, not wishing to elaborate further. 'It just came about.' As he raised his eyes he caught the disappointment in the lord's gaze. 'Why do you ask?'

'If you did the choosing I might have been able to free you from him; if you had taken him as a means of escaping Torrit.'

Jaron stepped back, Carna's hands slipping from his shoulders. 'But I don't want to be free of him.' He felt himself sway then and had to make a concentrated effort to stay upright.

Carna took his elbow and turned him back into the room. 'Time for you to rest. Sleep with your mother, I'll take the chair.'

'Well, if you're sure,' but Jaron was already limping ahead. He reached the bed and, stepping over Skite's neck, slid under the covers, forgetting even to remove his boots first. It was a relief to nestle his head against the pillow.

Rella was facing him, a strand of her hair across her face. He thought to reach up and brush it aside but instead he closed his eyes. Out of everything that had happened to him, it was the thought of that black kelpra back in the gorge that surfaced now in his exhausted mind. He was almost certain it was Caliber. *I'll go back to make sure*, the boy vowed silently. He owed it to the kelpra after Caliber saving his life.

'Jaron?' he heard his mother mumble softly.

'I'm here, Mum,' he whispered.

'Yes...' by her voice, he could tell she was smiling. 'You're here. You're... home.'

He opened his eyes. Her eyes were still closed. *Home.* He rolled the unfamiliar word round in his tired mind. 'Yes, Mum. I'm here. He paused. 'I'm home.'

Another smile stretched slowly across her face. Jaron closed his eyes again and in two shakes of a firedrake's tail he was fast asleep.

Book 2 of the Rillion is flying your way!

BLUE FIRE RIDER

Jaron now has a firedrake of his own but there's no denying Skite is different. Jaron's spirited blue doesn't always do as he should, and some people in Rakenar are not happy at all having a throwback to the wild firedrake of old in their midst. As Jaron tries to get Skite accepted, he learns more about the strange power that is inside of him and what it can do. But evil is lurking – hidden deep within Rakenar itself – and once again, Jaron's life is on the line…

ACKNOWLEDGEMENTS

Christine, my dear friend, I don't think any of this would have been possible nor taken wing without your support and belief in me over the years. Thank you.

To Red, who supported me every step of the way, provided advice, and who soothed my writer's nerves more than once. And to Curly, your pearls of wisdom always helped. To Amanda, for your excellent editorial mage skills and knowledge (I was a little stubborn on only a few counts). And Gel, thank you so much for being my first 'real' reader.

CPSIA information can be obtained
at www.ICGtesting.com
Printed in the USA
FSHW011659161219
65147FS

9 781999 324506